Mildred In Disguise
With Diamonds

Toni Kief

The Writers Cooperative of the Pacific Northwest Seattle, Washington 2017

Copyright © 2017 Toni Kief
All rights reserved. Except for use in any review, the reproduction or utilization of this work in whole or in part in any form by any electronic, mechanical or other means, now known or hereafter invented, including xerography, photocopying and recording, or in any information storage or retrieval system is forbidden without the written permission of the author.

This is a work of fiction. Names, characters, places and incidents are either the product of the author's imagination or are used fictitiously, and any resemblance to actual persons, living or dead, business establishments, events or locales is entirely coincidental.

ASIN: B06XXL53BJ

Toni Kief's website: www.tonikief.com
Cover design: Heather McIntyre, www.coverandlayout.com
Interior design: Heather McIntyre, www.coverandlayout.com

This book is dedicated to Connie Kreutzer
Baxter for inspiration

and Susan Brown, Alice Best Jackson and Roland Trenary for
their encouragement and support.

Acknowledgements

I owe extra thanks to Barbara Vericker and Joe Kurke my first readers, and I appreciate your invaluable input. The Writers Cooperative of the Pacific Northwest continually encourages in a multitude of genres and events.

Last, but not least, The Writers Kickstart pounding out 500 words at a time until it is possible to tie it all into a cohesive story.

– Contents –

CHAPTER ONE – New Direction
CHAPTER TWO – The Job
CHAPTER THREE – Ready Set Go
CHAPTER FOUR – Carry Out
CHAPTER FIVE – Building a Team
CHAPTER SIX – Interrogation
CHAPTER SEVEN – Two Days in a Row
CHAPTER EIGHT – Pondering
CHAPTER NINE – Raving
CHAPTER TEN – Fill the Night
CHAPTER ELEVEN – Fathers' Day
CHAPTER TWELVE – Turnovers and Plots
CHAPTER THIRTEEN – File Boxes
CHAPTER FOURTEEN – Different Program
CHAPTER FIFTEEN – Expanded Patrol
CHAPTER SIXTEEN – Team Member – 4
CHAPTER SEVENTEEN – Reports
CHAPTER EIGHTEEN – Check One Off
CHAPTER NINETEEN – Storage Part Two
CHAPTER TWENTY – Busy Day Off
CHAPTER TWENTY-ONE – One More Time
CHAPTER TWENTY-TWO – The Convention
CHAPTER TWENTY-THREE – First Day
CHAPTER TWENTY-FOUR – Ancient History
CHAPTER TWENTY-FIVE – The Past
CHAPTER TWENTY-SIX – Getting Lucky
CHAPTER TWENTY-SEVEN – Finally
CHAPTER TWENTY-EIGHT – Life Changes
CHAPTER TWENTY-NINE – Back to Work
CHAPTER THIRTY – Oliver
CHAPTER THIRTY-ONE – Police Ready
CHAPTER THIRTY-TWO – Gotcha
CHAPTER THIRTY-THREE – Pain Killers
CHAPTER THIRTY-FOUR – The Investigation Begins
CHAPTER THIRTY-FIVE – Truthing
CHAPTER THIRTY-SIX – Healing Continued
CHAPTER THIRTY-SEVEN – Question Popping

CHAPTER THIRTY-EIGHT – Casino Reboot
CHAPTER THIRTY-NINE – White Board
CHAPTER FORTY – Undead
CHAPTER FORTY-ONE – Background Checks
CHAPTER FORTY-TWO – Truth Be Damned
CHAPTER FORTY-THREE – Step Forward
CHAPTER FORTY-FOUR – Partners
CHAPTER FORTY-FIVE – Lucas Freeman
CHAPTER FORTY-SIX – Suddenly Tuesday
CHAPTER FORTY-SEVEN – Easy Night
CHAPTER FORTY-EIGHT – Ladies Lunch
CHAPTER FORTY-NINE – Night Shift
CHAPTER FIFTY – A Break
CHAPTER FIFTY-ONE – Night Crawlers
CHAPTER FIFTY-TWO – Kind of a Hush
CHAPTER FIFTY-THREE – Scare Tactics
CHAPTER FIFTY-FOUR – Moving Forward
CHAPTER FIFTY-FIVE – Unchained Melody
CHAPTER FIFTY-SIX – Safe
CHAPTER FIFTY-SEVEN – Family
CHAPTER FIFTY-EIGHT – Reception
CHAPTER FIFTY-NINE – B-I-N-G-O
CHAPTER SIXTY – Monday
CHAPTER SIXTY-ONE – Company
CHAPTER SIXTY-TWO – Clean Up
CHAPTER SIXTY-THREE – Double Turnovers
CHAPTER SIXTY-FOUR – Early Shift
AUTHOR BIO

– 1 –
New Direction

Seated in the third chair from the door, Mildred clutched her bag that held the folder of recommendations, and in her other hand, the completed application. It took effort to maintain a calm expression as her mind reeled with anticipation. Mildred never expected she would be looking for work at the age of seventy-one, but there was no denying her need when she had to consider hocking her wedding ring to buy groceries. She had loved that old man, but her grief had turned to anger the day they read the will. Then the bill collectors had started to show up.

The interviewer opened the door and called, "Mildred Petrie, please come in."

Maybe this was the time to stop obsessing over old Dick and to put on a smile. Mildred had sat long enough for her muscles to stiffen and her joints to creak. She hoped it wasn't too obvious as she limped in. Smiling through her discomfort, Mildred greeted the interviewer and sat in the single straight back chair.

Fifteen minutes later, Mildred exited decked with a genuine smile and an employee packet. The receptionist gave her the schedule for training classes on her way out. No one at the Ivory Winds Casino could know how grateful she was to be self-sufficient again. The casino was close to home and she could walk – saving money on gas – and with her erratic sleep patterns, coupled with desperation, she could handle any shift they might offer. Mildred was invigorated with hope on her walk to the retirement village.

Dick had decided they should sell their house and buy the small condominium just before his death. Mildred had assumed it was to cut maintenance, plus they would have the money to travel more. He had died the day they were to move in. This was when Mildred started to learn his secrets, including the massive gambling debt that didn't die with him.

Her new employer had promised to send more information, but in the twenty minutes it took her to walk home, her email had blown up. There were a multitude of forms, classes, and welcomes waiting for her. After an hour of filling in blanks, she checked the list of available positions: Server, Dealer, Cashier, Money Counter, and Risk Management. With fishnet hose over spider veins dancing through her mind, Mildred was positive she didn't want to serve food or cocktails. The recognition of the passage of time (and gravity) caused her to imagine how it would require science and technology to reconstruct a cleavage. After this flight of self judgment and fancy, Mildred considered the dealer jobs, but worried about the necessity for quick math skills. Finally, she requested Cashier, Money Counter, and Risk Management.

She pressed send, and the completed supplemental forms were out of her hands. With a sigh, she leaned back in her chair, proud of her accomplishments in a single morning. The reverie was interrupted when her phone rang with a recording. Mildred pressed one: yes, she would begin cashier training tomorrow at eight a.m.

Surprised at how excited she was for a simple job, she struggled through a fitful night and gave up at five. By seven, Mildred was dressed, fed and on her hands and knees searching for the box of orthopedic cop shoes. She hadn't worn them since her retirement from the department, but preparation to stand all day was always a good idea. She laced up the less than attractive footwear, as the memory of thousands of mornings she had put on this type of shoe in her thirty-five year career as a meter maid washed over her. She recalled the day when men joined, and the division was renamed to the Parking Enforcement Department. The Maids had joked, "Same money, no new benefits, and twice the danger – in the locker room."

Sadness and anger returned on the short walk to the casino. It took Dick's death to learn that the retirement savings were gone, along with the dream of a contented life's last chapter. Her greatest humiliation was not in being alone or old, but the need to turn to her sons for help.

The fresh air helped shake off the memories and anticipation. The irony of her employment at Ivory Winds Casino was the fact that – this was the same place that had been instrumental in

Dick's destruction. Almost everything they'd built over two lives was gone or mortgaged, and Mildred felt a smug satisfaction that she would recover on the same casino's dime.

She entered through the main entrance, a wall of thick glass doors held open by young and energetic parking valets. Mildred felt that she was passing from failure into a new life and was greeted with constant clanging and the smell of smoke. She was only slightly amazed that there was gambling at seven-thirty in the morning.

The first to arrive, Mildred took the seat next to the still-locked door marked Human Resources. Watching the younger applicants filter in; Mildred put aside her thoughts of the past and tried to look composed. An odd assortment of hushed conversations started to fill the waiting room. All of the trainees seemed prepared for a morning of rules, promises, and tests; Mildred was the only one envisioning the free buffet lunch.

– 2 –
The Job

Mildred sat in the classroom. The other applicants seemed nonplussed by the instructions, while Mildred made pages of notes. There was so much to learn, but she had spent a lifetime with rules, and this was simply another challenge. The break for lunch was just in time; Mildred thought her head was full until they turned her old self loose on the buffet. Nothing thrilled her more than a multitude of tiny servings. This job could be grand.

Revitalized, she returned to the classroom with the other new hires. She was about to sit, when the instructor called her aside. Her first thought was that the casino may have changed their minds on her employment. She tried to imagine what she might have done wrong as she approached the receptionist.

Instead, she was sent to report to security. With a hand-drawn map, she set her face to "determined" and started towards the innermost workings of the casino. Mildred continued to overthink the situation, and an inner bargaining began. Her first reaction was a feeling of guilt, followed by a quick review of her life and sins. Ever so slightly, she slowed her pace. The morning training had moved along smoothly. This must be a mistake. There are no warrants or records; they must have rethought my age. Maybe Dick owes more money.

She exited the noisy, bright, and shiny décor in the customer area to a stark and silent hall. She found the unmarked door exactly where the map described and reached for the knob. Oh no, it's locked. Mildred hesitated and then tapped gently. The door swung open, and a young woman in a dark suit answered, "Mrs. Petrie, I'm pleased to meet you. I'm Belinda, the office manager and agent supervisor. Please come in. Bud will be with you in a moment." Nervously, Mildred entered the large, dark room. There were banks of video screens that lit the faces of officers intently watching and typing. The room was warm, and the conversation minimal. They paid no attention to her and continued a constant scan of the black and white monitors. Mildred replied, "Hi Belinda. I'm not sure what this is about."

The young woman smiled, "No, no problem, we keep things discreet in this department. Please have a seat. It will be a moment or two; the boss wants to speak to you personally."

Mildred sat and watched the constant activity in the darkened room. She stared at the wall of screens and realized there was virtually no corner in the massive complex that was not under constant surveillance. *How do they watch continual slow action without falling asleep? I can't even make it through an entire episode of Law and Order without a nap.*

Over a very long fifteen minutes, Mildred's anxiety grew with concern over missing the cashier training. She couldn't afford to miss anything if she had to compete with the younger applicants. Finally, a young man – *hell, every man under seventy is young* – approached. Well-dressed in a severely pressed black suit, he reminded her of every police chief she had ever met. He made eye contact and waved for her to enter an office. The room was the size of a bathroom stall, and the vision of a commode, instead of a chair behind his desk, slipped into her mind. There was a single chair on her side, with no space for movement. The thought of a hasty escape was her first consideration and was immediately ruled out. Mildred glanced around the room and noticed a couple overstated motivational posters tacked to the wall. Maybe she'd got him wrong; he might have been a Marine recruiter.

"I'm Bud Moses, the director of the security for the casino. I'm sure that you are questioning why I called for you."

Mildred made a slight nod, "Yes sir, Director Moses."

"Bud works just fine."

"I am puzzled. Have I done something wrong? Was it the second dessert at the buffet?"

He smiled, "No, Mildred, we wouldn't bust you on the dessert cart until about the fourth time through. Human Resources flagged your application and sent it over. I am impressed by your resume and the letter of recommendation from Judge McCaffie. He is a valuable guest here at the casino and prominent in the community." He again scanned her application and letters. "The doctor's letter confirming your medical status and ability to work is a great addition. No one has ever done that before." He nodded and continued to read.

Mildred spoke up, "Well, I'm aware of my age, and when I applied, I decided to answer as many questions up front as possible."

"The reference from your supervisor at the police department was the attention-grabber, due to the demands of this department. Here is the deal. There's a new position we have been working on with the local police. Someone of your description was not the original idea. I've been on the phone with our police liaison, and now the original vision has changed."

Mildred's interest was piqued and she sat wide-eyed and silent. The pause was uncomfortable until she answered, "Oooookay, Bud. I'm curious."

His formality seemed to disappear. "Ms. Petrie, may I call you Mildred?"

"Sure. Mildred, Millie, late for dinner, they are all fine." She blushed with the use of the old worn out joke.

"We have been considering a security position with someone that can work undercover. The job would consist of roaming the casino, bars, shops, restaurants, hotel facilities, and to simply pay attention. That officer will have a radio and receiver and be in contact with the security office at all times. We do not expect him, or in your case her, to handle any confrontations. Security would be back-up and would handle all altercations. The hours would vary for the covert officer – to minimize recognition, and to cover particular events."

Mildred nodded her understanding and waited.

"What I like about you is that you would fit in with many of our guests. Now that I think of it, Judge McCaffie will probably recognize you. Just keep it casual with anyone you may know. I also like that you don't appear dangerous.

"Well, Bud, don't let appearances fool you."

He broke into a wide smile. "That's exactly the attitude we are looking for. If you decide to join us, you will name your hours, and have full input on the job description. We would provide whatever you need: gun, pepper spray, Taser. You name it, you got it. We will work out the details as we go along."

Mildred was slow to react as she tried to wrap her mind around what was being offered. "You are saying that I'll be in deep cover? I don't think I want a gun. A little old lady wouldn't carry one. I mean, I worked for the PD for thirty-five years, but it was in Parking. I had a gun, but I never shot it. In fact, I never took it out of the holster unless it was for inspection, and then I was told to dust it."

"Whatever you think is appropriate. Take some time to think about it, and once you let me know, we will set up a private meeting with the police and iron out more details."

She felt relief and relaxed a small bit, "I am interested and would like more information, but I don't know what to ask. When do you want me to start?"

"Right away would be great. If it is okay with you, I will set up the meeting with the police liaison, and we can go ahead and get you an employee badge. If this doesn't work out, we always have an opening in the control center with Belinda. I would like to invite you back here this evening at seven. We are having a security meeting, food and a film."

Mildred's mind squealed *yippee food*, but she responded simply, "I'll be here."

The interview ended with a map of the entire casino, event listings and some passwords. Mildred was sent for her photo badge and employment paperwork. She could barely sit still as she thought about the job. The timing couldn't have been better. With little thought of the details, she decided that watching a video screen for hours was more difficult than roaming freely.

Mildred went back to the main casino floor as she left for home. She stopped, looked around, and decided that, even with all of the lights and activity, this place, for eight hours, was doable. *As long as I get a paycheck, no problems.*

Mildred exited by the giant glass doors and made a left to go home. She fought the urge to dance as she walked, when she suddenly realized: there was no discussion about the rate of pay.

Yet most anything would make it possible to catch up on the bills and cover the increased condo association dues. Mildred unlocked her door and she immediately moved to the counter, pushed the bills aside, and opened her notebook. She made a list of questions and suggestions. After a few minutes, she decided on a nap to help her make it through the evening with some dignity. Living near the casino had caused the problem with her husband, but today it was an asset.

That evening, she drove and arrived several minutes early. Belinda greeted her at the security door and provided an additional pass card for security access. They chatted as they walked down the hall to a large conference room.

"Mildred, I'm pleased you are going to join us. I did your security screening, and Bud was really excited about your job history."

Mildred liked Belinda immediately. "Did you find any warrants or arrests?"

Belinda opened the door to the room. "You know better."

They entered a huge room already set up with soft drinks and a variety of hors d'oeuvres and boxes of popcorn. There were rows of chairs facing a giant TV screen. The two women sat together towards the back and watched the crew drift in.

Belinda whispered, "We decided it was important that you be able to identify staff, but there is no plan to read most of them in on your position. If asked, I will introduce you as my aunt or mother." They made up a simple back-story: she was considering a move from Dubuque to live closer. Hopefully they wouldn't need it. It appeared that, while Mildred had been napping, her new job had been expanded. "You will need to be discreet and available to observe all departments. For now, Bud and I will be your primary contacts."

The meeting started exactly on time and Mildred liked that. It was a casual get together — more of a reception. Bud spoke briefly, and then they moved on to 'officer recognition.' Next, they shared the month's stories of the strange and humorous casino life. She liked the thought of being part of this department, even though she shouldn't be recognizable.

Expecting a training video, she was surprised with *Paul Blart Mall Cop*. She watched the old movie with a room of security officers and found the humor magnified in the ridiculous film. With the laughter and kind welcome, she felt as if she were part of a community, and her worries dissipated. This may not be right, but it is all right for now.

The next day, she went downtown and met with Bud and Police Chief Nelson. They informed her that she would be both a casino and a city enforcement officer. Her pay would be divided between the two entities with an automatic deposit. The money and freedom were more than she expected. Enthused, she worked with the two men to formulate a plan. Chief Nelson offered several weapons, and after pondering the suggestions, Mildred spoke up. "I don't want anything that a nervous old lady wouldn't carry. I will take the pepper spray, a Taser, and absolutely no on the gun."

The men agreed. Bud pulled out a satchel. "Here is an earpiece for direct security contact. This button here is a direct channel to the police 911 operator." As Mildred tried it on, Bud continued, "Here is a Player's Club card, and feel free to use it for gaming machines. Gambling is free, and losses and winnings credit back to the card." He also handed her a debit card to use for necessary expenditures as an expense account.

Mildred picked up the cards. "Seems like you two have thought of everything."

Chief Nelson said, "We have thought about this for a while, but we also acknowledge that the position is still in development, and we will depend on you for input."

A tall, dark, and remarkably handsome officer, entered the room. Chief Nelson stood to give introductions. "Mildred, this is Detective Hampton. He will be your police contact. All reporting will be through Bud, Belinda, or Hampton."

Bud interrupted, "…and possibly Arnie Arnison, the night shift supervisor, but no one else at this time."

The Chief continued, "Detective, I would like to introduce you to your operative, Mildred Petrie."

As the two shook hands, it was evident to Mildred that the job had been a little more than an idea until she walked through the door. They repeated that the position was fluid and would develop as needs arrived. She would pay attention to, not only customers, but also employees and vendors. It was clear that the meeting was breaking up when the Chief added, "The last thing we need is a code name. Anyone have any suggestions?"

After a single moment, Mildred spoke up, "I'll be G-ma." The room broke into laughter and universal agreement.

Bud handed her a club pass. "This is good for any of the clubs with cover charges. I think you should start Thursday evening, then into the weekend. That is our busiest time. There are no major events scheduled for this weekend, so it is a good tryout for you. I'll make sure you are provided an up to date event list by email."

She walked with Bud to his car. He opened the trunk and gave her a laptop computer. "It is already set up with a secure email. You know how to use a computer, don't you?"

Mildred answered slyly, "I'm not that old. I have a computer at home. But there had better not be solitaire on this one."

There was no turning back.

– 3 –
Ready Set Go

Freedom to schedule her own hours was a benefit Mildred never imagined after a lifetime of shift work. She decided to stick to eight hours, five days a week for now. After arriving in the parking lot, she could text or message the office and later sign out the same way. Her experience as a meter maid gave her the confidence to stroll, amble, and saunter throughout the hotel and casino with ease. Even in retirement, she had maintained her habit of walking several miles a day, so that part of the job would be easy. That afternoon she had her granddaughter Glory come over to give her a crash course on the computer.

It was in her nature to start right away, but her first day on the job wasn't until Thursday evening, giving her a couple of days. Bud was clear that Thursday was the beginning of the busy weekends. In preparation, she went to the casino on Wednesday afternoon to get a feel for the layout before the weekend action. On Thursday, she started around dinner time. Eight hours would take her to two a.m. when the nightclubs closed. The Ivory Winds was open twenty-four hours, but they assured her it quieted down after two. She parked in the front lot, and on her way in, called the office.

"G-ma on the floor, north door."

Belinda answered, "10-4, I have eyes on you. Lookin' good. I'm leaving shortly, so your contact for this evening is Arnie."

"Does he know I'm undercover? Can he be trusted?"

"No question, he's been here since the casino opened. He even turned down Bud's job a couple of years ago. He takes care of his dad, and nights work best for him."

"I guess with the 24-7 business, you two couldn't handle all of the demands."

"We spend enough hours as is. I'll read Arnie in on you. We will arrange a meet soon and iron out the bugs."

Radio silence took over as Mildred started her first patrol, starting at the gift shop by the main door. Slowly she made her way through the gaming tables, slot machines, bars, hotel lobby, spa waiting rooms and back again. When she tired, she sat at a slot machine, or in one of the lobbies.

In the first week, she recognized customer types and identified regular faces. She knew that a set routine would be problematic. She stopped in one of the bars and found a quiet table at the rear of the room. She observed the frenzy of the day settle into an evening-out atmosphere. The clothing was less casual and the customers younger. She watched as the bar filled with couples and small, chatty groups. The employees slid into a dance of service, smiles and speed. She had brought a notepad, summarized things she saw, and worked up plans.

Back on her feet, she visited eight gift shops. In the last one, she bought a small recorder, using her new credit card. Flipping it on, Mildred made her first recording: "Testing... testing," then she slipped it into her pocket, convinced she had entered the age of technology. Hoping the purchase would simplify record keeping, she went back to the cigarette smell, noise, old music and flashing lights of the floor. For hours, she walked, studied and watched.

Around ten p.m. she noticed the older crowd start to thin. This was a good time for a break. Mildred entered the buffet and had a lovely dinner of baked chicken and steamed vegetables. The dinner hour was well over, and business was slow enough for her to identify the best tables for anonymity and a view. Since she wasn't paying, the drive to load up at the dessert table was hard to control. Mildred settled on a brownie and a piece of coconut cream pie with coffee, then off to the card rooms, sports venue, bathrooms and another spin around the floor.

She made brief notes on the recorder: "Mix up the hours and work split shifts. Order a Bedazzler from the Home Shopping Network, good to jazz up some sweatshirts. Conservative dress could be a red flag early in the evening. Do not drink coffee after nine p.m." Mildred sorely wanted to blend into the crowd. Every step was a learning experience. She called the office extension, and announced, "One a.m. G-ma signing out."

A deep voice immediately answered, "I'm on the floor. Do you need someone to walk you out?"

"Nope, I'm good, but thanks."
"Have a good night, G-ma."

– 4 –
Carry Out

Toward the end of the second week, Mildred had developed a system. She was a ghost around the distinguishable regulars and employees. No one had acknowledged her, which felt like a success. As she settled in for a late lunch at the buffet, she spotted her table in the corner on the upper level. This job supported her interest in people watching and provided access to unlimited dessert. Things couldn't be better. Setting down her chicken potpie and the brownie a la mode, she plunked into the seat. Discreetly, she inched off her shoes and put her feet up on the chair on the opposite side of the table.

At this time in the afternoon, the restaurant area was quiet. Most of the crew was busy in the kitchen getting prepared for the dinner rush, and there were only a few customers scattered about the large seating area. She needed a break more than food, and poked at the potpie as she stared blankly around the nearly empty room. Convinced that her surveillance had been discreet, she turned on the new cell phone. She tried to search for a Bedazzle kit on the Home Shopping Network, but there were too many apps. For a moment, she considered adding a cup of vegetable soup to her meal, and her eyes tracked over to the salad bar. It was more important to keep her shoes off and she gave up on the soup.

Mildred noticed a young man walk up to the serving area and scan the room. Not sure what held her attention, she watched him load a small plate with a variety of macaroni and potato salads. She saw him reach into the tossed salad bowl, look around the room, and drop lettuce on the floor near his foot. He stepped on it, crushing and spreading it around. He looked around again, and Mildred continued to punch buttons on her phone. He mashed the mess forward, making a skid pattern on the floor with his foot, and threw his plate into the air. He quickly lay down in the mess. Mildred triggered the silent security alarm and struggled to force her swollen feet into her shoes.

By the time she made it over, the cashier was at the customer's side. The man moaned and rubbed his shoulder and neck, he looked to Mildred pitifully asking, "Did you see anything?"

"Why, yes, young man, I saw you fall," she answered while glancing at the floor for the offending greenery. She patted his arm, told him not to worry, and began shooting pictures of the scene at the salad bar with her cell phone. He offered a weak "Thank you."

She took several close photos of the lettuce, and noticed it looked like it had been on the floor for a while. The way he stepped on it repeatedly caused it to smear into the tiles. Mildred took a picture of the large salad bowl, showing the original freshness. She was careful to shoot photos of the floor, additional salad bar offerings, and the young man lying in the mess of mayo and assorted bits. She avoided conversation.

Arnie appeared (looking official in his security guard uniform) and with an air of authority took over the situation. He glanced and winked at Mildred, then sent the cashier for a bag of ice. He focused on the young man, offering comfort and medical assistance. Hearing a weak response, Arnie radioed for first aid and then an ambulance. She was not surprised when the man refused emergency medical attention. Only then did the partner materialize. Mildred did not move from her guard post over the mess of macaroni and romaine.

Arnie finally looked to Mildred, and asked, "Excuse me, ma'am, did you witness any of this accident?"

She answered boldly, "Why yes, I saw the whole thing and took photos for him."

The man on the floor asked for copies as he struggled to stand in a schmear of Jell-O. He genuinely slipped, but the cashier steadied him in time. Arnie helped him to a chair and continued to offer full attention. Finally, he turned to Mildred and asked, "I will need your statement. Do you have time?"

With her best elderly voice, Mildred responded, "Glad to help. I'll go back to my table and wait for when you are ready. Sure, don't want my potpie to get cold."

Twenty minutes later, the man limped away leaning heavily on his friend's shoulder. Arnie approached, picked up her phone, closing the Home Shopping page and asked, "Tell me, what I'm looking at?"

"Okay, Dick Tracy, here are the facts. Your injured customer intentionally dropped the lettuce on the floor and faked the fall."

"How do you know that, Mata Hari?"

"Besides watching him inspecting the serving bowls, Sam Spade, I observed him take a handful of lettuce and mash it around before lying down."

"Genius, my dear Watson. How did you notice that?"ck."

In less than two weeks, Grandma Petrie, Undercover Security, earned her check and a coupon for the Friday seafood buffet.

– 5 –
Building a Team

Mildred continued to worry about becoming too familiar with the employees and regulars at the casino. She mixed up her hours, split shifts and often worked into the night to remedy the problem. Two weeks after the "slip-and-fall," it dawned on her to try a disguise. She decided it would be like job sharing with invisible friends, and she would keep all of the money.

There were a variety of clubs and activities. Most offered alcohol, which occasionally exaggerated the behavior of sad losers. There was sporadic evidence of illicit drugs, which she felt should be expected in this atmosphere. Lately, there had been a rash of credit card and prescription drug thefts from elderly customers. Mildred, vigilant as usual, still came up empty day after day. They had not caught anything on camera, and only had the complaints and the dumped wallets and purses. She decided to initiate a sting.

She didn't want to be spotted hanging out with security, so Mildred insisted that she and Bud meet at the McDonald's adjacent to the casino. She'd already unwrapped her fish sandwich, when he sat down with two #10 combos.

"Better be careful, boss. That is a lot of food."

He smiled briefly. "I'm taking one back to Larry. He is covering for Belinda today."

"Those fries should be tasty in an hour or two." Mildred shook her head in disbelief and immediately got down to the business of presenting her proposal.

"Bud, I have an idea for the prescription caper."

"Caper? Really, Mildred? What do you have in mind?"

"First of all, we can't meet so close to the casino. I thought this would work, but I see familiar faces, and I worry about your cholesterol. We don't want to blow my cover."

"Point taken, Mildred."

"Well, tonight is the Tom Jones concert, and you can guess what the audience demographic will be."

"True enough. There is a substantial probability of action. We have already scheduled additional security."

"Good. I would like to request a body camera." Mildred watched his face and saw a thoughtful nod. "Delilah Hopper will go to the concert on my behalf with a walker and a snap purse. I will keep the bag visible, hanging on the walker and then will rock out with Mr. Jones."

"Who the hell is Delilah Hopper? You know we can't have just anyone working. They need an interview and a background check."

"I'm Mrs. Hopper. You will have to wait and see. She is a work in progress. We can't have your undercover agent blowing an excellent opportunity."

Bud stared at her for a moment, processing the possibilities.

"Yes, ma'am, but be sure to let us know who you are before you arrive. This might work. I have a body cam that we are considering in my office. I'll run over and pick it up and give Larry his lunch. The concert starts at eight. Is there anything else you need?"

"Will my pass work, or do I need a ticket? That would be nice, or should I expense it?"

"No. Have a second cup of whatever that is you are drinking, and I'll get the camera and a pass. Text if you think of anything else. How about a T-shirt?" She rolled her eyes and went for the refill.

After the meeting, Mildred went straight to the dollar store for last minute details and then home to nap. Up at six, she strapped on the extra-large push-up bra and filled the semi-vacant cups with water balloons. By seven-ten, the fire-red wig, low cut black blouse and glittery elastic-top pants were in place. She applied all of the makeup she owned, topping it off with a sassy red lip. She secured the body camera into a scarf with a brooch, and read the operating instructions as she waited for her ride. Just as her granddaughter arrived to drive her over, Glory took a photo and sent it to Bud.

An almost instantaneous text came in: **"Incredible, Mrs. Hopper."**

Upon arrival, Glory struggled to get the rental walker out of the back seat. It was tangled with a backpack on the floor. After they had it out and expanded, Glory locked everything in place. Mildred walked around the parking lot a few minutes before they realized that the hand brake was still engaged. Finally, the two of them had it rolling and moving smoothly. Mildred never dreamed that she might need walker lessons.

On the stroll into the major event main doors, Mildred went deep into her Delilah persona. Once inside, she executed her first slow walker-about, looking for whoever didn't seem to fit in. She lingered at the bar and ordered a Cosmopolitan, which she only sipped. As the room filled, she took the opportunity to remove a medicine bottle from her purse. Mildred put the Tic-Tac on her tongue and washed it back with her cocktail. The combination left her breathless. She returned the faux prescription to her purse and hung that on the side rail of her walker. Mildred/Delilah made her way to her seat, and noted that the extra wide aisle had a walker at the end of nearly every row. *I'll bet the fine Mr. Jones is wondering what happened to his fan base over the past forty years.*

The overhead lights flashed just before the opening act, and Delilah settled into a second-row aisle seat in sweet anticipation of the performance. By nine, she was fully enveloped in the joy of her youth and closer to Tom Jones than she ever dreamed. Working undercover has many rewards.

After the show, the room of mature, giddy fans cleared slowly, while Delilah basked in the glow of sharing oxygen with Mr. Jones. Suddenly, she came back to reality, and decided it was time for Mildred to clock into work. No longer the breathless admirer, she watched the crowd leave and did not notice any suspicious action nor people who appeared out of place. Slowly she struggled to her feet and reached for the walker. "What the hell?" Her pocketbook was gone. Alarmed that she had missed the crime, she hoped that one of her errant breasts might have pointed the camera toward the theft.

Mildred registered no reaction and walked back to the bar. The area was still crowded with concertgoers closing their evening with drinks and excited conversation. She ordered a second Cosmopolitan, and as she reached for her bag, she exclaimed, "Oh my heavens, I was robbed!" The bartender pressed the security alarm, and the room buzzed like a swarm of locust as concert-goers began to discover their losses.

Officer Arnie arrived within minutes and ushered the growing group of victims to a room adjacent to the concert hall. The harsh light illuminated chairs filled with tired, overly made-up faces of vivid silver haired women and their ancient dates. Mildred's Delilah character commiserated with her peers. There haven't been so many female baby boomers gathered since the Beatles played the Ed Sullivan Show.

Bud entered, looking very professional, and offered instructions for the paperwork. He told them to cancel credit cards and phones immediately, then started the interviews as one of the ushers handed out incident forms.

Delilah asked, "How long will this take?" Knowing it was a question no one could answer, she winked at Arnie. Everyone in the room settled in, assured this would be a very long night.

About three a.m., Arnie came back in with a large box.

"We found some wallets and purses near the dumpster."

The few victims still waiting identified their personal property, and they tagged it with contact information. There would be notifications to recover property after the police investigation.

Mildred was the last called, and she let Delilah retire for the night. She pointed out her purse, and Bud opened it to see only pepper spray and a pair of lace throwing-panties. Her billfold and medications were gone. He was briefly stunned and lifted out the panties with his pen. He looked at her silently with an arched brow and asked, "For Mr. Jones, I presume."

"He didn't sing Sex Bomb."

Arnie shook his head and tried unsuccessfully to stifle a smile. He chose not to discuss the underwear further, but Mildred knew this might not be the last of it. She turned in the body-cam, and they decided to watch the video tomorrow.

Bud asked Arnie to give Mildred a ride home. She was so tired, she accepted the offer; glad she didn't have to walk. Arnie was unusually quiet, but she could hear him trying to suppress a series of snickers.

"I have a thing for redheads; they remind me of my grandma."

Mildred's exhaustion only allowed her to sneer at him as they passed the misty stand of trees at the entrance to the retirement village. Arnie parked in front of her unit and removed the walker from the backseat. He escorted her to the door and looked over her low-cut dress.

"Quite a night wasn't it, Miss Delilah?"

She unlocked the door and entered the apartment as Arnie turned back to the running vehicle. The last thing he saw from the corner of his eye was a double-E water balloon approaching his head like a missile.

– 6 –
Interrogation

Wearily, Mildred searched for the offending bleep. "Damn, I'll have to learn to work that phone." She groaned, picked up the transgressor, and called Security.

"Good morning, boss. Is that you rattling my cell phone?"

"Oh Mildred, glad you answered. I have been texting you for almost an hour. The police will be here any minute, and they want to talk to you and review the video tapes."

"Bud, have you had any sleep? I left before you, and I've only had four hours."

"None yet, but one day soon. Since you were the only officer in the audience, and the creep got your purse, they want you here. I hate to ask, but can you come in?"

"I'll be there as soon as possible, but don't expect a beauty queen."

"After last night, Mildred, you are beautiful in every form."

"Sweet talker, there better be coffee brewing. See you shortly."

The shower was a necessity to remove the last vestiges of Delilah and to wake up. With no time for serious grooming, she covered her wet hair with one of Dick's old baseball caps and mumbled: "Go Hawks." Within thirty minutes, Mildred was running, maybe more like fast walking, through the parking lot. As she swung open the door to the office, Bud was inside with coffee and donut in hand.

"Perfect Boss, I forget you have eyes everywhere."

He smiled broadly, gave her the cup and cruller and tipped his head toward the conference room.

"Processed flour and sugar, my favorites. No really, they are my favorites. Thank you, this may save lives."

"We don't want anyone to die." He paused and looked at Mildred. "You seem nervous. There is nothing to worry about; they just wanted to debrief you, check the video and see if you have anything to add. You had a different view from the audience, while everyone else was in uniform and patrolling the perimeter."

Bud added, "Belinda is stalling them with coffee and treats fresh from the bakery."

"You should pay her more," Mildred responded as she turned to enter the conference room.

The meeting started cordially with introductions, questions and discussion about what she may have seen, but not registered. The office phone kept Belinda hopping, as she processed more losses. There were over thirty claims by noon. Even with all of the precautions taken, the infiltration was bigger than expected.

Mildred watched the video footage, and they were confused about the continual bouncing. Arnie snorted and gleefully explained the real reason for the camera instability, with a wink at Mildred. Mildred added, "The camera would have been steadier if Engelbert Humperdinck were on stage." There was a lack of a sense of humor in the room (or they weren't old enough to remember) so she said no more. They spotted a light blue blur near the end of the concert video, the first vague clue.

Hours of questions, video and pastries passed before Mildred thumped her head onto the table repeatedly. Detective Hampton took it as a signal to wrap up. The officers collected the video drives, along with the rest of the donuts. Hampton expressed gratitude, patted her on the shoulder and explained, "The plan is to take the recordings to headquarters for enhancement. We'll share any evidence from the recovered personal property. Bud, we will follow up with you for arrangements on notifying the victims on the property recovery."

Brad volunteered to call the other casinos in the state to see if there were any similar problems. Mildred's only instructions were to keep her head down and eyes open. As the men discussed plans, she sat quietly for a moment processing the information. Whoever was pinching the meds and credit cards knew their way around. They appeared expert in dodging cameras.

Mildred's mind came back to the room as Hampton spoke.

"Wednesday, everyone will report on results and proffer their theories, and we will then have a better grasp of what is going on. Let's keep this quiet and no press. We don't want the perpetrators to know we are on to them."

Mildred was sure they were not dealing with an outsider, and there had to be more than one thief involved. She could barely stand after sitting so long, and the blood surged back into her body as she walked to the car, her mind racing with possibilities. It was too early to go home and sleep, so she started on a personal project. In her sleep-addled mind, she envisioned another disguise.

After an hour and forty minutes at the thrift store, she hauled two bulging bags of clothing to the car; then made a quick stop at Rhonda's Wigs and Cuts. Once home, she lined up three fake heads on her dresser. One held the red Delilah wig; the other two would become Oliver Brimstone and Bambi Hunter, the B-team.

– 7 –
Two Days in a Row

A day off. What is that supposed to mean? Mildred pouted as she toasted the last English muffin. *I pulled a short shift yesterday, which should be sufficient. Nothing I can do about it. The directive came down from the top. Well, maybe I'll buy groceries, wash clothes, read the newspaper. After that, who knows, I could run wild.* She hadn't noticed until that moment how she had allowed the job to consume her existence.

Don't they understand living alone is too quiet? While she munched absentmindedly and sipped tea, the realization struck: after thirty-five years with the police, this was the first time she felt like a genuine officer. The training from nearly fifty years ago seemed to be stored in her DNA. She was confident her reflexes were sharpening. No way would she waste any more life in that chair by the window.

When there is only one person who won't stay home, the housework took minutes instead of hours. A week's worth of dishes (four cups and a sandwich plate) took two minutes. One load of laundry and vacuuming – done. It was barely nine a.m., and the weather was perfect – maybe a turn through the neighborhood before the grocery store. Even though she walked every day at work, Mildred admitted there was nothing better than sunlight and fresh air. With so much time at the casino, she decided to increase her vitamin D and calcium in her supplements, Osteoporosis be damned.

Mildred slipped into her daytime pajama pants, T-shirt, and sneakers. In minutes she was out the door. A lovely stroll through the village to keep the legs limber should be enough, and maybe there would be someone else looking for a conversation.

Within twenty minutes, she found herself in the casino parking lot and was a little ashamed that she couldn't handle a day off. Admitting it was a sad statement on how empty she had allowed her life to become, she called her oldest son.

"Richie, I need to go to the store and would love to buy someone lunch."

"Mom, great to hear from you; it's been hours since anyone has seen you. I notice it is ten-thirty, and you want lunch? Hold on, I'll check with the girls and see if anyone is hungry."

Mildred sat on the bus bench in the rear lot and kept her back turned from the camera. If security spotted her, it would magnify her embarrassment.

"Good luck, Mom. Glory hasn't eaten, and she is happy to pull grandma duty – especially since it includes access to the car. It will take her about a half hour."

"You are a good man, with good children. Tell her I'm at the back entrance to the casino on the bus bench."

"The casino! Mom! You know what that place did to Dad. Be careful over there."

"Don't worry; I only gamble with their money."

"Didn't Dad say the same thing? I'll tell Glory to hurry."

She needed to tell Richie about the job, but not today. Mildred settled into the wait and soaked in the day's beauty. She started recording a shopping list, "English Muffins, no – bagels, tea, Lean Cuisine dinners, Oreos, apple turnovers, creamer."

She noticed the morning get underway as the retirement village tourist buses materialized along with cars and trucks. Damn. There will be a line at the breakfast buffet.

After so many years in parking enforcement, she was unconscious of her automatic scan of the acres of vehicles. Her cop sense tingled, drawing her attention back to a nondescript white van parked in the rear near the semi-trucks. Then it struck her that she had seen this vehicle before. It probably belonged to an employee or a serious gambler. She couldn't help but make a note of the '97 Ford van with tinted windows and evidence of a removed placard on the door. Then, only because she had time, she walked over for a quick look-see.

Mildred wrote the Oregon plate information on her hand (along with a note to buy a new tablet) as she turned back toward the bench.

Glory pulled into the parking lot in time to see her grandmother walk to the bench. "What you are up to now, crazy woman?" Glory was Mildred's favorite seventeen-year-old grandchild and the one that shared her face. "Come on, Grandma, hop in. We have places to go, women to feed."

"Glory, do you have paper? I need to make some notes."

"Paper, what the heck is that? Give me that cell phone. Okay, Grandma, see this app right here?"

"So, that's an app? I've heard about them, never knew I had one for sure." Now that she looked, there were several icons on the face of the telephone.

"It's called Notepad. You can put your notes and lists on here."

"Well, that's the nuts. Someday, I would appreciate it if you could teach me about texting."

"No problem, Grandma. Did you want to go to the breakfast buffet here?"

"No, no. Let's go someplace quieter." *And with fewer watching eyes.*

"I'll teach you about apps and texting then. We need to meet with Dad right after lunch."

They went to Jake's for a quiet lunch, and Mildred learned more about her phone than she ever wanted to know. Apparently, she hadn't needed to buy the recorder. They ordered sandwiches and toasted each other with milkshakes.

"Well Grandma, we have to meet Dad. He is already at the animal shelter."

"Animal shelter? That seems harsh. I don't think they will take me."

"Grandma! He worries about you being alone, and you don't call like you used to, so, we are going puppy shopping."

"That sounds fun, but I won't make any promises." Within minutes, they met Richie and Isabella, her favorite ten-year-old granddaughter, at the shelter. The four of them spent over an hour looking before Richie put his foot down.

"This is for Grandma, and a bunny is just not enough protection, Izzy. There will be no hare-raising in this family."

They all laughed and moved back to the puppies. Mildred decided a dog needed too much attention, what with her irregular hours. They ended the visit cuddling kittens when Mildred discovered a huge, white, older cat. Snowball had been brought in when her owner died, and the two females made an immediate calm connection.

Richie went to the store to buy cat accessories, English Muffins, and tea bags. On the way home, the women learned that Snowball was not a traveler. Within a block, there was a spontaneous eruption from the cardboard carrier. After a couple of screeching trips around the car interior, Snowball settled into a continual growl under Mildred's seat.

"Guess I'll need a stronger carrier for Snow, maybe something in steel." They all laughed, more out of relief than humor. The cat was calm, for now.

"I dread getting her into the house." "Dad can do it," Izzy offered.

"My dear girl, you are brilliant. He has no idea what he will be dealing with." Mildred sent her first text to her son:

"Buy cat treats, a leash and band aids."

Once the three of them finally got the cat into the house, only two were bleeding. Glory was the one that had brought out a towel, and they were able to wrap Snow and get her inside. The cat made a cursory inspection and then settled on Mildred's bed for a nap. Richie returned and set up the food and water dishes, and all three generations sat on the couch trying to recover from the thirty minutes of panic. Once the laughing was done, silence took over the room.

"Girls, I need to talk to your dad for a moment."

"Sure, Grandma. I have to use the bathroom anyway."

Glory went to the kitchen and Izzy walked to the bedroom area. Once they heard the bathroom door close, Mildred started. "Richie, I don't want you to worry anymore. I'm not gambling. I've got a job at the casino."

The man bit the inside of his mouth and responded, "Why didn't you tell me before? I can deal with a job."

Mildred answered softly, "Honey, I work in security, and I'm kind of undercover."

He looked at her, rolling his eyes to the back of his head. She continued to explain her position and duties until Izzy returned, and Glory asked about drinks and snacks.

That evening, Mildred settled in for television before bed. Snow came out of hiding and climbed onto her lap where they dozed until ten.

The cat would not acknowledge "Snowball": no head turn and no ear flick. She even seemed annoyed by it. The name seemed trivial for this confident creature, so the search for her real cat name began.

Mildred decided to let Snowball choose. "Isn't that right, Witchie-poo?" Nope.

All Mildred needed to do was keep the dish full, the water fresh and dip the litter box, because "Mrs. Brown is a very good girl." No. "Louise?" Sorry would greet her no matter what time she returned. "Lucy, I'm home. No." By the end of the week, "Petunia? Nope" had taken to sleeping at the foot of Mildred's bed. They silently agreed to the arrangement, and "Buttercup, No way" would save her cat bed for the extra daily naps. The cat dismissed all girly and flowery names with growls.

– 8 –
Pondering

The casino was quiet, and Mildred was bored. Even when the slots were slower, there was still a constant cacophony and activity. Tonight, she paid attention to the serious gamblers in the sports and card rooms. Seated just outside of the glass partitions, she caught a glimpse of Dick's reflection. She couldn't help but imagine the hours he must have spent behind the glass battling his games of choice. Dick loved sports, and never turned his back on a poker hand, so it could be any or all of these individual rooms. There was another card room upstairs for private, high-limit games. Her instinct continued to badger her. The money exchanging hands had to be a different issue with the high rollers than with the more public floor games. She had to do something. It was important to stay busy to stop the memories and obsessive speculation.

Mildred turned her back and called Richie. "Hey, Baby Boy, it's Chinese night at the buffet, and I know you love it."

"Mom, that sounds great. Lindsey made clam chowder and everyone is excited except me. How soon do you want to meet? I'm starving and can leave now."

"Now works. See you at the front entrance."

Mildred only had to wait at the lobby area a few minutes until her son arrived. They both enjoyed the rare time together as they walked through the lights and gaming area. She had always been close to Richie, and the noise of the casino faded as they walked with his arm around her shoulders. They settled in for multiple small dishes of food and shared good memories. Toward the fortune cookie and more tea, the conversation became serious.

"Mom, I'm worried about you being at this place. It was Dad's downfall, and all of the gambling scares me. I'm happy you enjoy your work, yet I can't help but worry. This place was a big part of Dad's suicide, and it is just too close."

"Honey, don't fret. I feel like the casino owes me, and I get no thrill from the games; it's like spending on nothing. The more

I watch, the less I'm tempted." She went on to explain the player's card, so she had nothing to lose and even less to gain.

Her son said he was relieved, but Mildred could still see the sadness in his eyes.

Mildred let him process for a moment and continued, "I have been thinking of Daddy lately, and I have questions."

Richie paused. "Not that he ever confided in me. He was closer to David, but you know I'll tell you anything."

"Was he into cards, roulette, slots or sports betting?"

"I knew he came over here, but I never put any thought into it until he died. He was always quiet, but I remember his enthusiasm for any sport on TV. He took David and me to local games, and I remember when he drove all night for the Super Bowl. It is my fondest memory of him; I never saw him so happy.

"You would have loved it – he was singing in the car and talking on and on about stats and the time Grandpa took him to the Colts and the New York Giants that was declared the greatest football game in history. He promised to take us to the Football Hall of Fame and then the Baseball Hall of Fame. The whole trip wasn't the Dad we knew.

"David and I were so happy that weekend. He gave me a Bronko Nagurski Football Immortal Card for my birthday that year, and I still have it. We were going to go to this big event to meet the stars of the '50s and '60s. I don't remember why, but we didn't get to."

Mildred responded, "I think you may be right, he was always a huge fan. I had thought it may have been horse betting. You weren't born yet when he took me to the Belmont Stakes, and he was so animated – not the serious, dependable guy I fell for."

"I remember him watching the Kentucky Derby and his yelling at the horses and cussing at the jockeys." Richie shook his head drenched in wistfulness.

"I get glimpses of his reflection off those glass enclosures by the gaming rooms."

"That's kind of creepy, Mom."

"Yeah, I guess it is. At first, I thought it was missing him, but then there are unanswered questions that nag at me."

"I know you had to cash in things to pay his debts. What was he thinking?"

"Apparently, nothing. I figured we bought the condominium to simplify our retirement, and then I learned it was so he could have the money from the house. There were a couple of collectors that showed up the day before the funeral." She did a hand gesture suggesting quotation marks. "But you know they don't leave business cards when they take the last nickel of your life. I was so angry with him when he died. I was distracted by the ugly details when I met those goons."

"Are you still mad? Ever see them around here?"

"No, I'm getting over it. The job keeps me moving, and it helps me heal. I think something was going on with loan sharks, and I believe the debt may have been what sent Daddy around the bend. I've wondered why I don't spend much time around the high rollers. Security covers them, but I think I should too."

"I know I can't persuade you to stop, but this could be dangerous. What are you considering, Mom? Please, don't be foolish."

Mildred smiled as a plan began to materialize. "Who do you think would know the lenders of choice?"

"I understand they find you." Clearly Richie was aggravated.

Mildred answered, "That probably isn't going to happen with my gambling patterns."

"Let it go. Mom, you paid them, and now it's over." Richie hoped this ended the conversation, but also knew it never did any good to argue with his mother.

Richie continued, "Change of subject. Lindsey wants to know if you are coming over on Sunday. She is cooking all the customary Father's Day favorites."

"Sounds good, I'll be there." They cleared the dishes to the trays and stood to leave, "I could use a ride home, how about it?" She signed out early, and they talked of Richie's daughters, his brother and the upcoming Father's Day on the way home. They both silently pondered Daddy's death. The final decision was Mildred would bring her usual covered dish for Sunday dinner and be there by three.

The next morning, Mildred's day off started on the computer; then she donned Delilah Hopper. She walked into the community center.

"My name is Delilah, and I have a gambling problem."

The room answered in unison, "Hi, Delilah."

– 9 –
Raving

Mildred had settled into a routine, when the unexpected diversity of her work became unmistakable. She tapped her microphone transmitter, "We've got a puker in front of the northwest men's toilet."

"Sending First Aid and housekeeping."

"Hurry, he's going down." Mildred sat at the entrance of the men's room, held the young man's hand, and tried to comfort him while averting her attention from the rainbow spew. She noticed his glazed eyes when he suddenly went into a seizure. Obviously, this was more than a bad clam. She fought back her gags from the aromatic vomit that covered man, floor, and her new pants. A quick scan of the area revealed a woman in a uniform pushing a housekeeping cart running in her direction. Immediately, the woman took over and waved, instructing Mildred to set up the wet floor signs. The housekeeper worked with confidence only experience could provide. She attended the man; cleared his airway, and with a gasp he started to breathe evenly. Arnie appeared with the first aid kit and gave it to the woman. Mildred was puzzled when Arnie said, "Great, Qaseema, you can handle this. I'll call 911."

Mildred watched as the man started to regain a healthy color and Qaseema softly sang, which calmed him as she cleaned his face and examined him further.

The EMTs arrived, and the housekeeper stepped away and scooped the vomit into a rubber glove, closed it with a clip and turned it over to the ambulance crew. Once they rolled the man out, Mildred watched as the woman returned to her employment persona, taking up the mop to clean the floor. Mindful of her need to slip back into anonymity, Mildred couldn't resist as she turned and asked, "How did you know what to do? You were amazing."

Qaseema didn't stop mopping. "In my home country, I am doctor."

"Why aren't you a doctor here?"

"I can't practice in the United States of America."

"That is a shame. You're good." Then Mildred's investigative nature kicked in. "Do you think those were vitamins or candy he choked up? It was so colorful; I couldn't look closely without retching."

"It was Ecstasy or another party drug. The amount was great, probably smuggling them into tonight's show."

Mildred pondered, "Was that a plastic bag you pulled from his throat?" Qaseema nodded, but didn't answer as she mopped.

"Do you always work nights?"

"Yes, I attend medical school in mornings." Drawn to this woman, Mildred wanted to know more.

"I will wash my pants and check out the concert. When do you take a break?"

"I lunch at midnight."

"Makes sense, not as busy then. I'll come to the lunchroom; I'd like to talk more." They walked separate directions, each with a slight smile.

An hour later, Mildred sat down with the young housekeeper in the employee lunch room.

"Dr. Qaseema, why didn't you warn me about DJs? I knew it was more of a show than playing records, but I'm feeling molested by an indescribable mixture of sound and youthful energy. I almost danced."

Qaseema covered her mouth and stifled a laugh.

"Arnie say you work here, but I'm not to tell anyone."

They settled into a quiet conversation; the two outsiders built an immediate alliance: Q, and Double-Oh-Seventy-One.

Fill the Night

Within a half hour, Mildred was back to work. She couldn't stop the ongoing anxiety about the drug culture and how it had changed, and yet remained the same. She realized that this job was so much more complicated than anticipated. Over the weeks, she began to expect petty crime, shoplifting, cheats, drunks, maybe an occasional prostitute. The thoughts of the brilliant candy-colored party drugs in a room full of virtual children saddened her. The thought of the new drug trends, and how they only added more ways to die. She meandered through the gaming floor, gift shops, and finally back to the show stage.

She stifled the smile when the door security chose to overlook her, which made it easy to walk in. The concert-goers tried to ignore her, but a few reactions made it clear she was outside of her element. Movement was impossible, with hundreds of young people dancing wherever they stood. The realization of how much dancing had changed since the last time Mildred was in a club decades ago, tickled her. It was much more demonstrative, and some of the kids appeared lost in the music. All the old boogie rules were off, and the thought raced through her mind about breaking a hip in a rhythmic collision. The restrictive crowd kept her patrol to the periphery in the flashing light show. With her gray head kept down, and her eyes always searching, the modern dance scene buffeted her. Unsure of who or what she was looking for, she kept moving.

Not the kind of music she preferred, but it was hypnotic. Her ears searched for a lyric, but it seemed lost in the driving beat. The energy of the audience controlled the auditorium. *Note to self, buy earplugs*. The music slowly quieted, and the DJ started to yell over the speaker. Mildred couldn't translate, but the crowd settled down, and when he left the stage, she had to assume it was ending. She leaned against the wall adjacent to the entrance and continued the survey.

She took note of blank, sweaty faces, and saw some who were agitated, and others disassociated. Clearly, most of the reactions were the results of the energy in the room, but it was evident in some cases there was something more. She made an additional mental note about a variety of possible enhancements that may be involved. She moved purposely to the chaos of the women's restroom, and it went silent as she entered. All eyes were on her, so Mildred turned and left with a sensation of being hundreds of years old. She returned to the periphery with the awareness of what she didn't know. Her ongoing concern for the young man earlier in the evening pushed her on, but she was now convinced that he'd intended to distribute.

Home after three a.m., Mildred cranked up the laptop and started a search. She made a list of over 250 names for club drugs, and she began to identify some of the references she had heard. There were multiple names for the same drugs; many were nonsensical. A lack of sleep complicated the inquiry. It had been twelve hours since her brief nap. Within an hour, she shut down the computer and went to bed, but her mind reeled with possibilities and an irritating, unnamed sensation. The rest of the night, and into morning, her dreams were haunted with mad scientists and a unicorn pharmacist trying to take over the planet by controlling the youth with rainbows.

Her hope for a decent rest dashed, Mildred was up after a couple of hours and called Detective Hampton. He could meet her in an hour at the café in the hotel. Mildred took a hot shower and dressed quickly. She arrived with a minute or two to spare and called in, "G-ma on the floor."

The boss responded, "Didn't expect you until later."

"I'm meeting Detective Hampton at the Serengeti Café. He is going to give me a brief schooling on the modern drug scene."

"What time? I'd like to come down for that."

"In a couple of minutes."

"Okay, I'll buy lunch."

"Thanks, boss. Breakfast would be better; I'll get a table."

Mildred arrived at the café and was able to secure the small private room in the back. Keenly aware of possible witnesses and her need for anonymity, she sat with her back to the main dining room. Within seconds Bud was there with the detective in tow.

Bud stopped at the door and waved over a server, and she heard him ordered three of the lunch specials. Hampton closed the door before they joined her. All were concerned about the importance of this meeting.

"Sorry, G-ma, but too late for breakfast." The three shared the usual polite greetings, and Bud asked for a quick rundown on the night before.

She nodded and started with the medical emergency and the fast action of Qaseema, crediting her with saving the young man's life. "When they took him away by ambulance, he was breathing regularly and was pale, but no longer blue. I have high hopes for his recovery. Qaseema told me the vomit looked like Ecstasy, and I decided to check out the Double Dog Spin Doctor show to see if drugs were passing around."

Bud found it humorous that Mildred went to the rave. "Really, you went in? Hope they didn't hurt you. Did they notice?"

"I haven't had so many second glances since I caught my skirt in a gun belt in 1986." Both men were silenced by the mental image. Luckily, lunch arrived, breaking the uncomfortable silence.

While they ate, Mildred continued and unfolded the list of club drugs. "My police experience had to do with overdue parking and non-moving violations. After last night, I need some serious education."

"When I went into the event, I wasn't sure what I was looking for. Due to the plastic bag, and something Qaseema said, I was sure the young man was on the distribution side."

As she talked, Hampton took a pen from his suit pocket and circled some of the names on her list. "I'll have Narcotics work with you. Do you know what hospital he went too?"

Bud lifted his hand radio. "Belinda, please check on the hospital the EMTs took the guy to last night."

Hampton also called the station and flagged Narcotics about the situation. Using the list Mildred had printed, he started to cross out some names, circle others and make notes. "The drug names are always changing, but many of these are only different names for the same thing. Some of the names are already outdated. I swear the terms are designed to convince kids they are harmless, but we see some severe side effects. Bud, do you have the Naloxone injection? It is for opiate overdoses, and it is effective."

Bud started his list on a small notepad. "I'll double check the first aid kits and arrange for department training." His phone beeped with a text, and he turned to Hampton. "He was taken to St. Mary's at 11:12 last night. Can Narcotics help us too?"

Hampton forwarded the information and arranged for a training session.

Mildred piped in, "Be sure you include Qaseema from housekeeping; she is a doctor."

"I heard something about that, but I don't know her. How do I spell her name?"

"You'll have to sound it out. Qaseema is someone you need to know. Her last name is Shadid and she works nights and weekends. She saved that kid's life."

They silenced as a server came in to check on them and began to remove plates and refill the empty coffee mugs.

Once the server stepped away, Mildred continued her report. They discussed her ongoing problem of recognition. Her need for obscurity was critical and grew every time she walked in the door. Together they decided she needed a direct contact with Narcotics, and maybe someone not so far outside the Disc Jockey and rave age bracket. They would meet again before the next monthly event, or more often if there wasn't a convention or larger program. A special early show scheduled for teens (in two weeks) was an added stressor.

They broke the meeting with immediate assignments: number one: they will not get together on site again. Number two: Hampton would call Mildred with a connection from Narcotics for training. Number three: They would plan for the upcoming events once connected., and number four: Bud was to update the first aid, schedule a training session, and meet with Qaseema. They went in three separate directions, focused on their assignments.

Since her first shift, Mildred realized the need to stay on top of the schedule. It was evident that shows and special events each drew a different clientele. With the addition of entertainment in the nightclubs, and live music in some of the bars, she had to map out a different plan every day. Bud was emailing monthly event calendars and hotel updates, but she took time to pick up the guest brochures at the customer service desk.

Feeling overwhelmed, it was time to go home and nap until evening. Just before she lay down, she called Richie. "Do you mind if I bring a guest to dinner on Sunday?"

He teased, "Heck no, Mom. Is it a gentleman?"

"No, silly boy. It is a new friend who doesn't have family here, and it would be nice to include her."

Fathers' Day

The days passed quickly, and it was already Father's Day. Dinner at Richie's was to start around three, and Mildred had opened the drapes to watch for her friend. She knew Qaseema was nervous about meeting the family. Mildred saw Q pull into the parking lot, and she stepped outside to wave. There was no delay, as Mildred loaded her dinner offerings into the back seat. These items were traditional, ever since the first holidays when Dick and Mildred didn't have the money for the usual holiday feasts.

Over the years, every holiday was wrapped in warm memories as Mildred stowed the crystal egg dish the boys had given over twenty years ago. Q brought homemade hummus with a basket of fresh pita bread. The two women shared talk of food preparation and memories of family and celebration until they arrived at the cemetery. Leaving the car in the lot, they walked to Dick's crypt. Mildred could see that her son had been there earlier. Fresh flowers filled the holder attached to the wall, and there were sticky notes left by each of her granddaughters. Mildred took just a moment and meditated with a bowed head. She then looked to the blue sky with a blessing to her husband. Q placed her hand on Mildred's shoulder as they walked back to the car, and they left for Richie's home.

Clearly, Q was nervous as they entered the warm, busy home. Mildred was pleased the family all came to greet them at the door. The guest captivated the middle granddaughter, Amelia, and she followed Q, staying as close as she could. As the day moved on, Amelia was the perfect emissary: she was shy, usually quiet, and intelligent. Before long, they sat whispering with stories about their fathers.

Glory finished her part of the preparations and joined them, choosing to sit on the other side of Q. The team in the kitchen listened to the conversation, as it expanded to include countries the girls had only heard of on the news. Before long, Izzy, the youngest, plopped on the floor at Q's feet. Izzy broached the unspoken questions about the headscarf that Q wore, and learned it was a hijab. Before long, all four were in Glory's room, and laughter spread through the house along with the smell of prime rib and roasted sweet potatoes. Mildred tossed the salad, and Richie finished carving the roast onto a large blue platter that had belonged to his grandmother. Lindsey filled the serving dishes, and the three moved the feast to the dining room. It was necessary to call twice for the girls to come to the table.

They came rushing into dinner as a kaleidoscope of color, with scarves tied in a multitude of intricate styles. They passed the food around the table with "oos" and "ahs," and the usually reserved Amelia was animated. "We were learning about women of North Africa and the Middle East."

Izzy added, "My name in Arabic is Lizabila. Did you know that people in other countries have Father's Day and a bunch of holidays at the same time we do? Some of them are just the same." A lively discussion of other cultures and differences in holiday traditions filled the dining room.

This dinner became one of those perfect days everyone would remember differently. Richie would look back with pride and describe this as his favorite Father's Day. The table was full of life, and he saw each daughter uniquely, brighter and more mature than before. For the first time since the funeral, the memory of the loss of his father did not darken the holiday. Mildred smiled, looking at the family she had made with Dick. No one had ever seen Amelia so outgoing, her razor-sharp intelligence evident, and clearly, she was in love with Q.

Qaseema was her usual reserved self, but the enjoyment danced across her face. She joined in, telling extraordinary stories of the world and many places the girls vowed to visit. This day was the happiest Mildred had been since losing Dick. She no longer felt haunted.

After dinner, the girls cleared the table and loaded the dishwasher, with none of the usual bickering. They were anxious to get back to their visitor. Q volunteered to help, but Lindsey would not have it. She was a guest, and the adults were eager to share time with her too. There was no denying the family was enamored with Mildred's exotic friend.

While Lindsey and Q talked about her job and medical school, Richie called his mother aside. "Mom, I've been thinking about the discussion we had. I was bouncing some ideas around with Lindsey."

He continued trying to keep the conversation private. "She remembered that Dad kept some boxes in our storage."

"Boxes? What are they? Did you check them out?" Mildred fought to keep her voice low.

"No, Mom. I'll wait, and we will go together. I don't want to do this without you."

"Where is the storage? Is it here?"

"It's at the storage facility on Broadway. I doubt if they're open today."

"Today isn't appropriate; I would hate to ruin the mood we have. Do you have any time off next week or so?"

"Yeah, I get Monday and Tuesday off." He promised to pick her up the next day at noon. They turned back to their guest just as the girls invaded the room.

By the time they were ready to leave, Mildred was exhausted with all of the youthful energy and too much food. Wondering where the luxury of a sugar rush had gone, she finished her slice of cherry pie. It was easy to tell that Q was worn down by the pack of excited girls. They said their mutual thanks and finished with goodbyes in five languages.

Once in the car, Q started the engine and turned to Mildred. "I owe you much gratitude for the invitation. I have not had such a pleasant time since I immigrated. If there is anything I can do to repay you, please do not resist. I am filled with love for you and your fine family."

Mildred sat for just a moment, tears of pride welled in her eyes. She decided it was time to ask for help. As they drove back, Mildred gave a brief update on the steps of the party drug issue and the upcoming training. Q confirmed that she was aware, that Mr. Moses had called her in.

Was this the time to expose the investigation into the shady lenders? "As you know, my husband Dick died about two years ago. It isn't common knowledge because it was a suicide."

Q stayed quiet and allowed Mildred to continue. "We lost almost everything due to his gambling debts. I wasn't aware of the situation, but he sold our house and stripped our checking, savings, and his retirement to pay them. The day before the funeral, some huge and menacing men came to me. They threatened to harm my sons and their families. I stripped my retirement and paid the remaining debt. I could have involved the police, but I was stressed and ashamed of what had happened. I knew he gambled, but I had no idea how deep he was in. I'm convinced he was driven to the suicide by the debt and the shame."

When they arrived at Mildred's, the two women sat in the car for a few more minutes. Mildred thought better of inviting Q in, but she needed a nap before she had to go to work. Mildred was slow to bring up the seriousness of the investigations on such a great afternoon. Q was her usual quiet self as Mildred gave a quick overview of her investigation. She had an idea to contact Gamblers Anonymous (GA) to see if there were any possible victims.

Q added nothing, only small affirmations, to indicate understanding. As she pulled open the car door to help unload she answered. "I have no information, but I will continue to pay attention and ask some women I trust. Please use care. Do not place yourself in danger."

Mildred watched her pull away and then went to the files on the kitchen counter.

Turnovers and Plots

She intended to research further, but Mildred wanted to go straight to bed. Her feline roommate would have none of that silliness; it was time to pet and play with the feather and ball. Too early to sleep and too late for a nap, she sat in her chair holding the TV remote with the cat draped across her arm. Lost in thought, they were both startled when the cell phone rang.

"Hello."

An unfamiliar woman's voice answered, "Is this Mildred Petrie?"

Mildred was curious, "Yes, it is, and to whom am I speaking?"

"Melody from Narcotics. We need to set a meet. I hope you can do this now. I'm on assignment and nearby. Hampton briefed me and stressed it is important that we get together ASAP." Within seconds they agreed Melody would come to Mildred's home, the safest place to avoid witnesses.

Mildred put some Pepperidge Farm apple turnovers in the oven and set out coffee cups and small plates. Concerned about coffee this late in the day, she also heated water for tea.

She heard a quick knock at the door. Mildred opened it to a very young woman with a purple Mohawk haircut and immediately appreciated the officer's camouflage. Melody was not much bigger than a wish, but had the confidence of a drill sergeant. With a brief introduction, they settled into the kitchen and got down to business. Melody was part of the narco-undercover team, and she confirmed Mildred's theory.

The room filled with the sweet smell of turnovers and hot coffee. Once out of the oven, the sweet treat relaxed the woman and changed the tension. Mildred, still uncomfortable from dinner, was not hungry and watched as Melody wolfed down two turnovers and eyed the rest. "The head of Narcotics and Detective Hampton went to the hospital to question your puker. They are to call me with anything of interest, and I've heard nothing so far. My department will handle that part of the investigation."

Mildred put another warm dessert on Melody's plate, as the two women studied Mildred's map of the casino. Melody unfolded a detailed schedule, and they worked up crowd profiles. Once they identified the most probable events, they developed a plan. Melody would go to the youth events and handle the floor.

"Melody, I could set up a table for some charity, so I would be able to cover the door and lobby."

"Like a charity or some other appropriate task where you could have a good vantage and not be out of place." Melody seemed satisfied by the idea.

"How about the Salvation Army?"

"No, Mildred, my dear. We need something else. Something they could ignore. We have to remember these are kids."

"How about voter registration? We could get some names and addresses." Mildred pondered the idea.

"That is so cute. So, you think you can get the distributors to register to vote? We need something that is appropriate, but they could ignore."

"Girl Scout Cookies!" Mildred was really digging for an angle.

Melody shook her head, "That would be too busy, and those kids are drugging and dancing. All you could do was sell cookies and not be able to a watch a thing."

They decided to let the angle work itself out, and they mutually agreed that Mildred could work a few of the older events alone with Security as back up. If there were a strong possibility of drugs, they would meet in advance.

Mildred added, "We can't ignore the nostalgic bands from the '60s and '70s. Those were times of heavy drug use."

"That was back in the day. They are all doctors and lawyers now and not serious threats."

Mildred laughed, "Those are the events you would have to work the cookie table, and I'd go inside."

They were in total agreement, and decided to make plans as needed. The women agreed on a series of signals for communication so they would not break either cover. They agreed it was important that the casino employees not know

Melody, and the police would not know Mildred. Everything moved quickly and purposefully when Melody's cell phone rang. She spoke briefly, but mostly listened. Melody disconnected, and put the phone on the counter, "It appears the puker checked out of the hospital on his own last night. They have a name, but need a warrant to dig any further."

The discussion continued as Melody slowly picked at the third turnover. Mildred decided next time she would offer a sandwich. "I think we may find it necessary to bring in a male officer so we can cover all corners of the event venues."

"Wait a minute." Mildred went into her bedroom and brought out the manikin head with the balding hair piece and goatee. "I would like to introduce you to Oliver Brimstone. He works for me sometimes."

The young agent laughed out loud. "I thought my Mohawk haircut was bad; this is outrageous. Hampton didn't fill me in about any cross dressing." They shared some bizarre possible scenarios, and decided there might be a time they might need someone bigger and without osteoporosis. As the meeting wrapped up, Melody gave Mildred her cell numbers and agreed to speak before the teen rave coming up.

Melody blew out of the apartment as she had arrived. The only evidence of her visit was a few crumbs, a hastily drawn blueprint, and a cell phone number. Mildred, completely re-energized, decided it was a good time for the eight o'clock Gamblers Anonymous meeting. She tucked the outline in her underwear drawer and slipped into her Delilah persona, and made a note to buy some more size EE breast balloons. The frequent meetings as her alter ego had used them up times two.

Mildred had spoken only in her first meeting, and she regretted the decision to keep quiet. Tonight, was her fourth session, and she hadn't yet made any friends. She spent the last two meetings listening and building a mental catalog. The leaders were evident. Apparently, they had put in years of recovery. She listened and noted that each story told was uniquely different, yet shared a commonality with varying degrees of destruction: lost marriages, children, homes, and debt from the allure of easy riches. She noted other addictions fed the gambling, and several members attended alcoholic or drug anonymous groups. There was so much to learn, and her previous knowledge of dependency was limited, and shamefully, judgmental.

The last speaker finished and Mildred remained seated, lost in thought in the circle of emptying chairs. She tried to organize her next steps. One: follow up Wednesday with Dr. Q. Two: Approach Arnie, he had been around longer than anyone else, and he works the desperate night shift. Three…

"Earth to Miss Delilah, come in." A friendly voice shattered Mildred's reverie. "A couple of us are going for dessert. Would you like to tag along?"

Mildred's eyes fluttered as she mentally came back to the room. "It is kind of late for me, and I need to go home." She questioned her immediate response. *I need this connection, there are answers here. Why would I say no?* "But don't forget me. Next time for sure."

– 13 –
File Boxes

Richie was early, but Mildred expected that. After all, she had raised him, and there was no denying they were a lot alike. She was ready, dressed in jeans and an old shirt. Not sure what to expect in a storage unit, she was willing to dig. They didn't speak much on the ride over. Finally, Richie started the conversation, "I'm sorry, Mom, that David blames you for Dad's death."

Undoubtedly, this was the last thing Mildred wanted to talk about. The pain of David's accusations still rang in her ears. "Richie, this is how he is dealing with loss. David was close to Daddy, and he feels betrayed. It was unexpected, but in his heart he knows better. He will be back." She brushed her hand over her eyes in an attempt to hide unshed tears. Memories and heartbreak filled the quiet car as they both acknowledged the reason for today's mission. After a moment, Mildred spoke of the Father's Day celebration, the joy of her granddaughters, and the good food. She blathered on about the history of the macaroni and cheese and finally shared the recipe. The instructions (with pasta choices, Velveeta cheese, and sour cream) brought back the happiest recollections of a family.

Richie realized, "Mom, all of Dad's favorites we had on holidays became mine too." Clutching the new happiness, they fought off a shared pain of the suicide. "I wonder if Dad would have liked the hummus." Each member of the small family buried unnamed emotions, and her investigation filled the car as they privately searched for explanations.

Mildred had never noticed this facility before. The area looked like acres of metal Quonset huts from World War Two. Richie punched in an entry code that opened a metal gate and drove to the back of the facility. He parked in front of unit number 927. She noted it was one of the largest storerooms as he shut off the car. Mildred asked, "When you rented this barn, did you think that you might have too much stuff?"

He smiled and looked at his mother with a guilty smirk. Mildred caught herself giggling like when she was a girl. With a shared deep breath, he took the key that was fastened to a giant safety pin from the driver's side ashtray. They walked to the closed door, both depending on the other for strength. Once he unlocked the padlock, he pinned the key to his shirt pocket. The door slid open and locked into place overhead.

The room flooded with a harsh light from a giant bare bulb. He took her hand and they stepped into the refuge of bicycles, old furniture, and lifetimes. He stumbled around searching. After a few minutes, he found four storage boxes that his father had entrusted to him. Mildred sat in the wooden rocking chair that still felt familiar to her backside. Her body recalled how she had lulled the man standing in front of her to sleep in this same seat. This was her mother-in-law's chair, and Mildred wished she knew where Nana had obtained this cherished heirloom. Richie placed the first box on top of the hope chest Lindsey had received on her sixteenth birthday. The room filled with ghosts who whispered to Mildred, *everything is as it should be, life carries on as it always has.*

Richie sat on the floor next to his mother and opened the second box. The closeness gave Mildred the courage to remove the lid. Once in, the first thing she noticed was a small, worn gift box full of Dick's badges and commendations from the force. It was approaching three years since his death, and she hadn't once wondered about the medals and badges. She thought of her own awards in the bottom drawer of the jewelry box at home and assumed his was in the nightstand next to his side of the bed. She often dusted it, but never moved any of his things, or even opened the drawers. They had always honored each other's privacy, and to this day, it still seemed like an invasion. As she dug further, there were bundles of newspaper articles about Dick and many of the cases he worked. There was a brittle two-by-four-inch piece of newsprint, so delicate, she feared touching it. Holding it by a fragile corner, she was surprised to learn that Dick Petrie came in second in the statewide spelling bee when he was in junior high school. She went through each clipping and slowly let the realizations and recollections flow over her. Over an hour later, she discovered the yellowed engagement announcement fastened to the wedding photo from the Daily News. Taped on a piece of cardboard, even the tape had yellowed with time. "Wow, Richie, look at this. See how young we were?" While he read the article, Mildred decided one day soon she would put everything in albums for the boys and their kids. It was important they remember his life as part of their own history.

Her trip into melancholy was halted by a loud hoot from Richie, "Mom, look at this!" He had opened a box of old photos. He held up a black and white picture of his dad. He couldn't have been older than a few months. Mildred put the news clippings aside and joined her son on the floor. They got lost in the archives of Dad's childhood. Mildred was able to identify his sister and some of his brothers. There were other group pictures, and she didn't know everyone, but she did recognize his parents. Richie found one of an old woman with a newborn baby.

"Honey, that is you, wrapped in Grandma Petrie's arms on the day you were born. She brought us a new Brownie camera as a baby gift. The first photo taken with it is in your hand."

Richie laughed aloud. "I didn't know we had met. I was very rude and self-involved at that age. I remember the camera; you would think I could remember her." He found the small plastic camera in the box and gave out a childish squeal. Lost in treasures, she shared story after story that Dick had shared with her over the years. His parents died not long after Richie was born, and they never were able to see David. Dick was the youngest and didn't stay in contact with his siblings. "Remember his sister, Susan, who came to the funeral?" Mildred made a mental note to get in touch and share the childhood snapshots.

"Mom, do you think this camera still works?"

"I'm sure it does; they were very simple. You keep it, and good luck finding film."

"Film, what's that?" They both shared another joke. They hadn't noticed it had grown dark outside and suddenly realized they had only searched the first two boxes. Lindsey texted that dinner was almost ready. They had found no clues, but they agreed to come back next week and continue the search. On the way home, he pulled through a fast food restaurant for drinks.

Both were severely parched from all of the dust and conversation. Richie spoke as they waited in line.

"Thank you, Mom. I didn't realize until this afternoon that my girls are growing up in a digital era; they will never have the joy of finding a box of photos. They can only look forward to a picture disc, and they will miss days like this."

"I have to agree with you. They would also need a computer that accepts whatever delivery system was in use at the time the pictures were taken."

"Can you imagine your whole childhood saved on a floppy disc? The way everything changes, it's not only possible, but also probable. I'm going to fix this and have everything printed. My girls deserve it."

"Maybe I could get them to help me put Daddy's and my photos in albums, and we can label them the best way possible."

"That is great." For the third time that day his eyes misted. "I would like to take the badges and commendations to have them framed if that is okay with you."

"I'll look after that, my brilliant son. I will divide them between you and David."

"Mom, I know you have some too. Please include them."

"This is going to be great. You know, I had no idea your dad had this stuff. I have a box of our photos and clippings, and I naturally assumed it was everything. Somehow, he surprised me from the grave." Nice one, Dick. She had forgotten his sentimentality.

Richie said, "Yeah, it felt like he was there with us." Mildred nodded in agreement as the cashier handed a large Sprite and unsweetened tea through the car window.

Once home, Mildred showered and microwaved a frozen dinner. She settled into her chair for the evening. Only then did she consider that they found nothing about Dick's gambling. The thought had slipped away for the afternoon, and the discoveries warmed her. Opening the drawer, she pulled out the notepad from the end table next to her chair. She started another list. Number one: buy photo albums. Number two: check out framing store. Number three: get Dick's Aunt Susan's address from Lindsey. I hope she still has the contact information from the funeral home. It would be good to make contact with Daddy's family, and Susan would know more of the people and help label the old images. Number four: buy one of those file saving things for scanned photos for Susan. Surely, she can share with the brothers. Number five: get uncles' addresses for the boys.

The same evening, Richie also took steps. He checked online and located a photo service, and then he submitted forty dollars' worth of files from the family computer. He also ordered three round floral hatboxes for his daughters' memories.

Mildred went to bed unaware that this was the first time in over a year she looked forward to a future and not just surviving day to day.

– 14 –
Different Program

Most of the week was quiet: no drunks or confrontations, not even a shoplifter. The first walk-through, Mildred plotted out her pattern of surveillance for the night. The main stage had the Glen Miller Band, which guaranteed an entirely different crowd and music. She remembered Glen Miller dying in World War Two, and her mind imagined a ghostly venue. Even though this was the same stage used for the DJ shows, the room had transformed to a different century. There were circular tables for four, covered with white linen tablecloths. A centerpiece with flowers and candles added a romantic glow. Directly in the center front of the room, the dance floor gleamed. The bandstand was already set up for the musicians, reminiscent of the 1940s. Fortunately, the show started hours earlier than the Double Dog events, another benefit of an older crowd.

Mildred made her rounds, and then settled at the Cleopatra nickel slot and inserted her player card. She played slowly with minimum bets. This machine offered the best vantage point to the entrance of the main stage, and with a turn of her head, she could see the central gaming floor. The room filled with a better-dressed crowd than usual. The rows of slots were busy, and she watched the machine migration. A few gamers sat at a single slot for hours; most roamed anxiously looking for the winner to draw them in. There was an almost endless flow with the constant noise of bells, chimes, mindless tunes, whistles and the occasional shout of success. Many winners made no sound at all as if they were afraid a celebration would cause the payout to disappear.

Eventually, the recorded sound of *In the Mood* drifted through the open door. She relished the smooth sounds of the 1940s and looked forward to the show.

It was crowded, and Mildred blended in with no effort. She stayed in the back with a virgin Mai Tai. Like in a time machine, the couples danced arm in arm. A flow of romance filled the room, and she watched guests mouthing the words along with the blonde band singer. There were no drunks, no drugs, only the memories of a bygone era. When the clock approached eleven p.m., the show was over and the crowd disbursed. Mildred slipped off to the employee lunchroom. It must have been due to the slow night that allowed so many employees to take a cherished break, and they filled the long lunch table with chatter. There were too many witnesses, and a meet up would be apparent. She would catch up with Q after the midnight lunch break. Mildred nodded a brief acknowledgment to her friend and continued with her duties.

Skewered chicken from the snack bar with an herbal tea would serve as her dinner while she walked toward the hotel. The gift shops had closed earlier, and the hotel lobby appeared abandoned. Even the card rooms had started to thin out. Only the die-hard gamblers hung on. The security line was unusually quiet, with only minimum communication. It was after one a.m. when she looked for a seat to watch the last of the concert-goers straggle toward homes.

She heard an unfamiliar voice on the earphone, followed by Arnie's clipped confirmation, which was a comfort. There were no notices of any thefts this evening, even though the crowd would have been prime.

Suddenly she was shocked to hear her name coming from the cashier area of the Timbuktu restaurant. "Mildred, Mildred Petrie. Is that you?"

Aw no, I'm busted. She turned towards the voice. It was Judge McCaffie and a young, very beautiful woman.

"You winning anything? I haven't seen you in a dog's age. How have you been, Officer Petrie?" He acted thrilled to see her.

Mildred smiled and tried not to leap to any conclusion. "I'm doing fine, not much new, and you?"

"I'd like you to meet my wife, Brittany." He turned to the young woman and explained how he knew Mildred.

Mildred fought back a strong desire to ask about the wife she had known for twenty-plus years, but decided to stifle that urge, as she extended a hand, "Nice to meet you, Brittany. Are you here for the Glen Miller show?"

Brittany didn't answer and rolled her eyes as she looked away. Judge McCaffie paid no attention and continued the conversation. "No, Brit isn't into the old music like I am. We are here for dinner and a little dice; she likes the Timbuktu; the curtained private tables make her feel like royalty. Are you here with someone?"

"On my own, I live nearby, and now that Dick is gone, it is nice to come over to soak up the energy and dining choices."

"I do understand. We enjoy the nightclubs, and I've always had a weakness for the tables." He chuckled and winked at Mildred, which told her more than he expected. "Are you still working? I heard you were working here."

Mildred had to change the conversation and quick, "No, I did work part-time at a hair salon for a while, but I quit when they moved downtown. Not up for an hour commute three days a week for minimum wage."

"Great thing about being a judge, besides the money, I don't have to hang up the robes until I choose to. Or die."

"Consider retirement. You could travel and join the mall walking club, all kinds of useless activities."

Luckily, the conversation drifted away, so Mildred excused herself and went back to her glass of tea and watched the old man and his trophy exit toward the roulette and crap tables. She couldn't help but feel a bit of sadness for both of them.

She turned toward the Day Spa area. She was able to locate Q, finishing buffing the dressing room floors. Her new friend thanked her again for the dinner, but it was a quick conversation, "I'm thinking of inviting Arnie Arnison to join our investigation, what do you say?"

With no time to ponder, Q answered, "Unquestionably. I have worked with him for over a year, and he is trustworthy."

"That is what I thought too." They both continued with their work. Mildred detected a new security routine and a couple of black suits she didn't recognize. There was only one call out with the code for drunk and minor dispute, but nothing that involved Mildred. Good time to leave, so she sent a text to security. "**G-ma out.**"

The office responded quickly, **"C U on camera 3. need a ride?"**

Slowly she typed her response, **"Yes - slow night."**

As Mildred waited for his answer, she heard Arnie's voice behind her "Must be no moon. The crowd was well-behaved for a weekend. My van is by the south entrance."

Mildred had driven, but this opportunity to talk to him privately was too good to pass up. She put a speech together as they walked. She was confident he was the right person. The ride was worth the walk back to pick up her car tomorrow. They started about the new hires, moved quickly to the drug issues, and she offered her dead-end on finding the supplier. Arnie's years as the night supervisor provided him with more insight to the unsavory aspects of the casino. She moved the conversation quickly on the short ride. They ended up parked in front of her home still talking. They bounced ideas and concerns about drugs, and then she moved him to the dirty loans. She was surprised Arnie admitted he knew her husband, but hadn't put them together. "I'm so sorry, he was a good man. I considered him a friend and one of the regulars. I'd heard he passed, but I didn't know any details."

Mildred explained the blue wall of silence and how the police protect their own. The information about his suicide was quashed. She shared an abbreviated description of the debt and the collection crew that appeared the day before the funeral.

Mildred started to get out of the car when Arnie suggested that they work together. He proposed they could come up with some answers. Mildred had been uncertain how she could open this discussion. This was a turn of events that was better than expected. He waited as she unlocked the front door and turned on a light. Just as she closed the door to the silent home, Arnie noticed a giant white mass run to Mildred and weave between her feet. He hoped it was expected.

– 15 –
Expanded Patrol

The next day she met with Bud at Mickey D's. He brought her up to date on the thefts over the weekend. "Security found discarded bags and wallets in two of the men's restrooms."

Mildred responded "That should narrow the suspects by half."

"In the review of the video, we were unable to identify any obvious activity," Bud added. The evasive nature of the robberies caused her to reconsider employee involvement.

Mildred nodded, "I was thinking along the same lines, whoever seems to know a lot about the security systems." Together they decided she would mix up her hours and appearance. They worked out some simple text abbreviations she could send to Bud, day or night.

Mildred resolved to go deeper undercover using one of the new personas. A quick trip to the beauty shop, and Mildred had the last of the detail with a thin mustache and theatrical glue. *It's time for Oliver to visit the casino.* The cat (Prima donna – nope) watched with the usual feline disinterest and a bit of judgment. Mildred discussed her issues with Carmen, who merely growled at the name. Mildred slipped on a pair of old suit pants, but they seemed a little tight in the butt. She took them off, and tossed them towards her donation box where they fell to the floor. The cat walked over and laid down on them. Next it was jeans, "Well, Miss Kitty, what you think?" The cat turned her head and snorted. Mildred had to agree blue jeans seemed to be wrong with the checkered sports coat. Standing there and pondering, she pulled out a pair of Dick's cargo shorts from the '90s. After a quick zip, she nudged the cat, "What do you think of this? Do they work?" With no discernable answer, and no other choices, Mildred exited the walk-in closet to a look of disgust from Princess Margaret (no way). She kicked off her slippers preparing for the proper shoes and went directly to the kitchen. Too tired to think of any new cat names, Mildred noticed a note on the kitchen table.

Dred, Where are you? Supposed to meet dinner, and you aren't answering your cell. Your neighbor let us in to check on you. When did you get a cat? Fed and watered the beast. She isn't very friendly, is she? Call me. Sissy.

Mildred called her sister, but there was no answer. She left a short message with an apology and suggested rescheduling. With a cup of coffee, she returned to the bedroom and the three wig heads and continued. No matter how long she talked, none of the manikins helped.

Slowly, she finished the preparation for the early evening shift. Thoughts of the meeting with Bud played through her mind. Clearly the older crowd was the target, and the crimes were more intense with concerts and events. Mildred made a mental note to cover the times for the mature crowd. She was confident that Oliver Brimstone had better access to the men's restrooms, where much of the personal property was dumped. She tied down her breasts, much easier than she liked to admit, and wrapped up her hair in a leg from an old pair of panty hose. She smiled into the mirror impressed by the balding gray hairpiece, and especially with the wispy mustache and goatee. Mildred sent a photo text to Ruby at the salon: "**Good work, Ruby, old gal**."

There wasn't an answer, so Mildred finished the last details, and it was time to try out Mr. Brimstone in public. She stared at her reflection at the full length mirror on the back of the closet door. Cargo shorts that reached below the knee, a Tommy Bahamas shirt, black socks, size nine Nikes stuffed with cotton balls, and she was set. She slipped on the sports coat and picked up her bamboo cane. She had to admit the makeover was startling. Mildred didn't recognize herself. For a fleeting moment, she mourned the loss of her husband and remembered how he always dressed up to go out. Turning towards the door, the phone beeped with a message from Ruby. "**OMG, you handsome dog!**"

Mildred strapped on the fanny-pack, and Oliver was off to his first assignment. Security had no clue about the new character, and she gave them no warning. Initially, she was nervous, but once inside the casino, the discomfort evaporated in a puff of smoke. She tapped, **"G-ma on the floor."**

It had been a long, hot summer day, and the air-conditioned casino was filling earlier than usual. Oliver walked the card rooms as Mildred disappeared into the new character.

She strolled the floor like a burned-out playboy, as she continued to build Oliver's background. After a few trips around the playing areas, she found a Sheik's Harem penny slot machine between the two men's restroom and the buffet. She plugged in her gaming card and made her first minimum bet. She loved the idea that, once Security noticed her card was active; someone would look for her on the camera. She was sure to keep her new face turned away. The face is the real test for Oliver Brimstone.

Two hours later, and three extended trips to each of the men's restrooms, Oliver considered a move to another area. The machines in this section weren't paying, and the slot players had relocated. Like the animals on the Serengeti, there was a regular migration as the bored-looking guests searched for the life-changing pot. Mildred's card took a hit; nothing seemed to be paying. She was grateful it didn't cost her to gamble. Nonetheless, she paid attention to the win-loss patterns.

Maybe another walk around to see where the players have wandered off to. There hadn't been much traffic to this men's room, other than those sprinting from the buffet; Mildred waited for the last dinner victim to leave and she would walk through one more time on her way to a new post. She walked in and the familiar stench of burritos and sanitizer greeted her. Luckily, the stalls were empty, which made rifling through the trash easier. She noted that men don't use near as many paper towels, and they were barely damp. As she dug through the trash container, about a foot down, she found a wallet and some personal identification. Immediately she checked the time, and activated her connection to security, "Code EV – Men's room – buffet."

She was unable to figure out how or when this had happened, since her last inspection was less than a half hour ago. Amazed she hadn't noticed anyone, she tried to run a check through her memory. She logged her location and the time, they could check the video.

Oliver took a seat at the machine adjacent to the restroom and waited. Within five minutes, Bud arrived looking ominous dressed in his usual black, and he was talking into his radio. He entered the men's room, and Oliver followed. Bud didn't look up and announced, "Sorry, this bathroom is closed. Sorry for the inconvenience."

At this point, Mildred spoke. "Bud, it's me, Agent Double-Oh-Seventy-One."

"Mildred? Look at me. You have done it again!" His smile seemed to cut his face in half. "So what did you see? Get eyes on anyone?"

"No. I last checked the restroom approximately twenty-five minutes before, and I logged the time. I was about to move on to another area and made a final inspection. That is when I found the personal property. I handled it briefly, with a paper towel. I'm hoping the video gives us someone, and hopefully, we will get prints."

"This discovery was so recent, there haven't been any complaints — yet. I'll have Belinda page the guests on the IDs and find out where they were over the past half hour."

Bud removed more paper towels from the can, as Mildred/Oliver turned to leave "I'm going to slip out; I don't want to be associated with you."

"Well, Mildred, old pal, my brother feels the same way about me."

"Oliver, Oliver Brimstone, dear sir. I think I'd like your brother."

"Hey! I'm your boss, Mr. Brimstone. By the way, good work. Where to now?"

"Brimstone works in mysterious ways; we will have to wait and see." She left the restroom trying to remember which leg needed the cane. After another turn through the slots, she settled at the Nairobi bar near the fireplace. There were several people on the couches, deep in conversation. The bar wasn't busy and only had a couple of customers. Mildred took the seat at the back corner of the bar with the best vantage point. The bartender came up almost immediately.

"Yes sir, would you like a drink?"

Using a slightly deeper voice, Mildred answered, "I would like a Grey Goose Vodka, straight up with water back." *That sounds like something Oliver would drink.* "And a menu."

The bartender reached below the counter for a menu, "Good. I'll get your drink while you decide on food." The employee was perfectly groomed and proficient, as they were trained. Ivory Winds was strict on grooming, and being professional and friendly. She made note of his name.

"Tyler, I'll have the Prime Rib dip and instead of fries, may I have fruit or a salad?" Again, the thought of Dick came to mind and his love for prime rib. Maybe it was dressing as a man that brought him back to her.

"Absolutely, I'll get this right away." While he turned in the order, Oliver poured the vodka into the water and then back into the drinking glass. It was necessary to be alert and in charge. Mildred decided that Oliver has been a widower for the past eleven years, and his only son is career military, based in Guam, no, Germany. If there were a need for more background, it would come to her as necessary. She would be extra careful not to change anything. Simple and consistent, the only way.

The sandwich arrived as she heard the announcement for three people to report to customer service. Mildred made a quick check to see if Bud had texted any more information and the screen was blank. For now, it was time to watch, eat and water down drinks.

The decision to hit the high-roller areas next got her moving again. The areas had been quite full earlier, and her focus had been on the card thefts. Bud had tonight under control as she heard the notice to floor security. This would be a good time to concentrate on the possible loan sharks. The casual gamblers had started to drift home or go to the nightclubs. She was able to identify tonight's losers and noted trends. Always good with faces, she scanned the bar before she walked away and thought of the two collectors, not sure what she would do if she saw them, but she would deal with it when it happened.

– 16 –
Team Member – 4

It was hard to wake up after three nights of men's room potty patrol. Still nothing solid on the thefts, but they had cleared a few suspects. Mildred had prepared folders for the three cases, and they were on Dick's side of the bed. Before she made a firm commitment to getting up, she pushed aside the red loan shark and blue kiddy drugs lists to make notes to the yellow coded medication and credit card theft file. So far, they hadn't picked up anything certain on the videos. It nagged at her that it had to be someone who knew the layout of the casino and how to skirt the massive video web. Bud promised a list of employees, and they would start ruling out people the first of the week. The job continued to expand; luckily there were no thefts last night, and the van wasn't there either. It might mean nothing, but it vexed her foggy mind. Combined with a stretch, she reached for the red case file on the far side of the bed. Her intention was interrupted by a nap attack.

She roused again about ten to a loud knock at the door. No matter the motivation, leaping out of bed was no longer an option with the aches and cracking of age and joints. She approached the door and heard a UPS truck pull away. It had taken nearly a full minute to get to the door. Mildred found the small package from Tango Tattoos. Today's plan changed with the excited arrival of the black and blue tattoo sleeves. She went back to her room, tore open the box and unfolded the delicate material. At this point, Mildred decided a late shift was in order, and she began to finalize the details of the next character to join her team. Giving up on napping, she left around noon, ready to shop.

The search was for leather jackets at the thrift store. Mildred searched the disorganized racks in the women's and men's sections, then back to the heavy jackets along the back wall. Finally she finished in the winter boy's jackets. With two black, well-worn T-shirts, Mildred's bill came to seven dollars. She was disappointed, but nothing else fit her new character. Mildred was inching out of the full parking lot and finally admitted, as much as she hated the idea of full retail, the only choice was the Harley Davidson store on Highway 22. Turning north at the light, she was on her way. At the edge of town, Mildred noticed a pawnshop, and she stopped on a whim. It was the perfect choice as Mildred searched a rack of biker leathers at the rear of the store. She didn't find the jacket she had in mind, but scored a heavily worn vest and leather chaps. Continuing to browse with an open mind for any other possible disguises, she worked her way to the counter. There was only one other customer in the store, but apparently they decided to check out at the same time. Mildred then found a vintage leather cap and a bandana. As she waited, Mildred noticed a men's diamond wedding ring exactly like Dick's. Nearly hypnotized by the similarity, when it was her turn, she couldn't stop and asked the clerk, "Do you mind showing me the ring?"

"No problem, ma'am. It is fourteen carat gold and real diamonds."

The touch of the gold felt familiar and warm. She held it in her hand, almost afraid of the possibilities. She stared at the sparkle of the three tiny diamonds. After a moment, she turned it so she could look at the worn inside of the ring. It was difficult to see, but there were familiar initials and her wedding date. Mildred couldn't speak for a moment, and when she asked her voice was weak. "How much for the ring?"

"We've had it a while, but it is marked four hundred dollars."

It was more than she should spend, but there was no other option. "Well, I want these leathers."

She turned to put back the hat and bandana when the clerk spoke up. "What do you want to offer?"

Mildred was still clutching his ring and her eyes filled with tears. "I can give you four hundred dollars for everything."

The clerk, an older gentleman, stared at her. "I don't know. That is kind of tough. The ring seems to mean something."

Mildred regained her composure, knowing that the negotiations could be difficult if she wasn't strong. "Reminds me of someone from a long time ago."

"I can do four-fifty." His grey eyes looked directly at her.

Mildred decided on strength, "Sorry, that won't do. I have four hundred and no more."

The clerk smiled, "Deal. You are a tough negotiator, but it has been a slow day."

Mildred slipped the ring on her finger, *I'll pay the electric bill next week.* She loaded the rest of her disguise in the trunk of the car, and wondered, *What did he have on his finger when we buried him?*

Mildred was about to turn towards home, but feeling lucky, decided to check out the Harley store. Once there, she picked up another T-shirt and had the bonus shock of the price for new leather. She started to consider that maybe Dick had directed her to the pawn shop.

Once in the car, Mildred made a quick call to Ruby to check on the long black and gray wig. She stopped by to pick it up, and Bambi Hunter, biker widow, was set to ride with an old wedding ring on a gold-fill chain.

Once home, she knocked back two yogurts and settled in for another nap. Once up, Mildred entered into the world of the night. Positive her road warrior character craved darkness. It was around eleven when she arrived at the casino and slipped in through the side entrance.

During her initial walk through, she texted her arrival, **"G-ma on the floor."**

Confident the backup wasn't anyone she knew, she chuckled at the thought of the eyes searching the monitors for a little old lady. While establishing her newest character, Mildred worked up her backstory. Her first stop was to the smallest bar located near the card room. With a bad-girl swagger, Mildred slid up to the counter and ordered a Bud Light. That seemed appropriate for Bambi's drink. Luckily, she was next to a banana tree planter, and she fed it the brew.

After an hour, and two trips to check the women's restroom, she needed to move on. The bartender Ray, was too friendly and kept making conversation. She feared he would notice her drinking pattern. Bambi was stoic and tough. Mildred played her as smart as a crash test dummy. She needed her eyes and ears available, and Ray was just too open and sociable. Mildred checked Ray off the suspect list as she left the bar. Walking down the rows of slot machines, she could hear music emanating from the Elephant Lounge. She slipped in and found a seat at the far end, ordering her newest usual. The band was loud, and the energy fed the crowd with dancing and loud conversations.

With a faked sip, she watched the bartender, bar-back, and two servers always in movement. It took about a half hour when she noticed some cash going into pockets instead of the till. She tapped notes into her phone app with names from the ID badges. Lounge and nightclub closing time, Mildred called it a night. On her way home, she decided to do the report so Bud would have it first thing tomorrow.

– 17 –
Reports

She aroused to a continued beeping from her computer. Mildred sat up and found fifty-seven pages of aaa-sss-ddd and a few fs. The late night clubbing had caught up with her, and her biological clock had taken control with both fists. The last thing she remembered was a warm cup of chamomile tea and pulling up a chair to input the notes from last night with a cat on her lap. She hadn't thought she was tired, but the next memory was when she awoke face down on the keyboard. The tea was untouched; the room was light with the morning sun, and the cat was sprawled across the bed without her.

She was grateful she hadn't fallen off the chair and was aggravated about waking up at seven from a restful sleep. Only for a moment did she consider sleeping in this position regularly. Mildred stumbled from stiffness into the bathroom, feeling like the third chapter of a dreadful book. She rinsed her face and studied the red welt on her forehead and evidence of drool on her cheek. *This can't become a regular sleeping arrangement.*

Relieved that it was Sunday, and the casino didn't get busy until after church, she appreciated the absurdity. She peeled off the fragile tattoo sleeves, setting them aside on a towel for reuse. Slipping into one of Dick's old shirts, she scooted the cat to the side. Mildred knew she needed more than three hours of sleep and decided on a nightcap. She knocked back a giant swig of Nyquil and turned towards the darkened room. With a laptop and charger in hand, she settled into the comfort of her bed. The cat immediately settled against her leg, purring loudly. Once the coded notes finished the upload, she decided Bud could unravel the mystery of last night.

Within minutes, maybe less, she laid back to rest her eyes and drifted into several hours of over-the counter, drug-induced slumber. Her last conscious thought was of the bartender and server. Once the report was read by the head of security, their lives would change, and they would never suspect the lonely, old biker.

– 18 –
Check One Off

Mildred arrived at the new fast food restaurant a couple blocks south of the Ivory Winds for her weekly meeting. She arrived early, but Bud and Detective Hampton already had everything set up. She approached the counter, when she heard them laugh, and Bud called her name. "Mildred, Double Oh! Over here." He pointed to her Big Breakfast Combo. These men seemed to believe she ate like a logger from the Northwest.

She acknowledged and calmly walked over to join them. Mildred was hungrier than she expected and was about to start the usual greeting when Hampton laughed, "There is our top secret agent!"

"Hush. Haven't you ever worked undercover, Detective?" Mildred puzzled over their cheerful behavior. She picked up what appeared to be some kind of fried potato patty, "What's up? Did you catch any new information?" In the first bite, she was surprised at how good the food was.

Bud took over the conversation. "We called in the bartender and the server and searched lockers. We fired the bartender, and the server is in lock up."

Hampton took over. "Yeah, the search found his locker clean, but hers had credit cards and... hmm, what else was it, Bud?"

Mildred joined in. "Could it be, oh let's see, medications?"

They answered in unison "Yes, prescription drugs."

Hampton continued, "Narcotics will get a search warrant for her car and residence. We think the bartender is a thief, but clear on the credit cards. We will check further."

They all toasted with their paper coffee cups and smiled. Mildred was feeling quite proud. "I thought they were just skimming, I hadn't tied them to the thefts. What luck!"

"Narcotics suggest they are hopeful she might cooperate and they can find the deeper connections. It doesn't appear that she was distributing, but she had a large stock of painkillers. We ran her background, and no surprise, she has gang affiliation and some petty crime."

Bud spoke up, "She used a fake name, and we are reviewing how her background check got through human resources. The second server and bar-back don't appear to be involved, but we will be watching them. We ordered another surveillance camera when they were off shift. This one should cover the blind spot."

As the meeting broke up, Mildred sat alone for a few minutes to finish her breakfast and watched the men leave. She was feeling cocky with one case possibly solved. *I couldn't be so lucky to have this connect to the club drugs too. Guess I'm getting lazy.* She held the smooth wedding ring that was still hung around her neck. For now, she could focus deeper on the red file; the loan sharks could offer some insight to Dick's suicide.

When she got home, all three granddaughters were laughing on the couch. They had a laser pointer, and the cat was dashing through the room in erratic patterns, focused on the elusive red dot. Izzy squealed with joy, and immediately said, "Look what Amelia bought with her allowance. It's a laser pointer." Mildred was immediately pulled into the merriment and squeezed onto the couch with the girls, "I can see. Miss Cat seems to love it."

"Oh, and Grandma, we know her name! It's Popcorn! I thought of it. I asked Glory to make me some popcorn, and your kitty came to me and started to purr. It makes her cat happy."

"What an excellent relief, Iz. It was a lot of work and a bunch of names for that sweet kitty. Popcorn it is." Mildred noticed the cat's ears twitched when she said the new name. It was only then that Amelia remembered to tell Mildred that their dad wanted to go back to the storage tomorrow.

The afternoon filled with girls shopping, and two expandable photo albums. There were a lot of giggles and chatter, with an additional financial hit that included milkshakes.

– 19 –
Storage Part Two

Richie called early and apologized that he had to put off the trip to the storage unit longer than he planned. They agreed to meet about ten in front of the U-Haul office. Mildred waited in the parking lot and then followed him through after he put in the code. They immediately got down to work. She loaded the boxes that held the news articles and old photos in the back seat of her car. She had a plan to save the memories for her boys.

"Richie, hope it is okay with you, I talked to the girls, and they will work with me on this. We bought expandable albums to save everything for you and David."

"Of course, Mom. They'll learn about the family, and I'd score the best stuff, especially since David is such a jerk."

"Now, now. I plan to be fair and treat my boys equally. I do understand his pain; he adored his daddy."

Richie answered, "Yeah, I loved him too. I know, he hasn't gotten over it, but I'm your favorite. Just look, I'm the cute one. Besides, I'll instruct my girls to bully you."

Mildred smiled, "Okay, you have me there." They both laughed and pulled out the last two boxes.

They were silent for the first few minutes. "Richie, I didn't notice this before, but this is an evidence box." She opened it and found a file, notes, and photos. "This was a case he worked on twelve to fifteen years ago. He was never satisfied with this one. There are notes and reports in here." She held up a bag wrapped in a towel. "I'm afraid this may be the murder weapon." Mildred held up a wicked looking knife in a tagged evidence bag. "He shouldn't have this. I won't ever forget how hard Daddy worked on this case, and it ended up in McCaffie's court. He was upset when the Judge decided that there wasn't enough evidence and closed the case."

"I remember, Mom. Didn't he claim that there was some additional information? He connected some big shot business guy. He was worried about us being in danger."

"You're right; I mostly remember the case itself and forgot about any threats. We talked about this case on several occasions. He was obsessed with justice for Lucas Freeman." Mildred visited her memories with her lost husband. "He often got caught up in the details of cases, but this was the one. He was sure that he had everything, and when the attorneys took over, it was declared a suicide and thrown out."

Richie sighed, and she could see his mind racing back in time. "This box proves he couldn't let this go."

Mildred answered his concern, "That is an understatement. He was sure Freeman wouldn't cut his wrists and his throat. That was overkill, and he had a lead on a possible hit man; there was a very distinct message sent with the murder."

Richie eagerly looked through the box, "I remember him talking about a pattern, but mostly he tried to keep us away from his board he had set up in his office."

Mildred added, "That is when he started locking the door and would cover the board with a sheet. I guess a lot of detectives have that one case, and this was Daddy's."

Richie looked through the box, and said, "What are we going to do with this?"

"I'll call Officer Hampton and make arrangements. So let's put this in the trunk of my car."

Tears reflected in Richie's eyes. "In a minute. I need to look at some of this stuff. Almost feels like Dad is here."

"I can feel him, too. Be careful, and try not to handle too much, but go ahead." Mildred then turned her attention to the fourth box. It was full of receipts, and the sales information on the homes they had owned over thirty years. There was a pack of letters she had written to him before they decided to marry. She was touched that he saved so much, along with a stuffed K-9 dog she had given him when he graduated from the Academy. He had the birth announcements for each of the boys and notes she thought were long gone. She applauded his ability of hiding the sentimental part of himself. She was touched to witness it now.

He had the kennel club papers for his first K-9 dog, Gypsy, and she shared it with Richie. They sat there for hours swapping stories of the dogs he had grown up with, often forgetting they weren't pets, but trained professionals.

"Oh my God in heaven! Look, Richie, he has your report cards and both of our graduation certificates from the Academy. I thought I had mine in the box at home."

"Let me see, this is so cool. Mom, what time is it? How long have we been here?"

Mildred hadn't noticed the passage of time until that moment.

Richie started packing up, "I have to go make dinner. You know how my girls get when they haven't been fed."

They came to an immediate stop and were putting everything back into the boxes. "Richie, do you mind if I take these two boxes home? I can go through some more where I have chairs and hot tea."

"Better pop the trunk, old woman. I have to go." He took out the first one, just as she finished packing the second one. He picked it up and scooted his mother out to the car and shut off the light. "I'll come over tomorrow and help you haul them in."

"No need, Richie. I can handle moving a box. I'm not that old."

Mildred arrived home emotionally drained, leaving the boxes in the trunk of the car. The discoveries and memories were exhausting. She was about to sit, when she noticed a message flashing on her answering machine. It was the insurance company for the casino. She called the adjuster back and learned this was about the slip and fall at the salad bar. They were able to complete a straightforward witness statement over the phone in about ten minutes. Mildred asked if Bud had sent the photos. They had them in the file, and thanked Mildred for the thorough scene inspection. It was made clear that the plan was to deny the claim and possibly take legal action for filing a false report. The call ended with the promise they didn't think there would be a need for a more formal testimony. If there was anything further, the attorney would contact Mildred directly.

This felt like a good time to start making the memory books for the boys. She hauled in one of the boxes and sat on the couch.

She began to divide the memories and news stories into two piles. Every item seemed vital for telling Dick's story to his sons and all those that come after. She felt proud of the man they would get to know; the man she married years ago.

– 20 –
Busy Day Off

It was a light schedule for a few days. Mildred/ Delilah decided to hit a variety of GA meetings at different locations. At the second meeting, she saw Rose and Karen, who had approached her the week before and extended an open invitation to join them for coffee. She regretted her refusal to go the first time, but today she was more comfortable with her back-story. It was a perfect time to make the connection, and she decided to join them after the meeting.

Mildred hadn't seen a couple of people before. They related similar heartbreak, with different names and details. When Chuck stepped up the energy changed. "Hi, I'm Chuck, and I'm a gambler and an alcoholic."

The group, as usual, answered in unison, "Hi, Chuck."

"I was a driver for Hope Transport. They are a commercial car ride company, and do a lot of work with medical transportation with nursing and group homes. I worked for them for several years. Do you remember that day last summer that broke all of the heat records?"

The group mumbled in affirmation, not wanting to interfere with his story.

"I had picked up a couple of older men at the clinic over on Forty-Second. I had another pick up in an hour-and-a-half. The grandfathers were napping, so I decided to stop at the casino just for a few minutes. I was just going to play a hand or two of blackjack. I parked the car near the door in one of the only shady spots and went in. Two hours later, I felt a tap on the shoulder, and when I turned, there was my boss and he had police officers with him. The car had heated up and the grandfathers almost died. One of the valet drivers noticed them and saved their lives. He broke the windows, and they pulled them out. When he called for an ambulance, the police came too. I learned later they paged me multiple times, but I was in a trance of cards and betting. I never heard the announcements, and time just slipped past." Chuck's face was awash in tears. "I almost killed them. They didn't do anything but get old." He had to stop for a moment to regain some composure.

"I was criminally charged with reckless endangerment. I spent two weeks in jail, and my driver's license was stripped away. I lost my job, and I don't know what to do next. Please help." He sat back down, drained, relieved and hopeless.

The circle responded, "Thank you, Chuck."

Karen spoke up first, "Does anyone else have something to share?" The room was silent.

She looked to Rose who stood, closed her eyes briefly, and started reciting the steps, "Number one: we admitted we were powerless over gambling, that our lives have become unmanageable. Number two: come to believe that a Power greater than ourselves can restore us to a normal way of thinking and living.

Mildred could tell they hoped Chuck would find solace and utilize what they were offering. The members joined the repetition of the steps one-by-one and at the end they finished in unison, "Number twelve: having made an effort to practice these principles in all our affairs, we try to carry this message to other compulsive gamblers."

Karen looked around the group and announced, "This works." She handed Chuck a laminated card with the steps and patted him on the shoulder.

Mildred felt bad about her first sharing; they were all awkward half-truths. Once becoming more of a spectator, she built an understanding of the organization and the people involved. Luckily, they were a welcoming group and allowed everyone to stumble without judgment. She sent a silent prayer to Chuck. When the meeting broke up, a couple of the members started taking down chairs. Most everyone else went back to the refreshment table. Mildred sat in her seat, mentally cataloging names and circumstances, when Rose approached. "A couple of the gals are going for some real coffee and not the rot-pot they serve here. Would you like to come?"

Thrilled at how her next step took care of itself, she answered as Delilah, "I would love to go. I can drive. Where to?"

Rose seemed genuinely pleased that Delilah agreed. "I'm riding with Karen. We are going to Collectors over by the old Penney's store."

"Great, I'll meet you there. I have to call my son first." Mildred pondered how her Delilah persona lied so easily. She needed to make some notes while the information was still fresh. Mildred knew she was smart, but was also aware her short-term memory was becoming a day-to-day challenge. She went to the car and quickly dictated some notes into her phone. She was about to finish, when she noticed the three women leave, waving their goodbyes to the men, who were still standing around with paper cups and handfuls of cookies.

She finished quickly and stowed the phone. Mildred adapted and became Delilah to follow their car to the mall. The parking lot was almost abandoned, and the women were able park and walk in together. Karen went to save a table, while the others stood in line and chatted. They were very comfortable with each other, and Delilah could tell that they had shared truth and secrets for a long time.

Once at the table, Delilah felt comfort from the warm smells of baked goods and fresh sandwiches. The heat of her latte felt like an embrace, as she held the paper cup to her face. She savored the first tentative sip, "Damn, I need this every day." The women all nodded in agreement. They included her easily, with questions and even more revelations about their lives. She was not sure if this would help the investigation, but she knew this was where she needed to be. The women fell into the usual conversation of kids and spouses with sighs and laughter. They were open and honest. Delilah/Mildred felt guilty for her guise. She mentally reassured herself that this was important, and would help many people, and was not just about her personal loss. However, with this group of honest women, her ongoing deceit stung.

Delilah/Mildred relaxed and mostly listened. Rose had spent nearly twenty years with Oscar and explained the dirty details of his alcoholism. She went on to describe how she started gambling, and the marriage was destroyed with secrets and lies.

"I started gambling to fill my time, and I was drawn to the energy of the casino. He was there in the bars; I couldn't get him to stop. So then, I hit the slots. At first, I ran up the credit cards, because you do win enough to think it is just one more deal, one more spin, and it will all be better."

The other women nodded, and someone whispered "Amen."

Rosie continued, "Then there are the payday loans."

Lydia piped in, "Fifteen dollars for a hundred doesn't sound bad, until you can't pay it back in time. I'm still digging out, and at one point, the rates added up to thousands more."

Karen said, "I've heard that some interest rates ran into four figures with those loans."

"It is a gateway drug for gamblers," said Delilah/Mildred.

Karen joined in, "You borrow on a paycheck, and then you borrow more to pay the electric."

"Then you get new credit cards and run them up on house payments and cash advances. Shortly you have borrowed more than the next check," said Rosie.

Karen added with enthusiasm, "All you need is one big win." Lydia sighed, "You get enough wins to keep at it."

Mildred could see the tears in Rose's eyes when she added, "Then it all collapses, and there is no escape. The bank forecloses, the credit dries up, and the payments escalate."

"That's about when I lost my job," said Karen. The other women nodded in agreement.

Rose continued her narrative, "Now I live with my two kids in the garage at my parent's house. I have daily battles with my drunken husband and his bitch mother for custody."

Karen said, "At least you got help, and we are here for you. Aren't we, gals?"

Two of the three women answered in unison, "Yes. We're here."

Here was the opening Mildred needed. "Did you ever get approached by those guys that lend money? I think they work over at the casino." Everyone froze for just a moment. Karen asked,

"Have they approached you?"

"No, I've never met them, but my husband did."

"I thought your husband had passed."

"He did, but they were there to collect while his body was still warm." Mildred coughed stifling a nervous laugh.

All three women nodded apprehensively. Karen sighed and said, "I've met them, and no matter what you pay, they want it all plus everything else. I had no idea how difficult the easy way out could be."

Mildred was tempted to talk honestly with these women, but the guilt over her identity continued to hold off the revelation. They kept with the conversation of debt, which tumbled into bargain shopping and finally tentative hopes for a future.

It was well into the afternoon when they broke and went their separate ways. Mildred had a lot to think about and strategize her next move. She decided that Rose was still too raw, and Karen would be the best person. Karen appeared to be the furthest into her recovery and a leader. Mildred resolved that truth time needed to be soon.

– 21 –
One More Time

"911 Man down, first quadrant Charging Rhino machine A-218. Isn't breathing."

Brenda answered immediately. "On the way."

Mildred tried to keep her anxiety out of her voice. "Brenda, send oxygen with the aid team. Call an ambulance."

Brenda, always efficient, responded. "Done and done."

Mildred turned to the woman on the next slot machine, "Ma'am, excuse me, do you know this man?"

The woman kept her eyes glued to the slot. "Yes, he is my husband."

"Ma'am, you are going to have to stop playing." Mildred began to administer CPR while searching for a pulse. The obviously distraught woman didn't stop. She reached over to spin the second machine. "But it's about to pay."

Looking up from the floor, Mildred counted the breath and chest compressions. "Ma'am, it will pay tomorrow, he needs you now." Mildred maintained calmness in her voice, aware her frustration could frighten the woman further.

The woman's eyes were full of tears, as she punched the buttons non-stop, "Yes, I can see that, but just one more spin. I don't know what else to do."

Mildred spoke, "I need you to hold his hand and speak to him. What is his name?"

Without hesitation the woman replied, "Jim, er, James. James Bradley."

"Mrs. Bradley, I need you now. Please, just for a couple of minutes; you can go back." Finally, the woman stopped playing the two slots and stared at Mildred, then she turned back to the machines and placed another bet. Mildred had seen the gambling obsession before, almost daily, but the avoidance was a sign of panic. "Mrs. Bradley, what is your first name?" Mildred continued to press on the man's chest.

"Simone."

It had seemed like hours had passed, but it was only minutes when Mildred spoke again, "Jim, Simone is here. Don't worry, help is on the way." Counting *two – three – four*, press. The Casino security team arrived, taking over the CPR and administering oxygen. Mildred whispered the couple's names, and slipped away to cover the door, so she could direct the ambulance crew to the location. The slot machines continued to whir, always taking more than they paid.

Within precious minutes, she ran back with the EMTs, and they took control. Mildred put her arm around Simone and patted gently. "You will have to go now; the ambulance is here." There was no answer, only the obsessive punching and playing.
"Simone! Stop! Jim needs you now."

The distraught woman pressed one more play on each and removed the players' cards and cash ticket. Mildred saw the pain in her eyes, and they both knew he might be gone. Something about stopping the game made it real. "I'm sorry, but I ah, I, ah…"

"It is okay, Simone. Go with Jim, and they will help you at the hospital."

"Please don't let anyone play our machines, I'll be back."

"Okay, sweetheart, I'll guard them." Mildred called housekeeping to put the two machines out of play; they could be reactivated in the morning. She watched the woman follow the stretcher to the side door, remembering how quickly everything changes. Once they were out of the casino, Mildred turned back to the bustling noise and acrid smell of desperation that filled the room. Even though it was time for lunch, she knew she couldn't eat, so it was another walk around the floor and into the hotel.

Mildred's favorite chair next to the fireplace was waiting. She sat soundlessly and watched the eager customers enter the hotel. She felt an ache for the sadness of their hope and expectation. She felt a need for her women at GA. Silently she offered a prayer for Simone and Jim.

−22−
The Convention

At the weekly Thursday meeting, Bud briefed Mildred over the usual pancakes and eggs. "Next weekend's convention is one of the largest events of the year. It usually stays subdued until after the parade on Friday. When they come back to the hotel, all Elvis breaks loose. We have briefed the security team and called in some off-duty police. Everyone is on for twelve-hour shifts all three days. The vendors are already arriving."

She sat quietly, and after a silence, acknowledged the upcoming event. Mildred had been trying to ignore this conference. "What are your ideas for my involvement?"

He presented her with a taped envelope of tickets, room card, passes and a Graceland T-shirt. He outlined the various events and scheduled guests, and as he rose to leave, she could almost see the stress surrounding him. She decided that next week will be soon enough to read him in on the loan shark investigation.

Mildred went directly home; first, fill the cat feeder and a roaster pan of water, and finish with extra hugs for Popcorn. Then she packed a variety of clothes for the weekend and went to the storage and brought in a box saved since the '60s. Well aware of this convention over the years, time had expired, and she had to face it this weekend. The long suppressed memories washed over her.

Hopefully prepared for a tough three days, Mildred went to the hotel and settled into the room. To shake off ancient recollections, she took a spin around the hotel and texted security, "G-ma on the floor."

Her earpiece buzzed, "10-4 G-ma, where are you?"

"You don't need eyes. I'll radio if necessary." Not recognizing the responding voice, she settled into observation mode and began to familiarize herself with the new set-up, starting with a banner at the front desk announcing *The New Heartbreak Hotel*. The lobby and conference rooms were filled with outrageous references and plays on words; this was going to be painful.

Everything was bustling, so she decided to cruise through the slots and card rooms. She was surprised to see the King's Cadillac in the main lobby. This was no minor conference. Mildred had brought two disguises and the assurance her advanced age would be the best cover. She settled into the comfort of the buffet and filled the first of two plates and then three desserts.

The gaming floor didn't change much; it was the usual crowd. The major action was the hotel. She patrolled and noticed new faces in the usual black suits of the security team. The posted menus at the smaller eateries had some kitschy changes. *Please, how many peanut butter and banana recipes do they expect to fry?* The Timbuktu was offering the Fools Gold Loaf, a sandwich that was not only expensive, but also obnoxious, just like the man they rushed to honor. Overall, the placed buzzed with additional activity, but no problems manifested.

The next morning Mildred's phone buzzed with a text from Belinda.

"B'fast at 8?" Mildred tapped in an immediate response.

"Where?"

"Hotel café." Clearly Belinda was hungry. Mildred rushed to find her shoes,

"C U there."

She was downstairs within ten minutes. Belinda was already at a table with a carafe of coffee and menus. She must have been in the restaurant all along. "Good morning; thought we gals in a department of manly men could use a boost."

Surprised, Mildred appreciated the simple get together. No planning, no plots, just eggs, toast, and conversation. Belinda voiced her concern about the temporary workers she would have to wrangle, and Mildred offered moral support. Everyone was pulling extra hours. Belinda didn't have a room, and Mildred offered to share if she needed it. Since Belinda had a home life, with two small children, she would probably not use it, but she was grateful for the offer.

Fed and ready to face the day, they left the café. As they walked towards the lobby, the women came face to face with two elderly men dressed in cowboy shirts and jeans.

The tallest man spoke, "Dred, is that you? Wow! It is! Look, Scotty, as beautiful as ever."

"DJ, Scotty! I thought for sure you two would be dead by now." They each embrace Mildred, and Scotty picked her up and swung her around. Immediately she asked about several names. Belinda looked as if she recognized some of them.

Mildred turned towards her friend, "Belinda, I'm going to go back and have another cup with the guys. See you on the monitor."

"Okay," then Belinda whispered, "Who are they?"

"Old band members from back in the day."

Belinda sputtered, spraying her shirt. "Mildred, do you have something to share?"

"It was so long ago, more like a book I read. Later, thanks for breakfast. I'll buy tomorrow."

As Mildred turned back into the café, Belinda reached out and took her arm. "Stop. Seriously, did you know Elvis?"

"It was a lifetime ago," Mildred smiled and winked at the dumbstruck associate. "Back to work, Missy."

Astonished to meet with the old band members, and even more that they recognized her, Mildred admitted she may not have known them so quickly, and the trio of lost friends laughed. Mildred was young when she got the part-time job at Sun Records. The studio was near her school, and she would walk over. It was a simple part-time after school and weekends, filling in for Marion. Little did Mildred know that many of the struggling musicians she knew would become icons. Elvis didn't record with Sun anymore, but he would visit often to see old friends. He occasionally sang back up and always wanted to meet the new discoveries. She had another coffee, and followed with two glasses of water while the men reminisced and ate omelets with toast, then they cried with shared recollections and the names of so many dear friends now lost. Scotty sighed "Time is a bitch. No offense, Dred."

There was a momentary silence as Mildred remembered the break up. Right after graduation, she gave notice to Sam. She explained her dad's insistence for full time work or college. About the same time she was reading *Seventeen* magazine about Elvis and his time in the Army. They had a story about Elvis and how he had met Priscilla, and there was speculation about the relationship. She sadly looked at the two musicians. "You guys don't understand how it is to be replaced by a younger woman, when you're barely eighteen."

The laughter was forced as they quickly tried to change the subject. Mildred didn't hear them as she thought of the letter she sent to his APO address. She ended the relationship, and made it clear that she felt used. He was lucky there were no emails back in those days, because Mildred still would like to yell some more. He sent back three letters, but Mildred burned them. Apparently, Priscilla knew about Dred, because the one time they met, there was an obvious hatred. Mildred bristled at the thought of sharing anything. It was easier to think about her second greatest heartbreak so many years later.

They guys started to pass photos of spouses, children, and grandchildren, which brought her back to the present day. Mildred made a promise to meet tonight in the Elephant Lounge well after the parade and before the impersonator contest. Mildred would reserve a table in the back, just like the old days.

The men had to leave so they could finish setting up their vendor table. They would offer autographs and sell classic vinyl records. DJ and Scotty brought their instruments to the conference; they always did. DJ said, "You never know when there could be a chance to play, especially at these events."

Before heading back to her room, Mildred went to the T-shirt shop on a whim and had a shirt made. She would wear it one time only, for breakfast tomorrow. Finally back in her room, Mildred dismissed the need for a disguise; her best cover was being Dred. She decided to take a few minutes to rest, her sides still aching from the laughter. It felt as if decades were erased. Clearly, the weekend will be a strange challenge.

First Day

Awakened an hour later to a changed feeling of energy, Mildred jumped out of bed, brushed her teeth and fought off an urge to tease her hair. She went to the lobby. It was packed, as were most of the major events based from the hotel and event center. The casino had also added several exhibits that increased the usual weekend hubbub. She leaned against the lobby wall to retie her new running shoes with a double knot, check the camera and transmitter, and then it was straight for the first patrol of many.

A couple hours until the first sign-in at three thirty, Mildred was surprised the lobby was busy with conventioneers. The faces glowed with pure excitement, and she watched men with terrible taste in grooming greeting others with similar fashion choices. She began her first pass-through with the vendors; a few booths were open, with many others setting up. The few that braved the early hours were cashing in. This area would demand much of her attention, and Mildred studied the layout. She identified a couple of vantage points where she could watch large sections of the room. She had to admit there would be no sitting for any length of time; most every inch was inhabited with souvenirs and trinkets. An indefinable sadness ached through her for the man, her first love, reduced to a sideshow and a velvet painting.

Out on the casino floor, that area wasn't busy yet. There was still the constant noise lit by the sun through the skylights, which reminded Mildred this wasn't her usual nights. Mildred noticed the increased security, all dressed in black suits or dark shirts, only visible to the trained eye. Overall, the team appeared serious and focused; none gave her a second look as she kept moving. The slot machines whirled, bells and whistles clamored, the room whispered its lies of riches. Mildred knew later in the day it would be screaming. Near the front of the main gaming floor was the pink Cadillac, the black Lincoln had been added, and both cordoned off. Best to keep the memories in the past where they belong and to get to work on this side of the velvet rope. It had become obvious that Priscilla supported the conference, too much money involved not to. Mildred didn't like the negative feelings of a girl from long ago; instead she sent out a mental congratulation for being an unexpected business genius. Still, Mildred didn't want to see her ever again.

Belinda called to cancel lunch. There was too much activity to walk away from her mixed crew and busy monitors. There was a disappointment in her voice, with a promise for tomorrow. Since Mildred was already on the floor, she was in full agreement. They both needed to be on the clock; it was going to be a red-letter day.

After a couple hours of constant walking, Mildred sat on the bench between the entrance of the casino and the hotel. She appreciated the marble seat making it possible to enjoy a mobile snack and a quickly cooling latte. The restaurants already had lines, and the crowd kept growing. A wish crossed her mind that Delilah, Oliver, and Bambi were real. She could use them this weekend. Much of the crowd were there for the conference, but some curiosity seekers added to the usual weekend gamblers and tourists. Enjoying a bag of churros, she watched new faces stream past. She could see out the door, and the valet parking crew was on a full run. Suddenly her attention was drawn to a young woman. She didn't fit into the crowd, and kept her head down, moving with an odd focus. After a moment, Mildred remembered, *That is the server we fired from the Elephant Club.* Mildred rolled the churro bag closed and stashed the treat in her fanny pack. She had to move and keep an eye on the woman.

She tapped the radio transmitter, "This is G-ma, who do I have on?"

"Yes, G-ma, this is Larry."

"Larry, check the monitors for the south main entrance by the car display. There is a woman in jeans and a gray sweatshirt with the hood up. She has her head down, and is walking towards the third quadrant."

"I'm looking. Yes, yes I see her. What's up?"

"I think she was an employee we fired for stealing. We suspected she might be part of the prescription drug and credit card ring."

"Are you sure?"

"Hell no, but she looks like her. Obviously, this woman is here for more than a couple coins in the slots."

"Can you stick with her until I have someone?"

"That's a plan." Mildred wasn't concerned about being recognized. Bambi Hunter had tagged the server the night before the firing, and Mildred looked nothing like her alter ego.

"Heads up, Larry. She has acknowledged three different people. It looks like they may have a crew. Not sure if there is anything to this, but I'm very suspicious."

"Damn, I've told Bud, and he is heading down."

Mildred recorded descriptive notes as she watched the group spread out. She would stick with the woman for now. Bud arrived within a minute and fell in step only slightly behind Mildred.

"Where is she?"

"Over there by the Timbuktu menu board."

"Got it. Difficult to see her face, but I think you're right."

"I've spotted at least four people she has recognized; they apparently have come in through separate entrances at about the same time. This one appears to be a leader and is coordinating the team. They are all relatively young, which makes them visible in today's environment. I've watched them communicate with clear signals. She was the one the others make eye contact with before they peel off in different directions. I think that they are taking advantage of the conference."

Bud answered quietly, "Sounds like they have planned this out. Are they all in the hoodies?"

"Not exactly, but they are young and dressed in jeans and dark shirts. They have different areas, and..." Mildred stopped talking, "Look, see that one by the Giza machines? Watch."

The young man made a subtle salute to the woman they were following, and she nodded. Bud whispered, "Got him. I'll follow that one. Check in with Hampton and see what he want us to do. Stick with her, and as soon as I can, I'll check back." As he walked away, Mildred heard him speaking, "Larry, I need Belinda. Have her come down. Patch me through to the 999 extension."

Mildred continued to follow and observe the woman. Both the hunter and the hunted kept their heads down and backs turned to cameras. Mildred spoke into her cell phone app:

"Suspect is covering the southwest sector of slot machines. She doesn't fit in... young, jeans, oversized sweatshirt, and not searching for that lucky machine."

Fridays were usually busy, but with the influx from the hotel, it was extraordinarily crowded. "It appears she's working the floor in a grid pattern, paying notice to purses and drinkers."

Mildred slipped into a seat at an end machine and plugged in. She cursed herself for using an old fanny pack instead of a big, open purse. The suspect walked past and made no notice. Mildred absentmindedly made small bets on the slot.

Bud returned and walked past, then stopped and looked away from Mildred. He appeared to be talking on his radio and reported to her, "We are to continue following and take action only if forced to. Hampton is sending two more plain-clothed officers. They should be here in ten minutes or less."

Mildred responded, "It appears they are casing the place, and I've confirmed a definite pattern."

"Good work. I'll take her for now. I need you to check in with the office and help Belinda get eyes on any others."

"On my way, boss. I hate to be identified by our crew, but I see the necessity."

"There is that; the regulars think you are Belinda's mother, but they are getting wise to your job."

"Okay, I'll be back as soon as possible."

It took about a half hour, but they were able to ID three, and possibly two others, connected to the suspect. They were easy to follow, as they were dressed appropriately for their age, and stood out in the field of Elvis fans and dazzling Bobby Soxers. They also didn't play any of the games, but hung back watching. Hampton arrived with a plain-clothes officer, who took over for Bud. There was a concern that the woman would recognize Bud, as he was part of her firing, and Hampton had been the arresting officer. Mildred watched the two men leave the main floor. She could overhear them slightly on her ear piece and overheard the reference about the woman's balls for returning to the casino, then they started to toss out guesses of possible criminal associations as she heard the sound of a closing door. "Hey, you two turkeys, I can hear you." Then the line went closed.

Her attention was pulled back by a minor commotion near the dice tables. Most of the guests didn't notice as the lights and continuous clamor of the room hypnotized them. Bud came back on the floor and turned quickly towards the table. The undercover officer waved him off, and Mildred's ear piece whispered for Mildred to continue with the primary suspect.

Mildred noticed that her subject only briefly looked, but didn't make any visible reaction to the incident. The suspect continued to move purposely and avoided cameras like a pro. Her target returned almost casually to the dollar machines. The next move was nearly indiscernible, as the woman picked up a designer bag that was within inches of the owner, while she stared at the rotating cylinders.

Mildred tapped out a request for backup and location. She noted a smooth handoff to another woman. Mildred decided to stay with the bag, and followed the second woman into the restroom and sent in a location code.

She entered and observed the purse on the sink with the thief digging through the pockets. Mildred spoke, "Hi, how is lady luck treating you today?"

The woman was stunned, "Ah fine, yeah sure."

"I'm doing okay myself; no big wins yet, just need a little luck. Cute bag, it looks like one of those fancy designer ones." Mildred smiled, keeping up the chatty old woman stereotype

"Are you here for the Convention?"

"No."

Mildred could tell the woman was nervous and aggravated at the same time. She turned on the water and began to wash her hands and face, stalling. "You from around here? I came in on the casino bus from Peoria." Mildred blabbered on, and wondered why she picked that particular city.

"Cool." Then the woman took the shoulder bag back to a bathroom stall, which gave Mildred the freedom to text security. She triggered the faucet to cover the sound.

Suspect – bathroom 6. Has bag in handicapped stall.

There was an immediate response,

10-4 on the way. Close down area. Get everyone out. Will watch the door.

Mildred moved cautiously, humming, and running the air blower, keeping her attention on the stall. She turned to leave as two older women entered. "Oh, hi, there you are. Come with me; I think it is getting lucky by the restaurant." The women were confused, but Mildred was able to usher them away from the suspected thief. Once clear of the room, she explained, "There is a plumbing problem, and you will want to use another restroom.

The two women spoke in unison, "Thank you." They seemed grateful and left unaware.

A uniformed security and one of the backup officers approached, and she waved them in. Within a moment, they exited with the suspect in cuffs and the purse in an evidence bag. Mildred went to the still unsuspecting victim, explained the problem, and directed her to customer service. Security would meet her there.

"G-ma on the floor." Mildred checked in with a feeling of immediacy to get back on the tail of the primary suspect.

Mildred's earpiece woke up, "Good work, G-ma. We have your woman on camera. She is on the bank of Jumping Jungle slots. She settled in as her team member was going down. No idea how many are here."

"Do you think she is aware we are on to her?"

"Hard to tell. Keep alert. We nabbed a second guy. He has gang tats."

"What's a tat?"

"Tattoo, G-ma. Got it. Over and out."

Mildred found her suspect quickly and settled into an adjacent machine like a sentry. The woman's anxiety was becoming evident as she checked out the area. It appeared that the leader's focus had changed. Mildred noted a purse she didn't have earlier and watched as she rifled through the bag. The culprit removed a wallet and slipped a prescription bottle into her pocket. *We have her.*

The adversaries sat for a quarter of an hour at their machines, feeding them just enough to avoid suspicion, and to let the previous activity settle. Finally, the young woman stood up and walked to the cash machine. She left the purse behind. Mildred watched as she took out a bankcard and a slip of paper from the wallet. After a moment, she swiped the card and withdrew what appeared to be the maximum of five hundred dollars. Calmly the suspect put the card and note back into her pocket.

Damn, when will they learn not to write down those PIN numbers and keep them with the cards? The woman eyes surveyed the room, looked past Mildred, and started calmly towards the door.

Mildred spoke to the office, "Suspect walking toward the main entrance. Check pockets for wallet and prescriptions."

"We have the door covered."

Suddenly there is an explosion of bells, whistles and alarms

"Aw no!"

"What's up, G-ma?"

"No, no, no. Hit the damned jackpot. Everything is going crazy."

Mildred looked instinctively to the suspect, and even she stopped to look back at the scene of flashing lights, as the numbers at the top of the machine rolled with a blaring recorded announcement

"WE'VE GOT A WINNER!" repeating with the fake sound of change surging into a metal tray. All attention focused on Mildred as she beat on the machine. Most took her action as enthusiasm, but she was trying to stop everything. Within seconds, there was a crowd of patrons and employees all cheering. Exhilaration filled the room as they began to count in unison as the total climbed. 5-6-8-10-12. It clanked and finally stopped at $37,526, with a cheer that filled the casino. Mildred searched for an escape; she found nothing and realized she was trapped. The floor manager brought tax forms and wanted photos,

not accepting her refusal. There was no stopping the celebration. They ended up with a blurry photo of an older, grimacing woman with her eyes closed.

"Bud, where the hell are you?"

The only answer she received was a breathless laughter.

"Stop it. This is serious."

"I've got eyes on you." Then she felt Bud tap on her shoulder and he murmured, "Nice covert operation, G-ma."

Mildred whispered back, "They have my name, picture, and social security number. What are we going to do?"

"Calm down, take off that Ivory Winds Winner hat for a start, and Belinda will clean up the rest."

Mildred tried to pull away from the crowd, "Did you catch our perp?"

"No, we didn't. We let her go..."

"What! We had her, why did you let her go?" Mildred was stunned.

"... and the police nailed her in the parking lot. Our crew secured the trash where she dumped evidence. We have her prints and video. Belinda is to email the employment file to Hampton while they process her."

Mildred answered, "Good work, Bud. Do I get to keep this money?"

Bud looked directly into her eyes, "Yeah, ah-no. Just like your gambling debt isn't real, your winnings aren't either." They parted as he continued to laugh, walking down the hall to the office.

– 24 –
Ancient History

"**G-ma heading back to hotel.**"
"**OK, are you moving on up to the penthouse?**"
"**No, Groucho, you are not funny.**"
"**Am too.**"

Mildred went back to her room and lay down for a short while. There was no sleeping, so she watched a talk show. Then she changed clothes, added a hat and called the office.

It was good to hear Belinda's voice answer "Good work! You buying drinks?"

"I will for you, but not for any of those other clowns."

Mildred responded, "Good deal. Rain check till breakfast. You have it. Any updates?"

Belinda gave Mildred a brief account of the accomplishments through the afternoon: three arrested and a couple of others identified with warrants issued. It appeared they were members of a local gang with suspected major affiliations. The two women spoke of concern about additional activity through the weekend. There was nothing new or pending, and as they closed the connection. *Time to sign in.*

"**G-ma in the hotel**"
"**Confirmed**."

Since noon, there were Elvis impersonators in every nook and cranny: men with poorly dyed hair, garish clothing, and a conviction that it must be attractive. She saw them work the room like ostentatious, imitation peacocks. After the previous excitement, Mildred's attention was on high alert, and she needed to find a subtle position. She walked through the busy lobby, and a seat on the couch by the fire pit opened up. She was able to sit comfortably and pulled out her phone to act as if she was reading. She could then listen and pay attention, without engaging in conversations. The conventioneers were exceptionally friendly. She had to stay on the outside and avoid distraction.

The thought of food was only momentary, as she removed the rest of the churros from her pack. The lobby stayed busy, but the crowd was shifting to the vendors in the conference rooms. It was getting close to time for the parade, so the costuming became even more dazzling. The women dressed as if they were from the '50s, and Mildred saw more poodle skirts and bobby sox than there ever were back in the day. The parade would start from the hotel and go through the business district. When they were back, the bands and participants would come through the casino and finish at the largest theater. Mildred would stay on site and visit vendors while the crowd was gone. She sighed, relieved by the simple plan. She mentally scheduled the rest of the day. The big event tonight was the impersonator's show, and there would be karaoke in the Ivory Coast nightclub. She was surprised at how much she was looking forward to a night of music from a previous incarnation.

The time raced past. She bought T-shirts for the grandkids and a figurine for herself. Now that Dick was gone, she realized she could honor her own past. He always acted as if anything she did before him was a sign of disloyalty. She had buried much of her history, and it was invigorating to remember.

She slipped back to the room to shower and change clothes for the last time that day. There was a burning need for different shoes. The radio quieted after the rush of arrests, even though there would be endlessly patrolling into the night. Neglecting the planned afternoon nap, she returned to the lobby as the attendees swarmed back in. They were loud and excited about the parade, and making connections with other fans and fanatics. The phone beeped; it was Belinda texting.

"Signing out. Glen is nite contact. C U – café at 7 A.M. I have?"

Mildred tapped, "C U then."

She began her cruise for food; there were meal coupons in the envelope Bud had provided. As usual, Mildred drifted to the buffet. It was seafood night, and Chef Mike knew how to do seafood right. While trying to balance a plate of crab cakes and lobster Rockefeller, Mildred spotted her old friends. "Room for one more?"

"We always make room for you, Dred. Are you here alone?" DJ pulled over a chair from an adjacent table.

"I live nearby, so I come over often; especially on Seafood night, Italian Night, and sometimes on Tuesdays too."

Scott spoke up, "Need to introduce you around." Mildred tried to focus on each name and face, hoping to remember a couple of them. There were wives, girlfriends, and later band members.

"My God in Heaven. Jerry Lee, is that you?" Her eyes made contact with the elderly man seated at the foot of the table. "I never dreamed you would be a survivor. Marry any little girls lately?"

His face lit up with a smile that filled the room. "Dred, we were just talking about you. Look at you, all grown up, but I still see the schoolgirl I knew. I've wondered many times where you disappeared off to."

"I moved to Nashville, hoping to get a job in music. Pulled a couple of office gigs for different labels, but you know how life shuffles your plans around."

Jerry Lee laughed, "Well, I know, darlin'." The table slipped into old stories and speculation about what should have or could have been. Jerry Lee admitted he occasionally did a concert, but wasn't working much. Occasionally, he would hit some events to pick up attention and the cash was still good. The years fell off their faces as they reminisced. The group sat for over an hour, eating, laughing and cataloging who was gone and how they died. The men referred to Mildred as the one that got away and kept her looks. Scotty teased her about surgery, and with enough money, her face could look as contrived as Priscilla's.

The women left first to get seats for the show, and Mildred stayed with her old friends. They would be part of the show, and Scotty's wife promised to hold a place for Mildred. Well-intentioned promises to keep in touch were shared, and the plan to see each other over the weekend was guaranteed. When she

got to the theater, it was nearly full. She walked down the central aisle, searching for three women with four seats.
A woman's voice called out, "Dred, over here."

Mildred squeezed down the row, and the women welcomed her. It was just like a musician to marry someone younger and beautiful, but Mildred found these women to be smart and comfortable with the life. Before the show started, Mildred excused herself to make a walk-through of the theater. In the back of the house, she made eye contact with Arnie. He nodded towards other members of the security team and approached her.

"Did you bring those throwing panties left over from Tom Jones?"

"Shut up, funny guy. Tom Jones is a fantasy. Elvis was a reality, so I'll keep my panties, thank you very much."

"Due to the arrests in the casino this afternoon, we have doubled up on security."

"That is a relief; my seating doesn't lend itself to any patrolling."

Arnie answered, "Enjoy the show; we have this. Are you going to need a ride home?"

"I swear I've been on my feet since breakfast. I'm staying in house tonight; Bud comped me a room," said Mildred.

Arnie answered, "Lucky you."

The lights dimmed, and Mildred hurried back to her seat and enjoyed the entire show. Great to hear the music, most of the impersonators were excellent, but having been with Elvis so many years before, she could imagine him spinning in his grave at $33^1/_3$ rpm.

Back in her room within a half-hour after the concert, she almost collapsed in exhaustion and warm memories. The fans were, unlike Elvis, serious drinkers, causing the night to exaggerate as time passed. She had not noticed any of the new party drugs, so she was confident security could handle the rest of the night.

– 25 –
The Past

Awake early, Mildred was surprised of how well she had slept in a strange bed. She sent a message to her granddaughter to check on the cat. It has been handy that Glory had her key. Even though she was sure there was plenty of water and food, it seemed inconsiderate to leave Popcorn alone. Mildred had time to shower and prepare leisurely for another day of walking and watching. Looking forward to the breakfast scheduled with Belinda at seven, she was in a great mood. Humming *Good Luck Charm*, the song Elvis said was hers. She wondered how many women he had given the same line. It was a conscious decision to believe him. She decided to wear makeup, with a definite feeling of anticipation about the upcoming day. Mildred was shocked to see her reflection. The remarks from old friends had convinced her she still looked like a teen. No time to question where all of the years have gone, a seventy-one year old woman stared deeply into the mirror. The only evidence of the girl was in the dark eyes and the curl in her hair. The woman wrestled the girl back from an old nostalgia.

There was nothing to do with the passage of time as she turned from the mirror. The T-shirt she had made yesterday cheered her as she slipped it on. She added a cardigan sweater to hide her arms and part of the shirt; then scurried off for breakfast.

"Table for two, please, something towards the back." She settled in with a carafe of coffee and two menus. She removed the sweater when she saw Belinda enter the restaurant.

"Good morning, Dred." Belinda had a huge grin on her face. "Bud wanted to join us, but I told him he had to buy the lunch. I want more information about your past, and I need you to talk freely. Hold on a minute. Let me see that shirt." Belinda stared at Mildred and read *I "KNEW" Elvis '63-'64*. "Do you mean like in the biblical sense of knew?"

"I'll leave all interpretation up to you." Mildred couldn't hide the suggestive smile as she raised one eyebrow and made a kissing noise.

"I think it does." Belinda stared deeply into Mildred's eyes and finally asked, "How did you meet him?" The question hung in the air as the server came to take the order.

Once they were alone, Mildred started to speak. "I'm originally from Memphis, and in my last year of high school, I had a part-time job at Sun Records. I was an intern and filled in for the receptionist. I have no idea exactly who I've met. There were some of music's giants coming through that door. Had to hand it to Sam, he is responsible for changing music as we knew it."

Belinda was stunned and thrilled to allow Mildred to speak of her youth. The names she mentioned were a catalog of history, and the stories were funny and amazing. Belinda felt excited that she was sharing pancakes with a historical treasure, someone who had been there. "What happened, how long were you there?"

"Once I graduated, I moved to Nashville, trying to get a full-time job in music, and ended up competing with musicians for restaurant jobs. I finally moved to California. I'd hoped for a career in movies. I'm still not sure how I ended up at the police academy. You know most of the story from there."

"Did you sleep with him?"

"Honey, we all did, and there wasn't much sleeping. I left when Elvis decided to bring Priscilla to Memphis."

"You met Priscilla too?"

"Oh, yes, I did. There are still harsh feelings between us. I was relieved to see she wasn't attending this convention."

Belinda reached up for a high-five salute and winked as Mildred returned the gesture and added, "No details to share, but I fondly remember the black Lincoln at the entry to the casino."

Belinda shivered and poured more coffee into each cup.

"Too much information, but I will walk past it before I go up to the office, to honor my new best friend."

"This is between us; I don't need Arnie giving me a hard time about Tom Jones and Elvis."

"Do you mean, Tom Jones too?"

"Hell no, Tom was, er, is a fantasy," Mildred smiled, and put the sweater back on; the shirt was for Belinda's benefit and only for her.

– 26 –
Getting Lucky

"**G-ma busy?**"
"**No, patrolling.**"
"**Check out roulette – crowd gathering 10-4.**"

Mildred turned and walked directly towards the center gaming tables. As soon as she entered, the boisterous assembly at the Big Six Wheel was clear. Most of the other tables emptied as people gathered in anticipation. There was a universal gasp from the spectators watching the action, and she joined the group.

The dealer declared, "Place your Bets," paused, and then the crowd threw down a variety of chips and settled into a mass of expectancy.

Immediately after the crush of betting, the dealer announced, "Bottle of water, jigger of gin, let's have a winner on the next spin." The wheel and the throng of gamblers lit up, mesmerized as they watched the spiral of lights and numbers hurling towards destiny. The room, in an anticipatory throb, watched the wheel slow and click-click-click. Pause.

"We have a winner," and the crowd cheered as the operator gathered the wagers and paid out a large stack of chips to a very tall, young Elvis.

Once the celebration calmed, the dealer said, "Place your Bets." Even more, people pushed to deposit wagers on the marked table. "Bucket of Whiskey, none of it rye, let's all give it one more try." Then she launched the wheel. The gathering hushed in expectation as the gigantic disk twirled. Lights blazed past in an anticipatory flurry, then click click click. "A winner!" The crowd went crazy. Several players and Skinny Elvis collected another payday amongst applause.

The dealer smiled broadly, and the mob's energy continued to escalate. Mildred tapped out a quick message to the office.

"**Elvis streak – Big 6. No problems.**"
"**10-4**"
"**Staying to watch.**"

"Place your bets. Shot of tequila, suck on a lime. Will he do it…" and the crowd answered in unison, "one more time!" The wheel propelled into a flashing revolution, and they tumbled into an excited hush as the spectators watched. Click-click-click.

It was just a moment in time that skinny Elvis would retell for the rest of his days. So close to a massive win, he forgot the odds on Big 6 and let it all ride one time too many. Mildred slipped away with the crowd as they dispersed, retelling the story and speculations on what could have been.

She ambled back to the theater for the amateur impersonator contest. The show started as she entered and luckily, there was a seat towards the rear. Many of the contestants were excellent, but she had heard the King, and it started to seem rude. She didn't realize how tired she was until that moment.

About an hour into the show, when another old Elvis entered the stage in the required white jumpsuit cut down to his rounded belly. It was enough. Understanding it was to be an homage didn't work for her, at least not tonight. She glanced around the room and noted visible security posted. Quietly she left the theater. Once in the lobby, she called in

"G-ma wrapping it up."

"10-4 G-ma, great day today."

She turned toward the elevator and her room. As she passed the Kasbah Lounge, it was a snap decision to spoil herself with a glass of wine. It would be welcomed, relaxing and could help her sleep. Mildred was relieved there were only a couple of people at the bar, and she found a booth. Being exhausted and not much of a drinker, it was hard to decide on a vintage, but settled with a lovely, large glass of house red.

"Dred, not at the show?"

She looked up looking for the familiar voice.

"Scotty! I couldn't take it anymore. How about you?"

"Yeah I know, I have a limit, and that ran out in 1985." They sat together for the nightcap, drenched in memory, light conversation, and exhaustion. "Sorry, Dred, I'd love to sit here all night, but getting old is a bitch."

"I'm done too. I want out of here before the Elvises get out. Not up to dealing with that insanity." Mildred picked up the check, to his objections, and they both walked to the elevator calling it a night. "Will you be around tomorrow?"

"Yeah, we will keep the booth open until two and break down after that. Lots of buying after check-out time."

"I'll find you before you leave." She left him on the elevator and walked to her door, entering the darkened room. She kicked off her shoes and wished for a bathtub. Once all elastic was removed, she pulled on one of Dick's old shirts. She turned on the nightly news and immediately fell asleep.

27
Finally

Rising early, she felt rested with a single complaint: aching and swollen feet. Mildred took one of the longest, hottest showers of her adult life. She dressed in the T-shirt Bud gave her with the same jeans. It was a little tight for a seventy-one year old groupie, so she decided to add her Bambi biker vest, and it was perfect. She packed her overnight bag, setting it next to the door and was glad this weekend was about to end.

As she started down for breakfast, she sent Belinda a quick text. "**B'fast #3?**"

With an immediate response. "**Table in the back. Pouring coffee now.**"

Mildred entered the dining room and could see Belinda waving at her. Bud was there too. *The man seems to have a fascination with breakfast.*

They ordered pancakes and eggs, but Mildred was more interested in a bran muffin. The three settled into a review of the day before. By the time, they finished eating, the café was full, and there was a line waiting to get in. Many of the Elvises now looked like middle-aged men with outdated haircuts.

Everyone was still in a festive humor, but apparently, the convention was winding down. Check out was at eleven, and the final closing ceremony and get together began then and ended at noon. The vendor tables would be open until two, in an attempt to harvest the last of the expendable cash.

Mildred left the café to set up surveillance in the lobby. She nested in the overstuffed chair to watch the parade of characters. Her timing was perfect, and she was able to kiss Jerry Lee goodbye. They were both teary-eyed, sure it was a strong possibility they would never meet again.

Jerry Lee spoke, "This might be one of my last conventions."

His wife snickered, "He has been saying since I was married to Rusty. He makes this announcement every event. He only came to this one because it fit into his concert schedule, and he likes getting paid."

Mildred was grateful he had. As he turned to leave, he stopped, looked back, and extended an invitation for her to visit his home in Mississippi at any time.

"That would be great." Mildred's enthusiastic acceptance was shadowed by the shared doubt it would ever happen.

Since it was nearly noon when she spotted her old friends, DJ, and Scotty; she rushed over for a possible final embrace. They laughed at her outfit and hugged her. She couldn't help but see in her mind's eye the young, hungry musicians from way back in the day. People waited for autographs and memorabilia, and she slipped away as curious eyes and whispers followed her exit. As the convention ended, she put her memories back in storage and returned to the present century.

"G-ma on the floor."
"10-4"

She was amazed how things turned back to the usual day-to-day as the convention passed like a dream. The floor seemed quiet for a Sunday, until she saw her picture flashing by on the Jumbotron video feed. THIS WEEK'S WINNERS – THIS WEEK'S WINNERS – THIS WEEK'S WINNERS. *Yikes, we need to fix this now.* A quick text to Belinda:

"Call me ASAP"

The phone rang almost immediately. "What's up, Hoochie Momma?"

"I'm on the video feed for the winner announcements."

Belinda answered, "Damn, that was supposed to be pulled. No one pays attention to those reports anyway.

"Yeah, right, I've just had my back patted with a 'Way to go.'"

"Okay, I'll call again."

Mildred answered, "Now!"

Belinda continued, "Here is Bud. He wants to talk to you."

"Since your cover is blown, why don't you go home? We still have the extra patrol going. You deserve a couple of days off," said Bud.

"Can't disagree. I'll go check out."

"You don't have to check out, just leave the key card on the dresser. See you in a few days." Mildred responded with a text: **"G-ma out."**

– 28 –
Life Changes

Popcorn met her at the door; it felt good to be home. As usual, the cat rubbed against her legs in a demand for attention. Mildred picked up the insistent feline and carried her to the couch for a cuddle. The memories were great, but Mildred had no regrets about her life right now. After a couple of minutes, she took her overnight bag to her room and found Amelia and Izzy asleep in her bed. Mildred realized that there was nothing more beautiful in the whole world than the sound of her granddaughters breathing while they slept. She quietly left the case and went back to the kitchen to heat water for tea. It made her smile to see Popcorn had a full feeder of food and two bowls of fresh water. Gratitude washed over her, as she looked out the window to see neighbors with canes and walkers in the afternoon light. Mildred realized her life now was exciting and new, the past will be packed away and only used for interesting stories. Gratitude to the universe and the people in it was extended, a feeling of satisfaction wafted over her, knowing she was not trapped in the day-to-day task of surviving old age.

Mildred turned off the bedroom television, "All right ladies, time to wake up."

There were grumbles and moans as the girls began to stir.

"What time did you go to bed?"

Amelia sat up slowly and stretched, "Oh Grandma! Glory dropped us off this morning to play with Popcorn."

"Yeah Grandma, we are taking care of our cat, and she is fine," Izzy added.

"Good job, girls. What are your plans for today?"

"Glory is to pick us up after her orientation for school."

Mildred felt a jolt of delight, "Orientation for school? Which college did she decide on?"

"She is going to the police academy in Los Angeles, and the promoter guy is at the Holiday Inn."

Izzy piped in, "She will be like you and Grandpa."

Mildred was overwhelmed with a contradiction of pride and concern. Police work was much more dangerous and challenging since her time on the force. She had a strong desire to go to the Holiday Inn and intervene. "Amelia, has she mentioned that kind of work before? Did she decide against college?"

Amelia took over, "She told Dad that she would go to college if this didn't work out. He isn't very happy about any of it."

"I can imagine he isn't. He grew up in a police environment, and there was a lot of pressure. It's a difficult job for sure."

Izzy went to the kitchen, and Mildred heard the freezer open. The cat followed her, and finally Amelia and Mildred wandered in. By the time they arrived, Izzy had already torn open a frozen pizza and was on her way to the microwave. Amelia switched on the radio and turned up the volume to sing along. Amelia then continued to chat about Glory. Mildred was relieved to learn her middle granddaughter planned to be a veterinarian or a teacher. They all fell into a pleasant afternoon. It was after five when Glory arrived to pick up the girls. Mildred stared at the young woman she had become, still only able to see a blonde toddler with a runny nose. *How could the Academy accept my baby?* Time, cursed time had passed, and it was difficult to acknowledge that the grandchildren were making life decisions more complicated than Popsicle flavors. "Well, Glory, I'm proud of you, but that is a big step. How did it go?"

Glory was filled with enthusiasm and questions for her grandmother. "Oh, it was great. This was just an initial interview and they will call for a follow up and a physical." There was no time for a long conversation. She wanted to take the girls home so she could get ready for a date that evening.

When the noisy carload of her greatest pride pulled away, the tears stored behind her eyes took over.

– 29 –
Back to Work

Once the girls were gone, Mildred had time to unpack the overnight bag and washed the T-shirts. As they dried, it felt as if her life had been only minutes long. Mildred lovingly folded each shirt and put them into the box of memories. She smiled with the tender thoughts of Elvis, the man that very few really knew. As she put the top on the box, she told him goodbye and returned those years to a long private part of her heart.

Slowly storing the box in the back of the closet, she returned it to history, the only story she never told Dick. She closed the door and came back to today and the responsibilities facing her. The girls had been helpful, but her biggest task was cleaning the litter box. She picked up the scoop and pondered. *Funny how people will put the food in the cat, and no one takes care of what comes out. I'll have to teach Popcorn to clean her own bathroom.* Next stop was to check the phone. There were two messages on the answering machine, both from Karen at Gamblers Anonymous with an invite, "The girls are getting together after the Sunday meeting for dinner. You are invited to join us."

It was almost time, and Mildred wasn't tired or hungry. *Might as well put on Delilah and show up for dinner meeting, but I'll have to hurry.*

Mildred arrived with a minute to spare, and found a seat in the circle of chairs next to Ed. She nodded to Rose as Karen started the greetings. Jack L. went first and relayed a weekend of old memories and temptations. His loneliness was palpable. The room gave Jack L. congratulations all around, reminding each other that it is one day at a time, and they were in it together. Karen led the group into a conversation about the steps and using them as tools to stay away from craps and vodka.

Ed D. spoke next about his ongoing divorce and missing his kids. The final court date was in two weeks, and he was concerned about losing his home. He understood that his wife deserved the house, but he was financially crushed, and this added to his feeling of failure and desperation. He finished with a string of swear words all aimed at cards and the NFL. Mildred made a mental note that he might have known Dick, since they were drawn to the same games.

Most of the people in the room spoke, but Mildred/Delilah stayed quiet. At the last, Karen asked if she wanted to share, and Mildred stated, "I'm doing well today, nothing new."

The meeting broke, and Mildred joined the women for dinner. They went to the nearby Denny's, and the chatter was comforting. It was a two hour dinner of old stories and challenges of the everyday life of recovery. Mildred stayed quiet, as the exhaustion of the weekend caught up with her. They divided with three of the women going to the restroom. Mildred paid, and waited to walk out with Rosie as she argued over the expiration date on her coupon.

– 30 –
Oliver

After a couple of days working as Bambi, Mildred thought it was important to go back in for the Senior Specials. They start early, and end promptly; funny how this change happened to the wild children of the '50s and '60s. The initial rounds of the poker tournament would kick off around seven. Mildred decided to be Oliver, mostly for the large loose loafers stuffed with cotton balls that completed his cover. When it came to footwear, men scored.

Mildred drove over, as she planned on staying late. Once parked, she made her usual scan of the lot. The white van was there in the loading dock area. She walked in the door just as a heavy rain began. It was late afternoon, and a poker tournament was set up, but wouldn't start until later. It was scheduled to wrap up on Saturday night.

Patrolling through the usual senior haunts for the first walk through, Mildred notice that the weather made a turn towards apocalypse. The sound of the hammering rain overpowered the din of slot machines. There was a weather warning broadcasted on the television screens that were scattered throughout the casino. Even though it was still afternoon, she looked up through the skylights and it was darker than night, with ominous threats of lightning. Quickly, a significant portion of the patrons bailed out, and employees started to gather in small groups to watch the news. Mildred thought about her cat waiting patiently at home. Concerned passed over her, worrying if the thunder was frightening Popcorn.

Her feet were tender from the two previous nights in motorcycle boots; she settled into a seat in the café to see if the weather would break. As the only customer, Mildred discarded her concern for the alternative personality. She smiled and contemplated her order and noticed each of her characters had different tastes. Oliver avoided Mildred's favorite buffet; he liked service and elegance; Bambi wanted quick and straightforward, and time would tell about Delilah. Mildred decided not to discuss this with any mental health professionals. Always best to avoid a diagnosis at this stage of life.

There was another crash of lightning and her phone buzzed with a text. Security ordered her home and asked if she needed a ride. Slowly she tapped a response, signed out for the shift, and refused the ride. The cell phone received a couple weather news bulletins and a notice of widespread damage with a traffic advisory on the 5th Avenue Bridge.

A friendly voice broke the news. "Do you mind if I join you?"

Mildred switched back to Oliver and looked up at an attractive, tall, older woman. Dropping her voice slightly to answer, "No, I don't mind. Please do." What else could she do? It would be rude to dismiss the woman, and Oliver was a gentleman.

"My name is Penny Dumple, and I'm staying at the hotel. I started to think I was one of the only guests left. Are you staying too?"

"Ah no, I live nearby. Just grabbing a little to eat." Oliver instantly liked this woman and had to pay close attention to maintaining character. Luckily, Penny dominated the conversation. She was from Lincoln, a widow, and when the storm started, her friends went home. She had won a spa voucher and booked a room to stay for what she called the end of the world massage and pedicure.

The waiter brought Oliver's tomato soup and grilled cheese sandwich with Penny's Greek salad. He topped off their coffee and disappeared. Oliver had to stay mindful of the fake facial hair as he ate the soup. The wail of the tempest intensified, and they felt isolated as if they were lone survivors.

Mildred could see Penny's concern, "Not sure what we should do when the animals begin to arrive two by two."

Penny laughed adding, "If they expect us to repopulate the earth, there will be some surprises."

Oliver agreed a little too enthusiastically, as she realized Penny was flirting. They ate and continued in a pleasant conversation. "Well, my dear lady, I have to go home while I still have one. Popcorn is waiting for me, and I'm sure the storm is frightening her." Oliver picked up both bills and prepared to depart. "Popcorn? You just ate."

"That is my cat and present love. She expects dinner to be on time."

"Cats do not forgive when their bowl is empty." Penny smiled.

It would have been easy to wait out the storm with this new friend. The conversation was light and easy, but Mildred knew Oliver needed a way out and fast. She stood to leave, as Penny reached over to slide a card into her hand. Oliver smiled, bowed and turned to go. *Oh my, I scored a phone number.*

Mildred walked through the casino towards the rear parking lot as the doors blew open. She had to grab quickly to save her wig and mustache. This storm was violent and in the past two hours had become almost biblical. She hesitated as she looked at the vertical rain and decided to remove most of the disguise before she made a run for the car.

Aware she would walk into the restroom as a man and out as a woman, she decided on the men's room, confident she could outwait anyone in there, besides there are often more bizarre happenings in there. Even better, she would do a quick check for stolen property. The worry was for nothing; the trash was empty. She wrapped the hairpieces and vest into a bundle with her blazer and fastened it with the fanny pack. There was a sudden loud popping and then complete blackness. Startled by her own scream, she took a deep breath, gathered her things and felt for the door.

As she touched the metal plate of the door handle, her pocket vibrated, which caused another involuntary yelp. She exited to the subdued light of the casino generator. Spooked by the storm and the soundless enormity of the gaming room, Mildred turned to the door. The automatic doors slammed shut, and the sound of the backup generator stopped. Once finished screaming for the third time, she answered the vibrating cell phone.

"Mildred, is that you? Are you still here?" She felt relief at the sound of Belinda's voice.

"Yes, I'm here. The doors just locked on me, what's going on? Do I need to find an escape route?"

"No, no, I need you! Meet me at the south steps." Belinda sounded anxious. Mildred knew something was up. Mildred did a walk/run to the meeting point.

Belinda appeared within seconds, out of breath and pale. "Mildred, come with me." She moved fast and continually scanned the surroundings. She pulled Mildred into a janitorial closet and searched it briefly before she closed the door. The absolute darkness engulfed them when Belinda pulled Mildred close, and whispered, "We are being robbed."

"What!"

"Shhhh. We think they are using the storm as cover, they cut the power, and they tried to shoot the security door to the counting room. Luckily, it has held so far, and the crew set off the silent alarm. At the same time, more gunmen forced their way into the cashier cages. They have hostages, and there were some gun shots.

"Bud and the guys are responding. Here is a gun and Bud's master key. He asked us to watch for the police and let them in when they arrive. The place is completely locked down; it is up to us to evacuate any players to a safe location."

"What's a safe place?"

Close to tears, Belinda responded, "I don't know. I haven't thought that through."

Mildred took a deep breath and said, "Okay, let's take them to the nightclub. It is Sunday and closed, and there would be no money for them. That should be the last place they would hit. We need to get employees in there, too."

As they started to exit, Mildred added, "Tell the employees to offer free drinks. That will calm everyone and keep them put."

"Brilliant, I'll take the east side, and you take the west."

"You may want to take off that name badge."

Mildred gave Belinda a quick class on the fine art of invisibility, and the two walked away like ghosts. One looked lost, and the other tapped her cell phone. No one noticed them, as they lingered at each door, eyes alert, missing nothing.

– 31 –
Police Ready

Caution be damned, she had to get the civilians under cover. Mildred edged through the darkened slot machine rows toward the card tables and gaming section. Her reflexes honed and ready, the only sound was the rage of the storm and the beating of her heart. Belinda had gone ahead to unlock the nightclub and gather employees to light candles and staff the room. Together they cleared the restaurants and bars. Hopefully, Penny had gone back to the hotel before the lockdown. Belinda told Mildred she would check the metal gate to the hotel and if it was quiet, close it off. Mildred overheard whispering on her ear piece with Belinda's instructions to the concierge. He had no out of the ordinary activity and promised to keep all guests out of sight. He signed off to lock the front doors and close down the front desk. The women cleared their sections, locked the safes and moved employees, too. Mildred moved to the private game rooms. Nearly running, she purposefully surveyed in every direction. There were some voices and laughter from the high roller card tables. Even at her age, people amazed her daily. *Guess you don't need electricity to hit on 16.*

Gamblers had resorted to illuminating the tables with the apps on their phones. "Excuse me, gentlemen, we have a complex problem here at the Ivory."

They laughed and turned toward Mildred in the pale light.

"The casino has asked everyone to move to the night club. This is an emergency drill, and we thank you for your orderly evacuation. There are free drinks, and we will let you know as soon as it is over."

The gamblers grumbled, but then she whispered to the nearest dealer, "This is important, no exceptions." The young woman nodded and left quickly, herding the perplexed card players. She promised them another hand at the nightclub.

Suddenly there was a commotion near the western entrance. Mildred ran toward the sound, fumbling with the passkey. She waved for the armed officers to stop as they started to breach the door with a metal battering ram. They pulled up short, and she was able to open the door. "About time you guys got here. We only have the Sunday Security team." Just as she finished turning the key, the S.W.A.T. team shoved the door and swarmed in like Mongols taking Persia. Mildred was pinned behind the large double door. They ignored her until the commander entered at the rear of the onslaught. He helped to close the door and barked, "Sorry Ma'am, we need you to show us where the breach is."

She straightened her clothing, "Your guys don't sneak worth a tinker's damn." He ignored her comments.

Forced to run to keep up with the invading force, she tried to give him the skinny on the areas under assault. "We have evacuated most of the civilians and employees; they are in the nightclub, over there. I understand the breach is in the counting room, with a second group at the cashier booths."

Not sure he was listening, she continued toward the assaulted areas, breathing heavily and giving all of the information she had.

"I suggest you consider the element of surprise!" With no answer, she assumed he planned on overwhelming force instead.

They surged through, Mildred noticed two buffet cooks watching wide-eyed from the front of the restaurant. Sternly she waved them over to the nightclub. "Get moving, you two! Everyone needs to go, now!" Mildred had to break into a full run to catch up to the invading force. They had guns drawn, and covered all directions, moving like a perfectly choreographed, deadly threat. Mildred was in awe as she struggled to keep up.

Mildred kept moving and called Bud. It was a spotty connection, she heard him, "Came in thr…the panic r…."

"Slow down, boss. Connection bad."

He continued, "I ha…the counting crew in…th.. safe room. Don't dare … move. Door jam…. Do ….h… passkey?"

"Yes, Bud, I have it. Once things clear, I will come down to let you out."

He tried to give an update status, but Mildred only heard isolated words. The connection went dead, and Mildred sped back up to a run as she stowed the phone.

She called out to the invading force. "Captain! Captain! I have information."

She saw her verbal message passed from the S.W.A.T. members to the front. The captain made some almost silent hand motions, instructing his officers, and came back to Mildred and demanded, "What do you have?"

She felt the need for efficiency. "Talked to Bud Moses. He has the counting crew isolated in a secured room. Right rear of the main room, behind a metal door. Moses reported he is unable to see or hear anything."

The captain relayed a brief message into a radio transmitter on his shoulder. Mildred noticed he continued a constant scanning of the area.

Mildred continued, assuming he was listening. "He said something about men and four."

The S.W.A.T. Captain only stopped long enough for the update and for her to unlock the access to the lower level stairs. In a low intense voice, he spoke to one of the apparent leaders. She watched six of the men disappear into the dark basement stairs. Their flashlights scanned back and forth. All she could hear were the boots quickly descend the stairs.

The Captain stayed back with three other officers and looked to Mildred for instructions. She pointed the way to the cashier cages.

In a glance across the lobby, she saw Belinda rush past with, hopefully, the last of the crapshooters. Their eyes locked, and she signaled Belinda to lock it down and pointed to the restrooms near the cashier's section. Belinda's face was serious as she shook her head no.

Mildred's police training was at 110%, and there was no stopping now. She slid into the ominous silence of the dark men's room. There was no sound, and she calmly said, "Is anyone in here?" The only answer was the echo of her voice. Using her cell phone's light, she confirmed the stalls were empty. Like a shadow, she crept to the women's room. Again, darkness and silence. As she started to check the stalls, there was the hint of a whimper.

Speaking softly, Mildred held her cell phone up to light her own face. "Hello, this is Mildred. I'm here to get you out." The whimper became a sob. Huddled in the rear stall was a cashier Mildred didn't recognize. The young woman was crouched on the floor. "Come on, honey, let's get off the Firing Line and go someplace safer." The young woman's legs offered no support as she struggled to stand. Mildred recognized raw terror and went for a damp paper towel to provide comfort. The smell of sanitizer filled her lungs in the heightened silence.

Mildred laid the cell phone on the counter, and she reached for the towel dispenser. The entry door crashed open. In the brief light following the intruder from the lobby, Mildred could tell she was face to face with a gun. The man shoved her against the wall, and she snarled, "Idiot, you really think the women's can is an escape route?"

"Shut up, you old witch. I'll get out now I've got you." He ran his hands roughly over her body "You're packing heat, old fool?" He took her gun with his free hand, missing her pepper spray and Taser in the fanny pack.

Suddenly and without warning, a woman's size eight Nike made contact with his genitals. The gunman screamed and crumbled. Mildred spun around, and her Taser finished him. As he convulsed on the floor, Mildred kicked his gun towards the young cashier. The woman picked it up and pointed it at the heap of punk on the floor. Mildred recovered her weapon, stood over him, and said, "Underestimating women; hope you like stripes, Butt Munch.

The two women were all business as they held both guns pointed at the floor in the dark room. The only sound was of strained breathing.

"Okay, Ninja Princess, we have to tie this guy up before he comes to." Mildred and the frightened cashier started to search for anything to restrain the unconscious Butt Munch. Once he was restrained, Mildred pulled out her phone and texted.

"Belinda, send biggest casino employee to women's room by cashier. Be sure can handle a gun."

There was an immediate response on her screen.

"10-4 Will do ASAP."

In less than two minutes, there was a polite knock on the door. Mildred peeked out to see a mountain of a man. "Chef Mike! Perfect." She pulled him in just as there was a burst of distant gunfire. Mildred took the gun from her terrified ally allowing her to collapse to the floor in a continued flood of silent tears. Mike took over the guarding the prisoner.

The thief slowly regained consciousness, to find he was restrained with his own belt, Mildred/ Oliver's breast-minimizing ace bandage and gagged with two dollars' worth of sanitary napkins. He was being used as the doorstop to the women's restroom.

His first sight was of a huge man dressed in white smelling, like cookies. The look of furious brown eyes squashed any fledgling escape plan.

Cognizant of the ongoing danger, Mildred called 911. "This is Mildred Petrie, Casino security. I need back-up in the main floor, women's toilet near the cashier cages. S.W.A.T. is in house." Staying acutely vigilant, the odd teammates waited.

The silence was broken by an occasional sound of gunfire. The only light was from the skylights and the minimal emergency lighting. Mildred broke the silence, "Thanks Mike. Where did you learn to handle a gun?"

The threatening man made a half smile, "Marines, ma'am. That is where I learned to cook, too."

The frightened ninja asked, "Which do you like better?"

Mike looked at the captive as he started to squirm, "Today I like the shooting," and the young thief stopped all movement and accepted his fate.

Mildred's phone rang. "Yes. West entrance, rear of the casino door unlocked. Sending someone to guide you."
Mike asked, "What was that?"

"More cops almost here. Ninja, you up to letting them in?"

The young woman began to tear up. "I don't know, I guess."

Mildred sized her up in the hazy light. "Let me try Belinda first." She tapped a quick message. The phone rang while still in Mildred's hand and she jumped. "Yes!"

She heard Belinda's voice. She was obviously in a take charge mode. "Mildred. More information, please."

"The police are sending additional backup, and we are still in the restroom, too much action nearby. Reinforcements will come to the west rear door."

"On my way, Double-Oh-Seventy-One." Mildred could hear Belinda shout instructions as the phone disconnected.

Minutes later Belinda appeared leading several officers, guns drawn and flashlights cutting through the shadows. Mildred buckled into Belinda's arms and they laughed, out of relief and nervousness. The officers jerked the captive off the floor, who also seemed relieved. Two took him back the way they had come. Mildred sent the others to back up police teams already inside.

It seemed like minutes, but actually hours had passed. The dim generator lights illuminated the haggard security team as they gathered in the Gold Coast Restaurant. Chef Mike brought out a pot of soup and sat down and joined them. In a collective meditation, they stared into the bowls, too tired to speak. The final count was: two robbers dead, at least two, maybe three, armed suspect escaped, and one, thanks to Mildred, captured, two cops wounded, one cashier supervisor shot, in critical condition, and five, including the ninja, were at the hospital.

The silence broke as Mildred revealed, "I've got a girlfriend." After the surrealism of the day, her simple statement broke the tension, and there was a universal exhale.

Bud looked at her fondly. "Whoa, you have had a full day. How'd you have time to include romance?"

Belinda snorted and added, "You folks have no idea about our secret agent's love life."

The tired group was able to relax almost in unison as Mildred told the team about Oliver's charm and meeting Penny. Only after the light-hearted story, could the employees relax enough to share their stories of the day.

Bud announced, "I want everyone to go home and write up what happened. We will work on formal reports on Monday. Clock in early and come to security before your shifts begin." There was a sigh of agreement.

Bud continued, "I'm passing my note pad around. I need everyone's name, address and phone for the police." Bud dug for a pen and wrote his name, title and contact information at the top of the list.

They were starting to break up when Arnie arrived. "Well, you folks had a challenging afternoon. I just watched the news."

Bud looked up surprised. "Oh, I'm sorry. I should have called."

"WOW, so easily forgotten, and all it took were bandits and bullets." Arnie exaggerated a look of dismay.

Belinda spoke up, "You are early."

"Figured you needed the night shift in as soon as possible. It wasn't easy getting past the crime scene tape."

Mildred joined in, "How did you get in?"

"Well, Agent Petrie, I have an ID, a pass key and know where the back door is. Here's my plan, I'll call the night shift and cancel most of them. Since we are locked down, and full of cops, I don't need a full crew." Arnie scanned the table and continued, "I'll take over for this haggard looking A-team. Mildred, you need to get some ice on that shiner."

"Shiner? I've got a black eye?"

Belinda smiled, "You have a beauty coming in. We have been watching it go from red to midnight purple."

Arnie took over, "Go home. I'm here, and I'll stay with the police through the night, and you folks get out of here. Give me that list, and Bud, can you introduce me to the head investigator?"

Bud handed the tablet with all of the contact information to Arnie, and he stood to leave. "They are interviewing the people in the night club and releasing them one at a time, so we will need someone there to walk people out. Larry is there now. The casino will remain closed until the scene investigation is completed."

Arnie nodded and made notes on another page of the note pad.

Bud sighed. "We will have to repair the bullet holes, and scrub up the blood spatter before we can reopen."

Mildred could see Bud's exhaustion as the two men turned to leave. Arnie put his arm on Bud's shoulders, "Don't worry about it, boss, we will get it all done. You aren't alone with this."

Belinda made a call and stood to leave. The young woman looked twenty years older. "My husband is outside to pick me up. He's going to take me to the hospital, and I'll check on our employees on my way home."

Mildred perked up and reached for her purse and a napkin.

"Would you give a note to the ninja?"

"You mean Lena Davis, right?"

"Yes, you know who she is. I want her to know she can call me for anything. She saved me from who knows what." Mildred finished the brief message with a phone number.

Chef Mike stood up and started to clear dishes. This was the signal for the rest of the casino warriors to head home before the police objected to their leaving. Mildred made a half-hearted dash through the flagging summer storm to her car. As she pulled from the lot for home, she noticed the white van in the abandoned delivery area was gone.

– 33 –
Pain Killers

Awakened to sandpaper kisses and a soft paw to a sore nose, Mildred tried to roll away from the sunlight. Her entire body burned, and movement was nearly impossible. Slowly, she tried to get out of bed, forced to respond to a clamoring need for the bathroom. Confident the stiffness would work out with movement, she struggled to take a hot shower. That was the instant she discovered she couldn't lift her left arm to undress.

She labored on, but couldn't open the drawer for her sweat pants, and it took several tries and slow gymnastics to realize she was helpless. She laid back her head when there was a knock at the door, followed by the sound of a key in the lock. Before she could react, she heard her son's voice. "Momma, are you here?"

Within moments of his arrival, a shirt was on, the cat fed, and Mildred was on her way to the ER. Relieved, she allowed him to take over; they were shrouded in silence. She tried to dodge an unavoidable conversation. He had heard the morning news and spoke of a body count. In a stall for time, she picked up her phone, and in frustration, Richie began the obviously planned intervention. "Mom, we don't know what you are thinking. Your job has turned out to be much more dangerous than expected. That place destroyed Dad, and now look at you. I didn't see the news last night. I… I heard about this on my way to work. The news about last night and now this? How did you get hurt? Were you beaten? What the hell went on?"

Mildred wasn't ready for this conversation, and could see the tears in her son's eyes. "Tell me when you're done with the questions, and then we can move forward." The short statement was exhausting, and Richie knew there would be no answers today. Her heart clenched as she failed to hold back tears. The sobs caused Mildred even more pain.

Richie's voice quieted in his recollection and with her obvious emotion. "That place is a jinx, and all of the Petries need to stay away. I've talked with Aunt Sissy and Lindsey. We have thought about this for a while, and my girls have agreed to double up. We want you to sell your place, and move in with us."

With a big sigh and more tears, Mildred knew this would never work. "Thank you, but no, not now. I don't gamble. It's not just a job. I can take care of myself." His mother's voice filled with defiance, and she could see his regret for starting the conversation at this time.

Mildred's phone beeped with a new text,
"Casino closed – can you come into the office?"
Richie found a parking space as she tried to respond to Bud's text. She was shaking when Richie took the phone and tapped in,
"At Dr. 2 call back."
After several agonizing hours, Mildred limped out with bottles of painkillers, muscle relaxants, and a sling. She reported to her son, "I have a hairline fracture to my clavicle, a sprained hip, topped off with contusions and lacerations to my face."

While he waited, Richie had picked up egg sandwiches and two cups of coffee at a drive-thru. They settled into the car in the parking lot, and he tried breaking off small bites for his mother. He didn't know if she wasn't hungry, or if she simply couldn't eat. The bruises were even more vibrant, and she sat with her eyes closed and whispered, "Casino first." He had to walk back around to help her with the seatbelt.

Mildred watched her son shake his head. He had learned from the years of living with his mother. If he argued, that would not stop her. Mildred spoke up, "If the casino is inconvenient, you can drop me off at home."

Richie mumbled, "And then you will just go anyway?"

"You know I can do it. I have a cane at home." Mildred croaked.

"Mom, I know you can't. But the word can't never stood in your way before. I'll take you and wait until you are finished."

He dropped her off at the employee entrance bus stop near the door. She sat at the bus stop until he parked and could come back to help her walk. Richie opened the door with her employee card. The casino felt ghostly: no valet, no cars, no flashing lights, even the incessant music was silent. The massive rooms stood vacant, gaudy and deserted. Slowly Mildred led Richie to a dark stairwell, and the injuries became more evident when she struggled with the first step. He picked her up and carried her back to the entrance. There he grabbed one of the courtesy wheelchairs, and he wheeled her to the rear elevator. The struggle was exhausting for both of them when they finally entered a door marked Employees Only. Lit by the blue-green glow of video screens, a single woman calmly scanned the monitors.

"Belinda, it is so good to see you. Are you all right?" Belinda turned with a painful look on her face,

"Oh honey, I didn't know you were hurt."

"Mentally, I'm great. Physically, we will wait and see." Mildred smiled.

"Do you want me to rerun the video?" Belinda reached for the switch. "I watched you come in and almost called an ambulance." She turned toward the glowing panels, and the reflection exposed her exhaustion.

"If you have a minute, I'd like you to meet my son." Richie noticed the women's connection. He had no idea that it was deeper than a friendship. They were a team built in a department of men.

A man's voice rang from a tiny office, "I hear someone I know." Bud entered the room and came over to hug her, but stopped in horror by the sight of the wheelchair, swollen face, black eyes, and the sling. "Holy crap, what has happened to my top gun?"

Mildred answered immediately, "Cosmetic surgery."

Richie shook his head knowingly and found a chair to wait. He was relieved as he crossed the bridge from worry to pride. It was obvious his mother had found her calling. Reassured, he saw she had good people around her who cared. He accepted his new task was to help her heal and to keep the secret.

When they finally returned to the retirement village, Amelia greeted them. Richie knew his mother would object to his helping her undress and had called ahead. Even though her body was damaged, she wouldn't change who she had always been. If she weren't so tired, Mildred would have insisted on privacy, but today she welcomed the help. In a few moments, Amelia and her dad worked together getting her settled into bed, then they just allowed Mildred to embrace the exhaustion and prescriptions. Enveloped by a strange world of fog and sleep, the afternoon and evening slipped past. From time to time, she would overhear television programs and sometimes felt a presence in the room. Another sip of water and more pills, she drifted off wondering why Amelia and Glory were the same person. As hours passed, the ice pack was always fresh, and food appeared on a tray next to the bed. Unsure who it was helping her to the bathroom, modesty was replaced by the comfort of a constant presence.

 Early the next morning, or maybe the day after, Mildred awakened fully. Her first notice was the reassurance and heat of the giant white guardian purring and snuggled against her aching hip. No matter how much she adored the cat, the pain made it necessary to move. Mildred slowly rolled to the right; she was surprised to find the other half of her bed was occupied. Rolled into a ball was her youngest granddaughter, Isabella, snoring softly. It was a struggle to move and not disturb the sleeping child. Settling into a position of marginal discomfort, she scanned the room. Everything seemed strangely the same, and yet different. The sun was peeking through the blinds, and her daughter-in-law was asleep in the chair by the window. Even though she tried not to disturb anyone, Popcorn arose with her movement, walked across the child and hopped onto the woman's lap. Mildred wanted to stroke the soft brown hair of her ten-year-old caregiver, but her arm was still immobile.

 Mildred watch Lindsey start to pet the demanding cat and opened her eyes. With a deep breath, she looked over at her youngest child and mother-in-law. Her eyes were greeted by her mother-in-law. Mildred mouthed "Thank you." Lindsey whispered, "Welcome back, Mildred.

 "How are you feeling?"

 "Pretty good, considering."

 "Do you need anything? Help to the bathroom? Drugs?"

 "Yes, but I'm good for a few minutes. I want to rest a moment and then maybe sit up for a while."

"Sounds like a plan. Izzy is your nurse of record this morning."

Mildred smiled lovingly. "I noticed. Hope I wasn't any trouble."

"Yes, you are trouble. We are worried sick about you. You had a terrible fall, and we all want you up and kicking again."

The girl aroused with a start. "Grandma, you are awake. I'll go get your pills and some ice."

"No, Nurse Izzy, I'm good for right now, but maybe a little later."

"Okay Grandma, you just tell me what you need. Are you hungry?"

"I hadn't thought about food yet. Are you hungry?"
Lindsey laughed lightly, "Izzy is always hungry."

The youngest nurse jumped from the bed and ran to the bathroom. Within a couple of minutes, the girl returned with a wet face and freshly brushed smile. The sound of the running water made the other two women need to start their day. There were errands to run and healing to address.

− 34 −
The Investigation Begins

With a need for clarity, Mildred had dismissed the pain medication that morning and slowly noticed the pain was constant, but improving. Before Lindsey left to go buy aspirin and a heating pad, she helped Mildred move to the chair in the living room. They raised the foot rest, and Mildred was able to sit almost comfortably, with Popcorn draped across her feet. It felt good to be out of bed, and the twosome napped in tandem. Suddenly Popcorn leapt out of the chair, walked to the front door, and started a patrol. The sudden action had roused her broken mistress. Mildred reached for the cup of tepid tea left on her side table, and wished it were either hot or cold. In no position to complain, she decided this was better than another cup of cold coffee.

There was a knock at the door, and Mildred, assuming it was one of the girls, called out, "It's open. Come in." Her boss Bud entered, carrying a catering box, followed by a tall, serious man.

"Mildred, old gal, this is Detective Elton Block. He is in charge of the investigation." They exchanged pleasantries, and he extended appreciation for her excellent police work. Bud reached over and took a sticky note off of her sling. "Looks like you didn't get the message we were coming over." Mildred blushed as she read the hasty note from Lindsey.

"So you will be here in an hour. Good to know."

The detective smiled, but seemed to be all business, and spoke up. "I'm so sorry for this inconvenience, but we need to talk to you. We haven't gotten much from your collar, but we will interview him again when I get back to the house."

As they spoke, Bud moved an end table to the side of her chair and opened the box. "I debriefed Chef Mike this morning, and he prepared this for you. He was concerned and wanted to come with me."

"So he knows who I am?"

"Don't worry; we had to read him in along with everyone at the table the night of the break-in."

"I didn't even think about it at the time. We were all kind of traumatized."

The box held a hot gourmet meal, a huge salad, and a variety of desserts, finished off with a carafe of coffee.

"I'll be the only casualty that gains weight. Bud, will you get some cups out of the cabinet and three forks?"

Mildred first concern when they arrived was what to offer, but the answer was in the box. The two men brought in kitchen chairs and sat near her. Each clutched a steaming cup and picked a dessert.

Bud asked, "Were you able to work up a written statement?"

Mildred answered, "No Boss, but it is on my calendar, and I can get on it tonight."

"No problem." Detective Block joined in. "I brought a recorder, and we can go ahead and take care of it now. If that is okay with you?"

Mildred gave an official statement to Block, which started with her arrival late morning. Privately, she was stunned this was over forty-eight hours ago. She didn't ignore any detail, well aware there was no telling what could be significant this early in an investigation. As she finished, the detective had a series of questions and clarifications.

"Please state your full name, and was your statement true and correct to the best of your knowledge?"

Mildred answered, "Yes sir. My name is Mildred Rhoades Petrie, and this statement is true and correct."

Once Block shut off the recorder, Mildred brought up the information on the white van. "This is only a gut feeling, but I've noticed odd hours, and it is usually in out of the way parking spaces." In the few minutes the statement took, she was exhausted. They helped her go back to bed, and she could hear them clean up the food box. Bud came back into the room with a glass of water and her prescription. "You look terrible, and I thought you could use a pain pill."

Mildred answered, "I really don't want to take them. They knock me out, and I want to be aware."

"How about half?" Bud broke the pill and she didn't argue any further. "Have a good rest now. We will lock up. Call if you need anything, Double-Oh-Seventy-One." Bud winked as they turned to leave.

Detective Block turned back and said, "I'm so sorry to bring this up, but do I recognize you? Your voice is familiar, and I think I remember you. Were you Officer Millie who went to the schools with McGruff..." and in unison they said "the crime dog."

The laughter hurt, but was welcomed. "I never dreamed anyone would remember me. McGruff was the star." A flight of memory took control as she wrapped herself in the warmth of love and pride. She had been so mad at Dick after the suicide, that she had let the good memories slip away. "Those school visits were some of the best parts of my law enforcement career. I was married to him, you know."

Choking back a response, Detective Block looked at her, dumbfounded, as she continued, "McGruff was Major Dick Petrie, and we worked the program together."

"I've heard about him; he was a decorated officer. I'm sorry for your loss. It was because of McGruff I wanted to be a cop."

She drifted into a drug-induced sleep as she heard the two men talking quietly and the click of the lock as they left.

Mildred didn't hear Richie come in, and she slept straight through the night with gentle dreams of her previous life.

– 35 –
Truthing

Whispers in the kitchen and the constant ache of her hip, woke Mildred. What she wanted most was to roll over to the black oblivion of painless sleep. Without the pills, moving anywhere was difficult. Focused on the voices, she heard her granddaughter Glory. "You don't have to worry, Uncle Dave. We have been here all of the time."

Mildred was shocked and called out. "David, is that you? What brings you to town?"

A familiar deep voice answered, "My mother is a klutz. and I thought I'd come see it for myself. Are you decent?"

"I'm decent enough. Get yourself in here. I need to put my eyes on your face."

Glory spoke up, "Wait a minute, Uncle Dave. I'll go get her up. Put your suitcase over here. Why don't you make coffee and then drink some?"

"No, I don't want to wait. It has been too long," Mildred whined, and her voice began to waver.

"Grandma, I'm coming in. I know your morning routine." Glory called out and entered immediately.

Mildred was relieved that she could go to the bathroom. The thought of David actually being in her home made the need to go immediate. She was able to brush her teeth before kissing her wayward son. She hadn't seen or talked to him since his dad's funeral almost three years ago. The two women moved quickly. Mildred decided on a washcloth over a shower. Mildred washed as much as her broken body would allow, anxious to see her youngest boy. "David, I'm coming out, and I need kisses."

Glory helped her grandmother walk into the living room, and David jumped up to help. "Holy Mother of... what the hell happened to you? Rich said you had a fall, but you look like your pimp kicked you to the curb."

"Nice. Who taught you to talk like that?" With full knowledge of her shocking appearance, she smiled. Mildred reached for him, and they stood for an eternal moment. Only after years had passed, Mildred was starting to accept she lost both her husband and youngest son in one gun shot.

Glory slipped into the kitchen to allow them time.

He had been so angry with her at the funeral. He blamed Mildred for his father's suicide, and she had prayed every night for his safety and hoped to see him again. She was nearly ready to accept the break until today.

He held on to her delicately and finally whispered, "I'm so sorry, Mom. I don't know what to say. I… ah… I…"

Mildred was so relieved to see David. "You don't have to apologize to me, ever." The feel of his body was a gift.

"Rich called and told me you had a bad fall. I'm sorry Mom. I've been a terrible son."

"David, you are fine. I will always love you, and I know everyone deals with loss differently." He struggled to compose himself and helped her to the chair. Mildred noticed how he had matured into a duplicate of his father. It brought more tears to her eyes to see that Dick lived on so clearly with David.

Glory came from the kitchen with a large tray and announced, "Breakfast is served." This was the break in the emotional roller coaster. They needed to come back to the present day. After they ate, David sent Glory home, and he cleaned the kitchen and took over the care of his bruised mother. He would look at her broken-heartedly and seemed to marinate in his guilt, as he watched her struggle with the simplest movement. He brought some water and two pills. Mildred refused the painkiller and only agreed to take one muscle relaxant. He shook his head, and she heard him mumble on his way back to the kitchen, "Just like my mother to trade comfort for control."

David helped her to her favorite chair, turned the occasional chair so they could look at each other, and settled in to watch the horror of daytime television. Mildred was oblivious to the programs, thinking of the past and all of the questions she had. She stayed quiet, deciding it best to start from today on. Mildred was startled when her phone rang. After a brief conversation, she turned to her youngest, "Ready to roll?"

He looked up and asked, "What do you need?"

"I need to go to the police station." At this point, Mildred decided the slip-and-fall lie was too flimsy, and better explain the truth of her work and injuries.

"Honey, I have to level with you about my fall."

David nodded. The feelings were familiar. He had been a cop's kid his whole life. He swallowed his concern and stood up. "Okay, I'll drive, but I have a little gift first." He went to where he had stowed his suitcase, and attached to it was a long thin package.

Mildred was flushed with emotion as she tore the paper and found an ornate cane. "How perfect! This cane is beautiful, and it will help with mobility." The one she had for the Oliver disguise was lost in the burglary. "I should be able to walk on my own." She shuffled over to her son and gingerly gave him a one armed hug.

David smiled, "Maybe not yet, but knowing you, soon. One more thing." He reached down the shaft of the cane and pressed a small crescent moon. The cover fell away to display a sword. They both laughed, "Rich already told me the truth. There is no need to explain your work. I tried to stick with your lie, but I've never seen anyone so injured in a fall."

Mildred's pained smile lit up, "I could have fallen and rolled."

He picked up on the joke, "Or fallen and kicked to the next county."

Mildred felt the years slip by as she recognized one of Dick's old phrases, "I promise no more lies. I just didn't want you guys to worry."

"I appreciate it if you recognize that both Rich and I are adults, and we can deal with truth, don't try to protect us ever again."

Mildred answered, "You're right. I accept the terms."

The two continued to talk about her work, as they drove to the police station. They had drifted into his memories of living with a cop. When they passed the college athletic field, Mildred yelled, "Stop! Turn around, quick." David flipped a U-turn, which caused her to gasp with pain, but she was too focused to complain, "Over there, back in the trees. Do you see the white van?"

"I see something. Let me try to get closer." David sounded excited.

As he drove around to the back of the field, she called Inspector Hampton, who was waiting for her at the station. "I think I found that van I've seen at the casino. We were driving past the University soccer field and bingo!"

"Keep your eyes on it, but don't approach. I'll get Block, and we'll have someone right over." Hampton ended the call abruptly.

"David, we are to stay back, but keep it in view. They don't want us approaching, just in case."

"That is good news. You aren't up to fighting car thieves. Let's try that apartment complex parking lot. Its close."

They discovered the van was invisible from the lot and guessed that whoever had hid it, misjudged the view from 12th Street. David spotted a rough dirt road, no, more of a path off the rear parking area. They were inching forward when a black and white and an unmarked SUV arrived. She could see Detective Block taking the lead, and he waved her over. Mildred couldn't walk, so she sent David on her behalf.

It was difficult to wait, and Mildred was relieved when she saw David walking back toward the car. "Do they have anything yet? What did you see?"

David nodded and answered, "I didn't see much. I stayed back until I got a chance to introduce myself. Detective Block said they were unsure if the van had been hidden or abandoned, but they intend to move it out of here right away."

"I noticed the black and white pulled out once they checked it. I'll bet they didn't move too far. I can feel their eyes on us."

"The detective told me the uniformed officers would keep it under surveillance until the tow truck arrives."

Detective Hampton approached. "Nice work, Officer Petrie. How did you see this, using those eyes? I heard you were injured, didn't realize it was this bad."

Mildred was touched seeing his eyes tear with sympathy. "You certainly know how to make a woman feel good."

"I'm sorry, Ms. Petrie. Just, when I saw you that night, it was just a black eye."

Mildred answered, "Basically, it is the wonders of adrenaline, my drug of choice. I didn't know I was injured until the next morning. Now the van. We were on our way in to meet you, and I just happened to catch a glimpse of it in the trees."

Hampton continued, "There is evidence of a lot of blood, and it is a mess inside; we are having forensics tow it in." They continued to talk like a primetime crime drama. Mildred noticed David watching, and realized that neither of her boys had seen her working like this before.

David helped Mildred into the car and she waited for Hampton to get off the phone. "Johnsen, I want to confirm the surveillance is set up. Okay, good. Once forensics has picked up the van, I need you to canvass the apartments. Do you need any backup? Keep me posted."

David and Mildred left for the station with the detectives close behind. Once they arrived, the office clerk took them to a small office adjacent to the interrogation room and offered coffee and ice. Mildred held the cup of ice to her shoulder and struggled to find some comfort when Detective Hampton came in. He broke down the strategy for the interrogation with the perpetrator. "You can watch from behind the one-way glass and use the intercom to offer any questions."

David had slipped off to the vending machines and joined them just as another officer came back in with a padded chair and a couple of car seat cushions. The two men silently moved her from the wooden chair and tried to construct a little comfort. She tried to hide the pain and never complained. David pulled a chair over and sat between Mildred and the intercom. Just as they were settled, the lights shut down and she watched an officer lead Butt Munch into a straight back chair and secure his hands to a metal hoop on the table.

He seemed different than from a couple of days ago. He was younger and bigger than she remembered. David leaned forward, and whispered, "Mom, that's the guy you captured?"

She merely smiled and nodded.

"That's the one who beat you up?"

"No, he was rough, but we took him down quickly." They settled in with a vending machine lunch to watch the show. David looked at his mother, smiled, bowed his head with a silent salute. Mildred had to admit she was impressed with herself too.

– 36 –
Healing Continued

The detectives weren't getting any information from the detainee. Butt Munch requested an attorney immediately and refused to give anything other than a series of fake names and countries of origin. After an hour with the officers, they had nothing of substance. Mildred and David rose to leave as Butt Munch claimed to be Truman Capote, New York, New York, and the last they heard, he was St. Bernard from Clair Vaux, France. He was a smug ass who seemed to have an education, or at least had read some books.

They drove away initially in silence. Mildred felt exhausted, when David finally spoke. "Mom, I'm confused, whatever convinced you to take a job like this? You are in your seventies."

"Early seventies, David. I consider it more like late sixties. The why doesn't matter, let's just say finances."

"But you have the two pensions and social security?"

"Not anymore, the pensions were used to pay off a debt. Period. End of discussion."

"I can help. You don't have to do this."

Mildred tried again to muffle the conversation. "I wouldn't ask my sons while I can still take care of myself, and I do that just fine."

"Obviously not so fine today," said David. Her laugh was hollow, and then she moaned. The trip continued in silence. Mildred was feeling defensive, and it was obvious that her son had more questions.

Once home, the silence continued. David helped settle his mother into her chair with a blanket and a cup of tea. He retreated to the kitchen to attack dinner.

The decision was made to utilize the moment alone, and Mildred took Penny Dumple's business card from the fanny pack still near her chair. Worry about her new friend had nagged her ever since the fiasco began. Once dialed, there was no turning back and the familiar voice answered.

"Hi Penny, this is Oliver. I wanted to check to be sure you escaped the drama at the casino."

"Oliver, I was worried about you, too. I was moved to the nightclub not long after you left. I hoped you got out before the lockdown. Do you want to get together for a drink?"

"I would love to, but I'm not in socializing condition."

"I can come over. Do you need anything? I'm free this evening."

Mildred had to smile about her new friend, but Penny didn't know the truth about Oliver. "Maybe in a couple of days; my son is visiting, and I have something else to tell you before we meet again." "Oh, Oliver, don't worry. I know." Penny teased.

"Penny, Penny, how could you know anything about me?"

"Honey, I'm a cross dresser too, and you were easy to spot." Mildred was stunned, "What gave me away?"

"The voice, always the voice, and you are pretty small in those big floppy shoes. I can come over, and we could work on it."

"You can call me Mildred, and your alternative name is…"

"Tim."

"So I have to go for now, Tim, but I'll call again, soon."

"Sweet dreams, Mildred."

David came around the corner, "Tim? Is he a boyfriend or a murderer you know?"

"Boyfriend? At my age, the term is laughable. She was someone I met moments before the robbery, and I was worried."

"She? I thought her name was Tim?"

"My dear boy, nothing is as it seems in this nightmare."

"Mother," David sighed. "I never forgot what you told me as a kid, a nightmare is a dream that got too big for its britches."

The laughter hurt, but it brought back the memory of her youngest son, crying in the night, and how Dick would wake her from the boys' room to get ready for work.

Mother and son settled in for a light dinner in front of the television. Resting was helping to resolve the all-day pain; Mildred again rejected the pain pill and explained, "I hate the oblivion of the medication. It is worse than the discomfort."

"Blah blah blah. If you want to sleep, think about how the discomfort makes it almost impossible," said David as he handed her the single muscle relaxant.

The evening passed with memories, small talk and watching TV's offering of cop shows. Before long, Mildred was asleep in her chair.

Awakened in the middle of the night, she couldn't remember going to bed, but then noticed she was still fully dressed. As she struggled to get up for the nightly trip to the bathroom, she saw David and Popcorn sitting in the chair by the window. He was reading in the dim light. "Pretty late to be up, Davey boy."

"Can't sleep, Mom."
Mildred sighed. "You know the couch folds out."

"Have you ever slept on it? I think you bought it from a masochist, or maybe a sadist; I get them confused."

"I should rest better knowing you don't know the difference. Can you help me up?"

David put the book down and moved the cat. "Do you want me to carry you?"

"Hell no, I just need help up." He walked over and offered his arm, and Mildred was able to struggle out of the chair. She noticed as they walked slowly towards the bathroom that his eyes were moist for the second time since yesterday.

Their eyes locked, and David spoke. "I always thought of you and Dad as indestructible. Now Dad is gone, and you need help to the toilet. This is tougher than I expected. I worry about how much time I missed, being a brat."

"No, honey, we can't change the past, only the present. Now get out of here, I have to go."

"Call me when you are done," and he closed the door.

Within minutes, Mildred was settled back into bed, and David shut off the lights and settled back into the chair. Then everything went silent, and she listened to him breathe. It felt familiar. It gave her comfort knowing he was there.

In the silence, David asked, "Mom, do you want any pills or something to drink?"

"No, I'm good." Then everything quieted down, and they settled into the quiet of the night. After a few minutes, Mildred heard a whispered question, "How much longer am I going to have you?"

Mildred, spoke a little louder than a thought, "David, honey, none of us get out of this alive. Rest assured I don't have any sudden exits planned."

"I couldn't deal with another loss like Dad." Mildred heard his labored breath, and then he continued, "I was looking at this book from Dad's nightstand, and I found a letter. I need to know more."

Mildred responded, "I don't know of any letters. There was just the note he left that day and it was only the one word, 'Sorry'."

David continued, "I'm kind of ashamed for reading it."

"No need for shame, he wrote it to be shared. What did it say?"

"You can read it yourself in the morning. It is a couple of pages long, and Dad wrote about regrets and his feeling of failure. He admitted that he lost the house. He mentioned his concern about borrowing from someone he met at the casino to buy this place, which only made his problems worse. Was it a loan shark?"

"Yes, I think so." Mildred answered. She made a promise to herself to answer questions, but to not add anything she didn't know for sure.

"He apologizes to you for not being the man you deserve."

Mildred was surprised by her own reaction, and the ache of loss that she thought was conquered. "I don't think I want to read it. Nothing can change what happened. I've learned a lot about the debt around the time of the funeral. I really, don't want you to think less of your father. He was a good man who had a problem. That is all."

"Is this what happened to your retirements?"
In the security of darkness, she could speak of the secrets.

"Honey, just before your Dad passed, he cashed out his pension to pay off his debt."

"A damn loan shark? That's what I thought."

"True enough. I cashed out my pension when they came back. They were threatening, and told me his death didn't clear the account. I just did what they asked, and they haven't been back. I still have my social security, but it is barely enough, and I maxed out my credit cards. Payments and groceries finally caught up with me, so I walked over to the casino to see about a part-time job." Mildred was grateful he couldn't see the humiliation and tears as she spoke.

David said, "I now see the irony in your decision. Rich and I talked, and we don't want you to work like this. We can both give you money every month. We will figure how much you need? Then you can quit that job."

"That job is one of the best things to happen to me since you boys." Mildred went on to describe how she finally felt like a police officer with the different challenges, and the good things she had been able to do. He seemed to soften as she spoke of the people she worked with and the bonds they had developed. The two of them talked in the darkness with no hesitation, until she heard David start to snore. Mildred laid back and felt both freed and comforted. She enjoyed dreams of the past until the room flooded with sunlight. When she awoke, Mildred heard David talking to Popcorn in the kitchen about breakfast plans. She found it funny how the cat had immediately bonded with her son, and shadowed him throughout the condo. To make things better, Mildred slowly got out of bed under her own power.

David called out, "Mom, want some cereal?"
Mildred entered the kitchen, leaning on her new cane.

"Sounds delicious. Is there coffee brewing?"

David's face lit up. "Hey, you're walking." He helped her to the table, and they sat next to each other enjoying the bowls of cereal. Mildred stroked the chain with both wedding rings around her neck, and couldn't recall the last time she was this happy.

– 37 –
Question Popping

"You're getting married!" Mildred spewed milk onto the counter. David blushed. "If she will have me."

"This is so sudden, but not unexpected. Is it Katie? The young woman you brought to the funeral?"

"Yes, Mom, it's Katie. We have been together almost ten years, and it's time." "A little past time, Romeo."

There was a light tap on the door, and they turned to watch Lindsey let herself in. "Hello, look who's up. I'm scheduled for this morning's routine." She stopped at the kitchen counter. "What's so funny, you two?" She picked up another bowl from the cabinet and joined mother and son for more cereal, questions, and good-hearted ribbing.

David's eyes filled with tears, and they could hear the mountain of regret in his voice. "Mom, I'm sorry. I didn't understand."

Mildred reached over and wiped his eyes with her good arm. "Don't you dare ruin this moment of joy. You have always been my tender heart. Get over it. You are here now, and even though the circumstances aren't ideal, we're good. It is time to start the rest of your life. Tell us more about this woman. I hope she deserves you."

"I don't know why I waited. There is no one better for me than Katie." The two women focused on David as he shared his plan. They put the brakes on his idea of a text proposal with looks of exaggerated disgust.

Lindsey reached over and picked up his phone from the table and said, "Stop. This question of yours will change both of your lives. She has put up with your sorry nonsense for ten years. She deserves a romantic story, and damn it to hell, she is going to have it."

David seemed overwhelmed, and Mildred understood his feeling of urgency to move forward. "But Lindsey, we never know what will happen tomorrow."

She smiled broadly, and slid his phone into her back pocket. "Did you hear what I said? That woman will have her romantic moment to tell her grandchildren."

Mildred waited as they continued to toss around different plans, and watched them work together cleaning the kitchen.

Lindsey laid out some clean clothes and helped Mildred into the shower. By the time Mildred called for help with her shirt, Lindsey had the home running smoothly and the first load of laundry was underway.

Mildred noticed a noticeable improved overnight. She still moved painfully, but her strength had improved.

Anxiously Mildred returned to the conversation, and collectively, they designed a script. When the two women left to help Mildred put on shoes, they continued to whisper excitedly, fine-tuning the initial plan. Lindsey pointed out, "You realize that some good came from you getting your ass kicked during the power outage."

Suddenly there was a yelp of glee, and they heard David hang up the house phone next to Mildred's chair. "We are a go, ladies."

Mildred sighed, "He is just like his dad, no patience at all."

"Damn it, David, you don't follow instructions!" Lindsey ran into the living room and demanded Katie's phone number. "I won't allow you to ruin this, and if I have to, I'll kick you in the head." Mildred could see that Lindsey was determined to make sure this was done right. "Okay, you sorry excuse for a man. This is how it works, once the asking is done and a ring paid for, you only have to show up, every day for the rest of your life."

Mildred hobbled to the open door. "All right, you two, is anyone up for an adventure? There is an employee meeting at the casino at three; they are reopening at six. We have time to go downtown."

David smiled, "So that is what you have been up to, hiding out while I get sassed? There is no way you are going back to work."

Mildred responded with a line from his childhood. "You aren't the boss of me. And if you would just pay attention, I only want to go in for the meeting."

The three loaded into the car, David said to Lindsey, "It is nice to see that, even though I left, my mother is still the woman I knew. Clearly she has a full life still ahead of her."

Lindsey nodded in agreement, "Yes, you are right on this one." She engaged the turn indicator and pulled out on the road to town.

By the time they got home, David had an engagement ring, with a larger diamond than he expected, a bouquet of flowers waiting on the windowsill and a plane ticket for tomorrow. Mildred no longer observed the wall he had built and hoped it was gone for good. Only twenty-four hours left to eliminate the rest of his guilt, and she was confident it was possible. While he was walking Lindsey out to her car, Mildred slipped the letter from the book he had been reading into his suitcase. She was confident it explained more than her words could, and he alone understood how Dick's battle with depression had colored everyone's life. Mildred consciously discarded those memories and chose the good times.

Mildred heard him come back in and she realized that David understood the battle, as she overheard him make two more calls before they left for the meeting. He renewed his prescription for anti-depressants and arranged to pick up a cocker spaniel puppy. Mildred knew her son well enough to recognize he had his own plan for a formal proposal.

Casino Reboot

Mother and son arrived for the meeting at ten to three. The rear employee entrance was propped open, and there was a stream of people on their way in. The rest of the casino would open a few hours. David dropped her off and went to park. While she waited, on the bus stop bench, Mildred texted:

"G-ma on the floor."
"10-4 G-ma on my way."

David helped her walk slowly to the rear entrance, when a man in a black suit ran up to them pushing a wheelchair. "I've been expecting you. I know there is no keeping our G-ma down."

Mildred quickly introduced her son to Arnie as they rolled to the auditorium. David took the book he had started reading the night before to the adjacent bar. Mildred noticed the stress in David's shoulders relax as he sat down at a table. He seemed to have appreciated the respite; his life had changed in the last forty-eight hours and would never be the same.

Arnie pushed the wheelchair as Mildred directed, and they found her a dark corner just off the stage. She wished to recover a little of her anonymity. She was able to study the growing crowd and before long, she could identify the employees that had been through the robbery. Their eyes were vacant and wary; many others were noticeably nervous. A group of cashiers sat in the front row; some still showing physical evidence of injury. Mildred continued to search the room until she spotted the Ninja. Pleased the young woman looked unscathed, Mildred dug out her sticky note pad and wrote a brief message. She stopped writing just as Chef Mike approached, and she covered the note.

"Miss Mildred, you look marvelous in black and blue."

"I beg your pardon, sir; my eyes have become a flattering shade of yellow."

He bent down to hug her, and she had to stop him. "As much as I'm glad to see you, my collar bone is just starting to knit."

He kissed the top of her head and pulled up a chair. He relayed his private meeting with Bud. "The security brass explained your position here and made it clear about the need for discretion."

Mildred started to respond, when he held his finger to his lips indicating silence. "I am grateful for the good work you do. Your secret is safe with me, and if you ever need anything, I've got your back."

Mildred spoke as he stood to leave. "That means a lot to me. One more thing, could you please give this note to the tall young woman in the first row?"

"I know who you mean. I feel the three of us are connected since that day." He palmed the note and left with a discreet thumbs up.

Mildred watched him walk over and saw the Ninja's face light up as he said hello. They chatted briefly, and he slipped the note into her hand. Not opening it right away, the Ninja looked around the room, but did not see the woman in the shadows watching her.

Bud and Belinda entered the stage with others of the security team. The program started with a pleasant welcome back speech and introductions. Mildred did not know some of the officers, so she studied their faces and noted names on the note pad.

Bud stepped forward, "I want to keep everyone informed on the investigation. The one arrest has not provided any information, and is now represented. The on-scene evidence gathering has been completed, and we are now in the process of finishing repairs. The cleanup is finished. In order to get reopened, we have expedited repairs, and I thank the maintenance crew. Thanks to them, we will reopen today. Now I would like to introduce command officer, Arnie Arneson."

Arnie stood up and joined them on stage. "We have additional updates and will expand previously planned technological and safety improvements." Mildred listened as she continued to watch the room. Arnie only spoke for a few minutes about computers and sensors, which was lost on Mildred. She had a strange feeling that there was something missing.

Bud then stepped forward, and Belinda joined him. "We want to take this opportunity to honor the accounting team. They followed the emergency protocols extremely efficiently: locking down, engaging the alarm, and even though the panic room wasn't completed, they were able to utilize it. Due to clear heads and following the training instructions, there were no injuries. By time the criminals gained access, the police were seconds behind."

Bud then called the names of each cashier that was on duty. They walked up to the stage and were awarded a citation certificate and gift cards. The reactions were pleasant, but Mildred could see the evidence of trauma. After the last name, she noticed a heaviness come over Bud as he continued. "Now for the floor cashiers. Their experience was even more traumatic. I would like to acknowledge an honorable mention for the cashiers who couldn't attend." He listed a few names as Mildred watched the small group of familiar faces that were sitting near the Ninja. Bud continued on. "This seems to be inadequate, but I would like to observe a moment of sorrowful silence for the death of the supervisor, Lillian Williams, who passed this morning. She had bravely stepped forward, placing herself between a gunman and her crew." There was a muffled sound of crying coming from the front row, which felt as if it spoke for the entire room.

The silence was too long, and at the same time not long enough to honor a life. When the room was completely silent, Bud called Lena Davis to the stage. Mildred watched with pride as her Ninja warrior stood up. "Lena was a relatively new employee. She was instrumental in capturing one of the robbers. Our gratitude is greater than this certificate can describe, we thank you for your action." He presented her with a framed award for bravery and a gift certificate.

Even from the darkened corner, Mildred could see her tear stained face. Lena looked to be a child as she faced the employees and gave a brief, obviously rehearsed speech. "I wish to thank you and the Security team. I witnessed teamwork and bravery in action. I had been paralyzed in fear, hiding in the restroom, and it was one of your officers that prevented any serious injury and possible death. Her action enabled me to also move when the ah, ah, robber came in." The Ninja took a shuddering breath, and her ordeal and continued fear, were obvious to the room. "I'm here because of the security officers. I'm sorry. I'm finished. Thank you."

She walked off the stage and returned to her seat amid a standing ovation. Mildred was honored and knew some of the applause was hers. She continued to examine the crowd with an unspoken suspicion. No overt behavior was displayed, but Mildred's gut told her that, whoever plotted the invasion had an inside connection. Confident they always let down their guard down, and if she stayed alert, it would be visible. Awkwardly she tried to photograph the room with her body camera, but she didn't have the mobility. She then used her phone to take a few more. Mildred planned to study the faces once she returned home. There would be no one above her suspicion. She watched the employees, and instead of associates, they were now suspects. A few left, but the majority moved towards the luncheon in the event dining room.

Her mind was documenting when Arnie brought David in to pick her up. Mildred looked at her son and once the room was clear, he started to roll the wheelchair toward the rear exit, she said, "Davey, do you mind? I need a whiteboard and some markers."

"You got it, boss. We can stop on the way home." She looked at David, "Are you hungry? Do you want to go to the luncheon?"

"You know me; I'm starving at a minimum of three times a day. We don't dare go to the employee buffet; I need to slip back into the shadows."

"Let's get out of here, and you can explain. How about pizza?"

She waited in the wheelchair next to the exit as David brought the car around. Mildred's mind was reeling with possibilities. Once in the car, she continued to make notes. David had his speculations about what was happening while he listened to her mumble, and the pen scratch on page after page. She waited in the car writing furiously while David went into the office supply store.

Over a Canadian bacon and double cheese pizza, she began to talk. Her frustration had grown since the meeting. David had known her as a mother, but saw her as Mom-cop twice in two days. He watched, asked questions and suggested some names she could rule out. Mildred shook her head. "The only people I'm ruling out are you, me and the dead supervisor." Her frustration turned to anger. "Those idiots wanted money, and people died. I can't let them get away with this."

"But Mom, it isn't all up to you." He tried to calm her, but from his experience growing up in a house with this woman, he knew it would only settle once she had answers.

The team of two started to draw diagrams on the back of placemats. David leaned over to another table and gathered additional supplies, taking notes and listing names as quickly as he could write. Mildred kept going back to the people who seemed out of place.

"I don't want you to do this alone. It is dangerous. Could you work with one of the police detectives?"

"They haven't passed my scrutiny yet. I am going to move deliberately."

"Mom, clear them first, please."

She didn't respond, but continued to think out loud. "The huge amount of money that flows through a casino and hotel can turn people. Somehow the crooks knew it was the deposit day. The deposit schedules change, but somehow they knew the date and were there just an hour or so before it all was secured and locked down for the armored pick-up in the morning. They process huge amounts of money through the counting room daily, but there are only a few times every month that events and daily deposits for the month come together. The amounts are staggering. How did they know that this was one of those days? Luckily the storm had helped clear out a lot of patrons, but they also had the weather to cover up. This was timed when the money was almost all counted and bagged for the armored pick-up. I have a nagging suspicion." Mildred stared at the notes. "I may be off my rocker, but we shall see." She slammed down her empty glass, and exhaustion took over.

David paid and ushered Mildred home. It bothered him how he had to physically help his mother as she settled into her chair. She had been doing better, but the fatigue came over her so quickly. He unloaded the whiteboard and other supplies, and tossed her a large pack of sticky notes to replace the one she had filled since the meeting. "Mom, I think I'm leaving too soon." He moved some family pictures and leaned the board against the blank wall. When he turned back to her, "I'm going to change my ticket." When he didn't hear a response, he noticed she was snoring softly. He went to cover her and found a large photo album on her lap. "How did you do this, old woman?" Mildred had just written David's name on the front.

He knew nothing of the saved memories in the boxes from the storeroom. He picked up the book, and she awoke gently. Mildred smiled as she looked at her youngest son. "For you to take home tomorrow."

"For me? Mom, this is wonderful, and I've been such an ass."

"Yes, but you are the ass I have loved for thirty-six years."

"This isn't a good time for me to go home. I'm going to change my ticket and stay a few more days."

"Don't you dare, young man! It is even more important that you go to Katie and start a life together. I'm fine."

He started to speak, but she cut him off. "Richie and I found some boxes in storage that Daddy saved. The girls helped me make books for both of my sons." He opened the dark green book that was filled with family pictures and news clippings, some she had and the rest found in the storage. He held it gently, almost feeling love from both parents. Mildred had slipped the letter into the last page of the album; she knew David needed the words more than she ever would.

White Board

Around eleven, Mildred woke to a gentle, yet insistent nudge from Popcorn. Her dreams had continued the investigation, and Mildred wanted to work some more and searched the darkened room. David had set up the white board while she slept. She then saw he had settled on the fold-out couch. He was so involved in the photo album, he seemed to ignore the lumps and metal bar that stressed him the night before.

"Honey, I'm sorry, but I need to go to the bathroom. I think I can walk if you help me out of this chair."

"It had been a very full day." He put down the book and went to his mother.

Mildred stared at his face. "You look terrible."

"I think the night of little sleep caught up about an hour ago." He helped her stand, and she hobbled into the other room. She came out of the bathroom dressed in a worn flannel nightgown. "Your recovery is a sight to see. You never give up, do ya?" David helped her lie down and tucked her in. "Sleep tight, don't let the bed bugs bite." Mildred remembered saying the same thing when she did the tucking in.

She watched him go back to the living room, hopefully to sleep. Mildred noticed that he was still clutching the photo book.

In the darkest part of night, David started awake and noticed the light coming from beneath the bedroom door. There were no sounds or indication of movement. He peeked into the room and Mildred was sprawled at the foot of the bed, marker in hand. She didn't fight when he gently removed the pen, left her at the foot of the bed and covered her with the blanket. Only half awake, Mildred watch him settle back into the chair by the window just as the morning sun began to light the room. David stroked the demanding cat and stared at the white board. There was a rough diagram with initials marking locations, and names written across the top.

BUD MOSES – On site, off hours – safe room – complete access. Aware of deposit schedules.

BELINDA JASPER – On site, off hours – total access – knows floor plan and schedules.

ARNIE ARNISON – works nights – location unknown, access all areas and schedules

LENA DAVIS – NINJA – New cashier – in restroom near assigned work station – background unknown. Minimal knowledge of layout. Get hire date.

DETECTIVE HAMPTON – Casino liaison – unknown knowledge of access and layout

DETECTIVE BLOCK – no known casino connection prior to burglary

ESCAPEES – one associated with BUTT MUNCH – guilty, has the $$ from cashier cages.

PENNY (TIM) DUMPLE – wild card

A tiny voice spoke from the blanket pile. "Are you asleep, Davey Boy?"

"No Mom, just studying the board."

"I need to get back to it. You were right. This is too big for just me. I need background information deeper than the internet and interviews."

David sat forward as he studied the list. "These are your friends. How can you do this?"

"I have to. People were hurt, and Lillian died. I'm convinced I can remove Detective Block. His only connection I know of is this case. I'm only fishing the shallows until I can access police databases."

As they stared at the list, there was a knock at the door. "Stay where you are, Mom. I've got this." Too early for a visitor, David took the cane with him.

Mildred struggled to sit up and smooth the blankets. After a moment, she could hear the soft voice with a slight, yet intriguing accent. "Q, is that you?"

The familiar voice of Qaseema. "Yes, Ms. Mildie, it is me. I came to check on you."

I have one person I didn't consider, and she shows up at my door. "What are you doing out so early?"

"I go to class after my work. Arnie told me you would be awake." Mildred could hear a whispered discussion between David and Q, but there was no stopping her friend. Q entered the room, and went straight to Mildred, giving her a box of chocolate covered cherries. "Have you been back to doctor?"

"No, I've been busy."

"As I thought. It is important, old woman."

"It is only a small fracture and a sprain."

"Only? Look at yourself, it is more." Her gentle and firm touch checked the right shoulder and she began to hum the song she sang to the puker months ago. She also examined the hip, and finally the battered face. "The nose is broken, but not badly displaced." At this point, firm and knowledgeable hands quickly straightened Mildred's nose with a crunching sound.

"Holy mother! What the hell! Let me know when you are going to do things like that." Mildred's shocked expression was exaggerated with the fading bruises and tears.

"No! Mr. David, can you please get the case from my car. I need medical tape. My keys are here." Q took some keys from her pocket.

Mildred also called out, "Davey, there is tape in the bathroom cabinet."

Q continued to feel the bones in Mildred's face, "I reset your nose, and this will help stabilize so heal correctly. We want your face to be woman we know. You seem to be recovering well, but you do need to see doctor. Why is my name not on your list?" Mildred blushed, "I trust you."

"That is foolish; you need to trust no one. I tell you I was not part of the break-in."

"I know. I don't think money motivates you, and you have too much to lose."

Q responded immediately, "I could be funding terrorists."

"True enough, but more likely it would be schools in countries I can't pronounce." They both nodded in agreement as Q taped Mildred's nose in place.

"I'm convinced that, due to the timing of the break-in, that there has to be someone from inside the casino involved. The big deposit days are rotated, and only a few know the schedule." Mildred struggled to stand and pointed to the diagrams"

"I have not thought of details. I think you are correct." Q stared at the board. "I usually work the ten p.m. to six a.m. shift, and I never seen Detective Block before investigation. I was off night of the break-in and have nothing more."

"Q, I didn't see you at the employee meeting yesterday. Where were you?"

Q smiled. "You are questioning me now? I was part of the cleanup and repairs, and they are anxious to reopen. I was cleaning blood, while men patched bullet holes. This may not be the time to bring up something else."

Mildred looked at her friend. "No, please go ahead."

Q bit her lip and continued, "I hear some talk about place to borrow money."

Mildred noticed David as he sat listening and looking confused. The questions were clear on his face, but he added nothing.

After further discussion, and a quick internet search, they all agreed that Block was clear. He had no connection or access until that day, had a successful career, and he had moved quickly through the ranks. David made a mental note to ask his mother about retirement sometime in the future. Certainly not now.

Q took the marker and pointed out the access housekeepers had to every corner of the casino, and would provide additional names for the suspect list. There was only a couple authorized for the counting room maintenance. Once Q left, Mildred and David continued with research. They started background checks into each suspect on the laptop computer.

"I like your friend. There is something about her that instills trust. She is very intelligent."

Mildred added, "And perceptive. I didn't see her look at the board, and she knew exactly what was going on."

"Meeting her will help me sleep. Not tonight, but sometime in the future."

They slipped into a conversation about prioritizing the names on the list. The discussion moved to the robbery, family, and then finally Dad.

After they spoke for a while, David broached the subject of the mention of loans.

Mildred explained, "Don't worry. That is a separate research into the dirty loans. That won't stop because of the robbery."

He could only roll his eyes with a deep sigh. "Mother, you are messing with dangerous people. I know you won't stop, but promise me you won't continue this alone. I'll be back as soon as I can."

Mildred laughed. "Okay, Batman, I'll flip on the bat light if I need you."

Richie and Glory arrived early in the afternoon and took David to the airport. He was excited to begin the next part of his life, but harbored worry about his mother. Glory stayed, but it was obvious that Grandma no longer needed constant care. The two women went to the grocery, and Glory saw her Grandmother still tired quickly, but she could move.

Mildred discovered that leaning on the cart took the pressure off the hip, and she could do the necessary shopping, although she didn't resist help. Still uncomfortable with driving, because of the shoulder, she was confident that would pass soon.

"G-ma on the floor."

There was a response in her earpiece. "Welcome back. This is Eddie. How are you feeling?"

"I'm good. Is Arnie on tonight?"

"Yeah, he is doing a walk-through. You might see him."

"Thanks."

Mildred started in the hotel, and then gift shops, restaurants and off to the gaming floor. She was using the cane that David gave her, and it helped more than she wanted to admit.

It was a typical Friday night: lots of activity and full to capacity in fine dining. There were no conventions or major shows this weekend, so it would be Double Dog Spin Doctor tossing out tunes. Mildred decided to check the main stage and watch for drug activity. They had popped some kids who were distributing, but nothing higher up, yet. As Mildred arrived, the banner over the door surprised her, ZOMBIE DRAG. Everything lately had been zombies, and she had started to miss mummies and vampires.

"Eddie, you didn't tell me about the Drag."

"Sorry, G-ma, I can see they are starting to arrive. Is that you in blue?"

"At least, I don't need a disguise to fit in."

"Shush, you don't fit. Need more rot."

"More rot? Nice. That makes me feel pretty. Do you know who's working this?"

"We have the door and patrol; the police have undercover officers inside."

Eddie was quiet for a moment. "I'll pay close attention; I pulled office duty all night so, I've got your back."

Even using a cane, Mildred found she had to sit more often and for longer periods of time. Sure she couldn't deal with the crowd nearby, she nested in a spot facing the Drag entrance.

Mesmerized by the gruesome parade and the unexpected smell of Axe body spray and cheap perfume, she watched.

A particularly decayed woman slowly crept from the entrance and directly toward Mildred. She stopped short, turned to the door and murmured, "Hey, G-ma, didn't expect you. Feeling better?"

"Melody?" She whispered, "Good to see you, looking lovely. You'll be busy tonight. How will you know the difference between undead and high?"

The decayed mouth struggled to smile. "It will be a mobile pot-staggering, ecstasy-snagging kind of night. I'll keep wobbling and pay attention."

Melody stumbled away as a server approached. "Ma'am, would you like a cocktail? We have a special on Blue Moon beer for the event."

"No, thanks, but a tea would be nice." Mildred watched the crowd of fiends flounder and moan into the auditorium. Approached twice, with a mantra of "Brains, brains," the casino filled with the loud mixed versions of songs she didn't recognize. When the door opened, she saw a black and white movie projected on a huge screen. She realized she was possibly the only one in the casino who knew who Lon Chaney was. The server returned with a small teapot and a cup, Mildred paid and continued with the freak show. An hour later, she was still having a terrible time separating over-acting from drug use.

Bam! There it is. She saw two zombies crash together and a hand-off! Mildred used her right hand to divert attention, fumbling with the cold tea bag while snapping pictures with the left hand from inside the sling.

First task was to text Melody and then she followed with Security.

"Eddie, drug deal going down at the Drag."
"I see the door. Which one?"

She tapped the earpiece, "The tall dirty male in rags and decomposition, and the shorter man in the gray shroud. I have a photo. Send someone before we lose them in the crowd."

Ten minutes later, the drug dealer was in the holding room. Uniformed officers were about to pack him off for the rest of the evening. She had to smirk, considering this demon's probable night in jail. Thugs and drunks don't take the undead seriously.

Background Checks

Detective Block dropped off a subpoena at Human Resources for employment records. On his way back to the station, he stopped at Mildred's condo and offered a ride to the station for a status on the background checks she requested.

On the ride in, Block apologized. "Mildred, I should have called, I'm sorry. I was at the casino, and it seemed convenient. I'll call next time."

"Don't worry. This seems to be to the price for living close to all the action." Mildred settled into the ride.

Once in his office, he turned his white board around and displayed a list just like the one at her home. Then he plunked down a large folder. "It is going to take more work to find connections; we are just not seeing it yet. I wanted to bring you up to date on some of our suspects. We have no large bank changes or new accounts on any of them, so far. It takes a while for so many people and all of the possibilities."

Detective Block started the checklist. "Bud checked out just fine. His birth name is Stone Francis Moses."

Mildred snickered, "Stone Moses? That sounds like a biblical command."

"He legally changed it when he was eighteen." Block couldn't help but smile at Mildred's glee.

Tears moistened her laughing eyes. "I don't feel so badly about my old lady name anymore."

Block tried to ignore her and continued on. "His parents have a bookstore in San Diego. He was an only child and went to school at California State. He majored in Sociology with a minor in Criminal Justice. Let's see... he had good grades and has been married to Becky for ten years. They have one son, Anthony, who goes to Highview Elementary School. His wife is a schoolteacher at Garfield High School. There have been no major purchases or suspicious activity. In fact, they applied for a loan on a relatively modest home, and that is pending. He has been above board, and we can almost do a genealogy search on him."

"I don't know why I was worried about Bud. I'm relieved, and it feels right. Now Belinda?" Mildred stood and erased the top name from the board.

"Belinda Lee Johnson, now Jasper, has lived here her whole life. Her parents are still alive and have a house on Oak in the old part of town. They are active in the Unitarian church, and she has been married for three years. Her husband, Brandon, is a firefighter, and they have two children: a two-year-old, and an older girl from his previous marriage. Nothing exceptional showed in banking records and debts."

"Next, Arnie Arnison, and there was nothing of note. He was born in New York, some college credit from City College. Never married, no child of record, no banking irregularities, carries an average amount of debt, and he is current on payments. He lives with a disabled father who owns the home outright. He worked security in college and then stayed in the field with temporary agencies for a few years. He started at the casino when they opened."

Mildred nodded, and checked his name off the board.

Block continued without hesitation. "Bud Moses isn't the only one with a name change, though. Lena Davis. She is an interesting one. Her full name is Magdalena Demiri."

Mildred marked the name change. "Demiri, I don't know that name. Is she from around here?"

He pulled out a sheet of paper from the folder and responded, "It's Albanian. Looks like she immigrated with her mother when she was three years old. There is no record of her father in this country."

"Is she married, or do you have anything else about her?"

"Married briefly, when she was seventeen. No further connection after a quickie Vegas divorce. She went to school here, but went back to Albania for a year, and got back two months ago. She still has extended family in Vaqaar, a village just outside of the capital. Paternal grandparents, I think. She takes bookkeeping classes at the community college; no other background of note. We have no criminal history. Requested any possible sealed juvie records, but that may take a while. The forensic accountant is searching for financial and other possible criminal connections."

Mildred stared at the report, as if digesting the information. "This is interesting. I'm not even sure where Albania is. How about other employees? I'd like to clear them as soon as possible. I catch myself pulling away and feeling distrustful, and I always liked my co-workers."

Block had to agree. "The more I probed, the more questions came to mind. This robbery was more sophisticated than it appeared." Mildred shook her head.

He continued. "I initially assumed it was a bunch of punks, looking at the one we caught. The more I learn, the more questions come up. We could start going through departments that would have access to the armored truck schedules."

"Then start at the top of each department and work our way down," Mildred said as she turned to a blank page on her legal tablet. The two brainstormed through the departments, and with the employee sheet, listed the supervisors and schedules.

While they worked on a new list of suspects, a uniformed officer came in. "Boss, I've got the enhanced photos of the guys in the ski masks as they spray painted the camera lenses. Not much more than eyes."

"That is great, Jacobson. No telling what will help. Stick to it, and keep me posted." Block picked up the large folder and studied the photographs.

"Elton, ah Detective Block, I have some housekeeping names that Q emailed over, and I haven't added them to the list. I'll print it out for you."

He nodded and said, "You can call me Elton, if you like. Save your ink; you can email them over. Another thing I couldn't find was anything on Penny and Tim Dumple. There are no records in a five-state area. Do you have anything additional on them? Do they work at the casino?"

"Not that I know of, and they are one person. I met him as Penny, and he busted me as a cross-dresser."

"What? You're confusing me. Do you have more to report on this?"

Mildred relished the suspense as she left his question hanging in the air while she went for more tea. She returned with a steaming cup and a sneaky grin. "Okay, Elton. I have several cover disguises I use for work. One of them is Oliver Brimstone. We have an ongoing investigation into a string of purse snatchings. I needed access to the men's room. Voilà! Oliver. The crooks used the trash to dump the personal property, and Oliver was my pass to the can. I was in that persona the night of the robbery. I didn't know Penny until she approached during the storm, about an hour before the heavy action. We shared dinner in the Nairobi Café. She told me she was there for a spa weekend, and I didn't question it. I've got her phone number, and I'll set up another meet."

"Give me that number and we can start research with that. Let me know when you schedule anything. You need to move carefully. If you have a lead into this burglary, it could be dangerous, especially with this Dumple wild card." He then scratched more onto his tablet. "Here is something interesting. The white van."

Mildred looked up from the list, her eyes wide open. "Oh, good. I am really curious about that. Was it involved? What did you find?"

Block smiled, and opened another folder. "It was stolen a year and a half ago in Michigan. The plates also appear lifted, and the registered owner didn't report anything. It is possible they didn't notice the plates had changed. There is a possibility of multiple changes to cover a trail. I have Detective Jacobson following with the registered owners. Forensics has the bloody clothing and the muddy boots we found in the field. I'm still waiting on DNA and a final report. Sure wish we got results as quickly as they do on TV."

Mildred responded, "That would be nice to have this solved in an hour."

"This would have been a two-parter." Mildred and Block both nodded in agreement. He went on, "There was nothing new on Joshua Waller, also known as Butt Munch. I wonder how a punk-ass kid could afford bail, let alone Thomas Conner, one of the top attorney's in the state. Conner rushed him through the court in record time and posted bond."

Mildred was stunned. "I thought he had a million dollar bond. Who? How?"

Block checked his watch and started to gather his files. "He just is. You need to take care, starting with taking your board down. We don't want any of this to come back on you."

"I appreciate your concern, Elton, but I won't step out."

"Somehow I knew that. Officer Jacobsen is going to give you a ride home. He will help you take the board down. We don't need people stopping by and seeing what and who you suspect."

Mildred had time to think on the ride home. Once they were at her home, she had him move the board and set it up in the walk-in closet behind her winter clothes. "Detective Block just told me to take it down. He should be all right with this compromise. Don't think it can be seen, but I'll check from outside as I leave."
"Thank you. I appreciate your help."

He walked around her condo, and tapped on the front window and waved goodbye. The door had barely closed when Mildred took out the business card from Penny Dumple and dialed the number. She could tell by the voice that it was Tim.

"Hello, is Penny there?"

"No she stepped away, may I help you?"

"Yes, I'm her friend Oliver, and I was hoping she could get away for a cup of coffee."

"Oh, that would be marvelous." Mildred heard the voice change slightly. "I could be available this evening. What is good for you?"

"How about tomorrow, after lunch?" Mildred stalled for time to talk to Bud and Block about backup. "I'm thinking the Nairobi Café at the casino, around two o'clock?"

Tim answered immediately. "It's a date. I'll be there, but Penny can't. She has to work."

"Perfect, you will know me; my arm is in a sling." Mildred answered.

Tim replied, "Don't worry. I'll recognize you."

As Mildred hung up the phone, she puzzled over the strangeness of the conversation. It was as if Mildred was talking for Oliver, who was still Mildred and Tim spoke for Penny, who was still Tim. *Oh, what tangled webs we weave, when first we practice to deceive.* The Sir Walter Scott quote would repeat in her subconscious until she walked into the casino the next day.

Around noon, Bud arrived as Mildred was putting together her disguise. She didn't have the wig or facial hair on yet, and he sat on the end of her bed so he could see the white board in her closet. He had checked on her during the recovery, but this was the first business visit since she was hurt. Mildred started with an apology.

"Bud, I have a strong feeling that there is someone on the inside on the robbery. You were the first one on the list, but you're cleared."

"You are sorry? I'm relieved. I don't want you after me." He smiled brightly and faked offense. "I agree with you, and Hampton, and we have been working up the same theory."

Mildred pondered for a moment. "One question, how did you get locked in the safe room?"

"The safe room was under construction and access code wasn't programmed yet. The only way in was from the back. I locked it all down once I had them safe."

"I think Belinda mentioned something like that, but I really don't remember all of the details."

"One of the first things we did was get it finished while everything was closed down. Now they have the extra protection and, the training will finish in the next couple of days about operation." Bud looked proud of the accomplishment. "The cashier cages now lock down with metal doors at the push of a button. When they slam shut, it is very intimidating."

"Good work. I've been working with Detective Block, and we haven't cleared Hampton yet. I don't know what Hampton knows about the casino layout and schedules, so he is still on my list. Block thinks he's clear and wants to include him with our progress."

"I agree with Block, he's good," said Bud. With the pressure off, they got into a brief rundown on the status of the underbelly of the casino. "The purse snatching has settled down. We still have a shoplifter or two, but no prescriptions have been snagged."

Mildred nodded. "Good news, sounds like it was the ex-employee and her clan."

Bud exclaimed, "Clan? More like a gang. Hampton picked her up, along with four of her associates."

"Associates. That's a polite term for thieving bastards," Mildred answered.

Bud looked up. "I pride myself in good manners."

Mildred took the conversation back. "This is just a thought; do you think they could be connected to the robbery?"

"Hmm, that is interesting. I hadn't thought of that – yet. We need to search into the crime affiliations too. I'll put Hampton on it." Bud continued to write in his notebook.

Mildred said, "Let's check with the server and bar back that still work at the casino, find out if there are any associates."

Bud turned the page and continued to write. "I'll have Arnie take care of that. They probably wouldn't tell you anything, and he manages the same shift, so they know him."

"We have cleared Belinda, and Arnie looks okay too," Mildred said.

Bud wrote another note. "We are in agreement. I forgot to tell you that you may be cleared soon."

Mildred faked alarm. "Damn Bud, I forgot about me."

"You weren't an easy one; we had to involve the FBI and the CIA," he joked.

"Next time check with the KGB too. Well, we are now to the reason why I needed to see you today. I met a woman the night of the robbery, and we had dinner together. She told me her friends had left because of the storm, but she won a spa weekend and stayed. Block wasn't able to find anything on her, and he even checked other states."

"Is this your girlfriend you mentioned the night after the burglary? I don't have anything on this."

"Didn't seem important at the beginning, but when I started outlining who was out of place, Penny Dumple came right up." Mildred went on to explain the Penny-Tim connection.

Shaking his head and smiling, Bud added the name to his list. "I'll check to see if she was registered, and if she really had a reservation. I'll ask around to see if anyone else knows of her."

"No need, I'm meeting him for coffee at two today."

Bud looked up with alarm. "Where at? Is Block handling backup?"

"We will be at the Nairobi, and I'm going as Oliver, as you can see, because that is who I was when we met. Besides, the truth be told, I'm not ready for Tim to recognize the real me yet."

"Makes sense. Do you want me to join you?"

"No, I'll handle it, just wanted you to know."

"Okay. Keep your camera on. How much longer do you need to wear the sling?"

"The end of this week, I'm getting another x-ray, and hopefully it will be healed. The pain has been gone for a while." Mildred completed the disguise during the conversation. He stared at the transformation when she added, "I need to go, and I want to be early."

"10-4, Mr. Brimstone. Are you working tonight?"

"Probably will stay on after coffee for a while. Trying to get back in shape."

"Good, I want a full report before I leave at six."

Bud left and as he closed the door, Mildred could swear he was mumbling. She didn't have time to worry about it; she had to feed the cat and finish preparation. She felt comfortable driving, as the shoulder seemed healed, but continued to wear the sling at least for the meeting.

She arrived fifteen minutes early. As she looked for a table near the rear, there was a subtle tap on her shoulder. She turned and looked at a handsome man who was probably about sixty years old. He looked her right in the eye and said, "Oliver, I presume. I wasn't sure who you would be." Mildred smiled and reached out to accept the offered handshake. "Nice to meet you.

Again." She slid into the booth he directed her to, stowing her cane propped against the seat.

Their conversation began quickly and then silenced when the server approached. "Would you like more time to look at the menu?" Mildred looked up to see Bud in an African shirt and a Kufi Hat. He was looking intently at Tim and smiling politely. They both ordered iced tea, and Mildred knew not to look at anyone until Bud left the table. It was hard to maintain the Oliver personality when she wanted to laugh so desperately.

The unlikely couple settled back into a pleasant conversation. Tim, like his other personality Penny, was a talker. Mildred chatted about her old job at the beauty shop, and he was entertained with the variety of hairpieces she described. He took over the discussion, and she learned that he worked in town as an engineer. He didn't share the name of the company and moved the dialogue away from anything identifiable. Mildred gained cooperation when she brought up her childhood. He lit up with stories of creeks, dogs, and long lost friends. She eventually knew that he was born in Virginia and went to school there too. Oliver began to share stories, constructing a sudden interest in genealogy in the hope of finding an identifiable last name. That ploy didn't work. After a half hour, Bud brought them two fresh iced teas, and Mildred noticed he took the used glasses gingerly and placed them on the tray. She had pondered the thought of fingerprints, but Bud took care of the problem. She watched how he only turned in one glass to the service tray. *This teamwork thing is great.*

Tim took a sip of the new tea and then checked his watch. "I have to get back to the office. This was nice, Oliver. I hope to see you again sometime. Maybe Penny can join us."

They both smiled and shook hands again. Tim reached for his wallet, and Mildred intervened. "I invited you, so this one is on me."

"Well, thank you. I owe you a meal and an iced tea now."

"I like it when people owe me food," Mildred answered, half flirting.

Mildred walked to the west exit. "Hey Bud, I'll be back to pay in a moment, I'm going to try and get a license plate."

Bud waved and answered, "I've got the tab; just go. Be careful, old man."

Mildred walked out and towards the exit. She saw him go to the east lot, and she followed. He walked directly to a new Cadillac sedan in the side lot, and she walked as close as possible without appearing to be following him. Mildred took out her keys and hoped the old pick-up truck she used as a cover didn't have an alarm. She couldn't get closer without being spotted. Tim sat in his car for a moment or two on the phone. He pulled out, turning away from her. She could only get two letters and a number; not perfect, but it was more information than they had this morning. She radioed Belinda with the info and told her she was going back to the café.

As she walked to the restaurant, Bud exited with a plastic bag in hand and waved her over to the back stairs. Neither spoke as he led her to the holding room. He set the glass on the table and secured the door. When he turned to her, she started to laugh, and he joined in. "Next time, Colonel, give me a heads up."

"Getting even. You aren't the only one with alter egos." He removed his hat, and they slowly recomposed.

"Nice work on snagging the prints."

"The more I thought about your meeting, the more concerned I was. I realized that prints could be the information we need. How else could you get them without being obvious?"

"It was smooth. Better than my attempt at the license number."

He pushed a tablet over to her, and Bud took out his notebook. "It is a relatively new Cadillac; I only got NA and a 9."

Not looking up Bud asked, "Did you get the state?"

Mildred nodded, "Here, this state."

Bud slipped out as she wrote furiously, making a list of phrases and impressions. He returned about ten minutes later and nodded. Mildred said, "I want to send a text to Block and let him know what's going on."

"No need; while you were busy, I checked the video feed, and it recorded. I called Hampton. He and Block are on the way over. They should be here in about twenty minutes. You hungry?"

"I swear you men will fatten me up to a healthy three hundred pounds."

"Well, I have to go back upstairs and change. Belinda is making a copy of the video. Do you want to wait here?"

"I think I'll go out on the floor and walk around a little. It will help me calm down and put things into perspective."

"Okay. I'll call when they arrive."

Mildred followed Bud out and breathed a sigh as she started to walk. It was oddly comforting in the jangling noise of slot machines and the ongoing smell of smoke and alcohol. She watched the early crowd as she strolled to the other end of the facility and into the hotel. She turned to start back when her earpiece announced softly, "Need you. Block is here."

– 42 –
Truth Be Damned

Mildred lay in bed after a rare night of uninterrupted sleep. No pain, no personal demands. She quietly cuddled and stroked the huge, purring cat. Slowly, the realization occurred to her that her obsession had calmed. She pulled the blanket over her shoulder to steal another hour of peace. She dozed, languishing with her unnaturally quiet mind, until there was a rude nudge into the morning. The bossy bedmate forced a furry head under Mildred's hand with a gentle but painful bite.

"Is someone's bowl empty?" Mildred slipped out of bed and padded into the kitchen. "I see that you still have food, but the bottom of the bowl is visible. We know that should never happen, isn't that right?"

Popcorn didn't answer; she seldom did. Once in the kitchen, Mildred made a single cup of coffee, using the fancy machine she received for her birthday. With a steaming cup of some unpronounceable exotic brew, she turned to go back to her room when the business card on the refrigerator caught her attention. She refused to ponder her action and called Karen from GA. *Today is the day; I'll tell the truth and explain my plan.*

"Hello, is Karen there?"

"Speaking and you are who?"

"This is Mmm – Delilah from the meeting."

Karen's voice changed with recognition, "Oh, Delilah, what's up? I haven't seen you in a couple of days. Do you need help?"

"Yes and no. Is there a time we can meet? Just the two of us?"

"Absolutely. Where are you? I'm just finishing here at the Dress Barn. I can come now."

"I'm moving slowly this morning. Do you mind meeting at my home?"

"I need an address, and I can be there as soon as I pay."

"I'll crank up the coffee. I live in the retirement village by the casino."

"Oh, I understand. You don't have a sponsor yet, do you?" Karen responded.

"No, I don't, but that isn't the issue. I just need to speak to you."

"See you then." Mildred wasn't worried. The mood of the morning held as she heated the oven to prepare a treat and went to get ready for her guest. *To tell the truth, I feel relieved.*

Her hair was still damp when Karen arrived. This would be the first time meeting without the disguise. Mildred opened the door to greet her. Karen scanned her face and then checked a note written on her hand.

"Hi, Karen. Yes, this is the right address."

Karen looked confused as she stepped through the doorway.

"Sorry, Karen, no 'Delilah' today, I have a lot to explain to you."

Karen raised an eyebrow and said, "Yes, I think you do. I recognized the voice, but was looking for blazing red hair." She followed Mildred into the kitchen, welcomed by the tempting smell of coffee and apple turnovers. They sat at the counter, and Karen stared at Mildred.

"I guess I need to start at the beginning. My name is Mildred Petrie, and I'm the widow of Captain Dick Petrie." She proceeded into the narrative of her history from the police department, Dick's gambling losses, her present position, and ultimately, the investigation. Karen said nothing and waited for all of the details. Finally, Mildred said, "I'm sorry for my dishonesty at the meetings, but my intention was good."

Karen slowly frowned at Mildred. "No offense to Delilah, but I don't want her back at the meetings. I appreciate what you are doing, but we base our group on anonymity and trust. It's a haven to tell your personal truth and not be judged."

Mildred felt shamed and asked, "Could I come one more time so that I can apologize to the group, and give them contact information?"

"I don't know right now. I have to think this through. I do forgive you, because you weren't familiar with our steps, but wearing a disguise was too much."

Mildred kept her head bowed, "I only did that so no one would recognize me at the casino. I didn't want anyone to feel the need to intervene."

"Yes, I understand, but it was a lie on top of a lie; and no matter, you betrayed us." Karen rose to leave, and Mildred wanted to stop her, but remained seated, not sure what to do next.

"I'll call you another time, Mildred." Karen walked out, shutting the door firmly. Mildred looked at her plate of untouched turnovers and two almost full cups of coffee. *Well, that went well. At least I've come clean.*

– 43 –
Step Forward

Feeling there was nothing to add to the loan shark investigation today, Mildred went to the closet and moved back the clothing. It was necessary to sit on the floor to add the list of housekeepers. Surprised by the exotic names of the ghost employees, Mildred realized the scope of access and knowledge was impressive. Planning a couple of internet searches, she would make a document for Arnie and Q and email a request for a Monday meeting.

The phone rang, and Mildred struggled up from the floor and tripped over a box on her way to answer. By the end of the fourth ring, she was able to catch the call. "Hello."

"This is Karen. I have thought about what you had to say. I will work with you, and if anyone has information that would help, I will give them the choice of telling you or not."

"Thank you so much, Karen, I…"

"You can come to the four o'clock meeting and speak first. No disguise, and then leave a business card. No staying for the main meeting."

As Mildred attempted to respond, Karen hung up.

This is fantastic, but I don't have any cards. Her first reaction was to call Bud, but decided she wasn't ready to tell him what she was doing. There is no way he could get her business cards in a couple hours. She called the printer over by the meeting hall. They had an answer to the dilemma. They would do a copy job on a light card stock in a subtle color. For just a couple more dollars, they would cut them. Mildred immediately went to her computer and designed a page she would cut into strips imprinted with Delilah, Private Investigator, and an email address. At second thought, she opened a new email account with the cover name and put that address on the cards, and sent the page to the printer.

In a quick response, the printer confirmed receipt and promised a pick up at three-thirty. This would give her time to design some real business cards and still make it to the GA meeting.

Once that emergency was resolved, Mildred went back to the closet and the box that tripped her. It was the evidence box. Remembering her initial plan to turn it over to the police, Mildred hadn't done anything uncomplicated in the past few months. She couldn't help wondering why he had saved it for all these years. It shouldn't take much time to flip through it and then drop it off. The box was heavy to lift, so she scooted it next to Dick's side of the bed. Lifting off the lid, she saw files, a rusty knife, and discolored clothing. There were some loose letters and notes in the thickest folder. She slowly set to organizing, stacking, and sorting. Mildred struggled to get up from the floor and went to her desk for more folders. Dick was a good cop, but his organizational skills haunted his entire career, and now they were plaguing her. It felt like they were working together, and in a little over an hour, she had three folders labeled Investigation, Notes, and Evidence. She wouldn't read the material until it was organized.

At three-fifteen she left for the printer for her makeshift business cards. At three-fifty she arrived at the GA meeting where Karen greeted her.

"Hi, what do you want me to call you?"

"Mildred is okay. I had these contact cards made up with Delilah and an email address. I am trying to protect anonymity, both mine and yours."

"I appreciate that. I want you to speak first, explain what you are doing and then leave."

"I'm not going to use my real name. I need to move carefully. Is that okay with you?"

"Yeah, I guess. I hadn't thought about the danger you could be in. Those people are called sharks for a reason. Everyone is settling in, so it is time to start. I'll introduce you first."

Mildred sat quietly, mentally trying some lines, deciding on a simple truth. Karen spoke and then turned the podium over to her. Mildred was nervous, but there was only one thing to do.

"Hi, everyone. You know me as Delilah."

They answered in unison, "Hi Delilah."

"I want to apologize to each of you. My real name is Mildred, and my husband committed suicide three years ago. By the time of his death, he had lost our home and retirement, and just before his funeral, a couple of men showed up wanting even more. That's when the cars and savings were liquidated. I was able to buy back a written agreement with my husband's signature. I wasn't thinking clearly, and I was frightened. They destroyed the note, and I don't remember any other information besides Dick's name. It is only now that I'm ready to find out who was behind it all. I know I came here under false pretenses. I hoped to learn more about the loan shark behind our destruction. I have begun to work with the police, but I don't have any valid information. I left some email addresses by the cookie tray with Delilah's name. If you have any information, I will honor your anonymity and hope you will do the same for me. We all know how dangerous these guys can be. Again, I'm so sorry for my ignorance and dishonesty. Thank you, I'll leave now."

Mildred picked up her purse from the chair, took out the blue contact cards, and left them on the table as they watched. She nodded at Karen and, without looking back, quietly left.

By the time she was outside, she took a deep breath. *Now, patience to see if this works.* Instead of going home, she drove to the casino. As she parked in the front lot, she tapped in the text on her cell phone.

"G-ma on the floor."

– 44 –
Partners

Sunday's activity was over earlier than the other nights, so Mildred was able to be home and in bed before midnight. Awakened early, her mind was racing with questions and ideas. Instead of fighting to silence the thoughts, she leaned over to reach the paper by the bed and made a list. Once she calmed the pestering internal conversation, she had to get ready for the meeting with Q and Arnie. She had the turnovers she made yesterday and pondered what else she could serve. Looking in the refrigerator, then the freezer and then back to the fridge, she found a frozen pie crust. Pulling out eggs, a tomato, and some frozen vegetables, she was able to construct a very impressive quiche.

She removed the breakfast from the oven just as she heard a quiet knock on her door. "That sounds like Q." Mildred opened the door to find her friend, and Arnie was walking up from the visitor parking.

"Welcome, you two. I assume you know each other." They smiled, and Arnie started into a narrative about Qaseema's first night. It was a relief that they were comfortable with each other. They moved to the counter for coffee, food and reports. Mildred had set out dishes, tablets and pens. Both Arnie and Q brought file folders. Mildred warmed up her printer to scan anything they decided to share and set up her erasable markers to use the refrigerator as a whiteboard.

Q spoke, "I am happy to have met you both. You have made my transition to America easier. I wanted to share that Human Resources has given me a promotion. I am still cleaning, but also tasked with night first aid and employee emergency training classes. There is more money, which relieves personal stress."

Mildred made a mental note to thank Bud. She was sure he was responsible. As soon as the quiche was cut and served, they moved directly to the mission. Q and Arnie had stories of violence, and five other deaths ruled suicides in the past six years.

Arnie reported, "There is also evidence of over-zealous collections and blackmail. I've changed my patrol with more focus on the cards and sports betting sections. The slots are more regulated and not nearly as noticeable when losses build up."

Mildred agreed, "No nickel, no spin. I think the social aspect would make the rooms more likely. Great angle, Arnie."

He continued in his update. "I'm also reorganizing the regular patrols with additional headings in nightly reports. During the night shifts, the struggle to recover becomes even more desperate."

"The old double down?" Mildred asked.

Q added, "This is exaggerated by the alcohol." The other two nodded in agreement.

Mildred started a list with her erasable marker and the front of the refrigerator. "Let us start a list of regulars."

Arnie knew a few names, but not all. "The victims would probably be frequent guests digging in too deep."

Q spoke up, "I will check with the night crew; they sometimes notice things."

The three decided to continue the investigation, considered initial contacts, and outlined possible behaviors that could flag involvement.

Mildred told of her foray into Gamblers Anonymous and shared her contact information. They all agreed this group could be a wealth of information.

Arnie stopped the chatter. "You recognize that this could be dangerous, and Mildred – you stick to a cover name. The new email is a minimum of protection. I will also get a separate email to keep this investigation isolated from the casino and my personal information."

Q admitted, "I don't have internet presence other than at library."

"Get a new email, with a different extension, completely separate from your personal. We will all communicate through the new address. Next meeting we can exchange the information."

Mildred started to clear the dishes, as it was obvious that the meeting was coming to an end. "It's time to present a profile for the notorious lender." She stopped and turned to the team, "I think we are looking for a middle-aged white man, a little overweight, wearing a fedora and a scar on his left... no, right, cheek."

"No, no," said Arnie. "He will have a very elegant suit with an Eastern European accent, a fur hat and an enormous bodyguard named Uri."

They all laughed when Q spoke up. "You are both incorrect. He is a tanned, slim man wearing a keffiyeh on his head and has access to explosives."

Arnie and Mildred stopped speaking and looked at Q for a brief moment, noticing the glint in her eyes, then laughter resumed. Mildred added, "I guess that tells us we must open up our preconceived notions. Probably won't fit the stereotypes, and we will have to be ready for any option."

Arnie stopped laughing and added, "This is organized and there is a shit load, pardon my French, of money behind it."

"What do you suggest?"

"Ladies, I think we need to gather local organized crime information."

"And gangs. Many of them are the new crime syndicates," Q added.

"How do you know that?" Mildred asked.

"I watch television news. It aids my English."

Mildred dried her hands. "Okay, time for assignments. When do you want to get together again?"

They decided to meet on Mondays, their day off, around noon after Q's class.

Mildred was first. "I'll put out some casual feelers with the police, since I'm working with them on the burglary."

Arnie went next. "I will see what I can learn about local organized crime and kick up the night watch. I'll also add a heading to the evening reports."

Q promised more research and wanted to buy a personal computer with her raise. She continued, "This would help with my school work and contacting my family."

"Don't forget to have separate emails!"

"Yes Mr. Arnie, I remember. I will make some subtle inquiries of other housekeepers. Not risk contact with every member of department."

Arnie said, "Don't tip your hand, only speak to a few that you know and trust."

Speaking up, Mildred said, "We all agree the housekeeping staff has some of the best access to every corner of the casino."

"And invisibility too," said Arnie. "I've watched lately, and most customers pay your workers no mind. Oh, and finally, before I go home for a nap, I think we should wait until we have something more than a theory before we bring in security and the police. Right now we only have speculation." He raised both hands for a high five, and the women responded making an unstated agreement.

Once her team left, Mildred cleaned the kitchen and wiped down the refrigerator. She had a difficult time removing the images and continued to talk to herself, *I need a second whiteboard. Even better, a second bedroom for an office and the occasional guest. As long as I'm wishing, that would be nice.*

As she let the luxury of a nap draw her to the bedroom, the phone rang. "Hello."

"Mom, it's me, David."

She loved how both of her sons identify themselves to her as if she didn't know their voices since the beginning of their lives.

"David, it's great to hear from you. I'm anxious to know how the proposal went."

"It worked perfectly. Katie loves the puppy, and she can't believe that I picked out such a beautiful ring, considering what she calls my stingy nature and lack of style." Mildred could hear the joy in his voice, and pictured his face.

"I hope you took credit for choosing the ring?"

"I did at first, but she kept pushing, and then I had to tell her about you and Lindsey making me do a proper proposal. Katie agreed my idea of a text would have destroyed her childhood dreams." He continued to chatter on, reminding her of his teen years. "We are getting married next weekend and..."

"Stop! Hold it, David Andrew Petrie! I don't know if I can make it, I have to get a flight and a gift and something to wear. Does Richie know?"

"Don't worry, Mom, this is for her family, and then we are coming home, well, my home, for the reception. Lindsey already took over the planning."

She stayed quiet for a moment, and after a deep breath, "Okay, David, here is the deal. I'll pay for your airline tickets."

"No, Mom, I know you can't afford that."

"I can decide what is affordable or not. You forget I'm employed. So don't worry about what I can or can not do. When will you arrive?"

David lost some of the joy in his voice. "Our plan is to come the Thursday after the ceremony, and we will stay until the first of the week. That fits into our vacation time."

"Congratulations, my dearest boy. Don't worry about anything, Lindsey is a planner of the ultimate degree, I'll still get a new dress and it will be memorable. I'm so happy and excited. I love you so much."

His mood seemed to recover some. "I love you too, Mom."

Once off the phone, Mildred called Lindsey, left a message and then left a message for Belinda as she walked to the casino.

Belinda met her at the front desk. "I'm sorry, the honeymoon suite is booked six months to a year in advance, but they are putting together an elegant suite with flowers and champagne for the happy couple."

Mildred nodded, not expecting things to pull together so quickly. "How much do I need for a deposit?"

The clerk smiled, and answered "There is no charge, but if you would like to leave a credit card as a guarantee, that would be great." Mildred signed to cover additional meal costs while Belinda finished the approvals.

They were about to conclude the final negotiations as Lindsey called. After a short conversation, Mildred turned back to the clerk. "I also need to reserve a private dining room for a reception." The three women looked at the reservation map, and discovered one of the larger rooms was available. Mildred was stunned that she was on her way back home within a half hour.

Once home, she collapsed into her chair in front of the window and sighed. It was only two-thirty, and already a full day. Retirement was exhausting.

Lucas Freeman

Mildred jerked awake after a few minutes, and even though she was hungry, decided to go to the clinic first. Monday afternoon was a perfect time. It was slow, and she could get right in. A quick x-ray confirmed everything had healed, and she could remove the sling.

The doctor came in and handed her a referral for physical therapy. "Mrs. Petrie, you are healing well for someone your age."

Mildred looked at the information. "I don't know if I have time for this." She stretched her arm and started to pick things up.

"Couldn't you give me some exercises or something?"

The doctor scowled. "To regain all mobility and strength, physical therapy is important, but I will have the nurse bring in some exercise worksheets, but this is in addition to the physical therapy."

While waiting for the nurse, Mildred worked out some exercises on her own. She was stretching and flexing her left arm when the nurse came in with some printed sheets of paper. "The doctor wants you to have these, and I can see you are intent on recovery." She smiled and shook her head.

"I think I'm doing pretty well, and there is no pain when I lift and stretch. My mobility seems recovered, but I'm a little weaker." Mildred added, "Now that I have two arms back in operation, I feel pretty powerful."

She stood up, gathered the papers and started for the door. "I understand, and I'll behave. Do I have to come back?"

The nurse answered, "Mrs. Petrie, don't overdo it. Take things slow, as the healing takes a while. We do want to see you after the physical therapy completes. Please call in for an appointment."

With a wave good-bye and a roll of her eyes, Mildred left. As she drove home, she privately admitted that age and the demands of the job were creeping up on her. She considered using the AARP discount for a membership at the gym on State Street.

Once home, she finished the last cold slice of quiche and made some iced tea. Measuring her options for the evening, Mildred voted against playing mind numbing Mahjong on the computer, and television shows could wait. She moved to the bedroom, sat on the bed, and started to go through the investigative folder. The memory of Dick's frustration with this case returned. He was positive that Freeman didn't commit suicide. The records brought back his anger when Judge McCaffie ruled insufficient evidence and dismissed the case. The months he obsessed with this problem replayed as she handled the things he had touched. This was over fifteen years ago, and Mildred assumed he had resolved the case. She was so busy with two teenaged boys and a full-time job. She didn't follow up with him and the guilt brought tears to her eyes as she studied Dick's reports.

She read and reread the victim's history. Lucas Freeman was a young man, first in his family to finish high school and college. He was getting an advanced degree at night and working construction during the day. Married for three years. They had one son and another on the way. *Why would he kill himself when his life was taking off?*

Mildred read on. There was a lot of debt with student loans, credit card balances and payday advances that had multiplied. *Well, that is one thing to consider.* Many of the people at GA had mentioned payday loans.

Dick had circled a lump sum payment to the hospital for his wife's previous delivery bills and a bank deposit. She studied an emergency room visit for a fall, but the stories were inconsistent in explaining his head injuries that included, a fractured nose, orbital socket, and a dislocated shoulder.

Mildred reached over for the sticky notes on the stand next to the bed. *Follow up with Mrs. Freeman* and stuck it to the front of the folder with an old phone number. The light was starting to fade, so Mildred packed it in and went to find a real meal and some television to finish out her evening. While her frozen dinner cooked in the microwave, she dialed the number. There was a recorded announcement: "This number has been disconnected, please recheck the directory." Things were never easy, but Mildred felt it was necessary to talk to Mrs. Freeman.

Her dreams that night were filled with memories of her husband and sons. Towards morning, they morphed into Lucas Freeman with the baby he never met. Subsequently, it became a vision with camels and Krispy Kreme donuts in the desert. Once awake, a line from the television show from last night kept traipsing through her brain: follow the money.

Still in her nightgown, she started digging through the box, spreading the investigation across her bed. *There is something here, but what?* An answer was somewhere, and she knew it was in front of her. Maybe it was her irregular hours, maybe the stress from the robbery, but she began to combine all three investigations.

– 46 –
Suddenly Tuesday

The hours slipped past as she worked her way through notes and crime scene photos. Popcorn had settled in the box to nap. She ran her fingers over the remarks written in Dick's handwriting. Sort, read, and stack. She had no idea what to look for, and fought to keep her mind open. Suddenly the cat leaped out of the box and ran to the living room, followed by a knock at her door. Mildred felt a short panic and embarrassment, she hadn't gotten dressed. *Oh damn. I forgot it was Tuesday.* She grabbed a sweater and went to answer the door. It was Detective Block standing on the porch with a folder and a paper bag.

"Hi Elton, the morning got away from me. Please come in, and I'll be right back."

He laughed gently, as the cat greeted him with a leg rub and a purr. He went straight to the kitchen. While Mildred slipped into her day pajama pants and a long sleeve T-shirt, she could hear him making coffee and searching through the cabinets. She had to smile at how comfortable the team members were in her home.

When she came out, he had two small plates with steaming breakfast sandwiches and the coffee was brewing. He laid out the contents of two files, and she blushed as she entered the room. "I got sidetracked and time got away from me. Thought you were going to start calling?"

Block smiled and pointed at the huge file folder on the counter. "Not when we are pre-scheduled. I understand completely about distraction, I do the same things. I apologize I'm a little early. But for now, sit down, and I'll get the white board. We are going to need it."

"No, no, I'll..." But it was too late; he was already in her bedroom. She heard the closet open, and she grimaced, hoping he didn't pay attention to the piles of paper and the box by her bed. Then the realization of the markings on the box and he was, after all, a detective. Mildred started to search for an excuse, but she knew better. If he asked, she must confess.

He pulled out the board and propped it against the wall, then sat down and took a deep sip of the coffee. He spread the papers from the first folder and then turned to look at Mildred. "Is it the old evidence box that was consuming your morning?"

"Yes, it was a cold case of Dick's I found in storage, and I was just going through it."

"Find anything interesting?" he asked.

Mildred answered, "Hell, I don't know. I was going to give it to you, but once I opened it, there was a need to get to the bottom first."

"That's the detective itch. There has to be an answer to every question. Happens to me every, single time. To be a good investigator, there must be degrees of obsessive compulsion."

Mildred said, "Nice when a personality disorder is a job requirement."

Block continued to study the board and added, "From what I see of you, we wasted your God-given talents checking parking meters."

"I'll take that as a compliment, Elton." That went better than she had expected. "I guess we need to leave the fifteen-year-old case and work on something current."

He explained there were no connections with the list of housekeepers, but he was intrigued with their free access to all corners of the casino. He checked off the list on the board, photographed it with his phone and erased the old list. He started a chart, with the different departments displayed. At the bottom was housekeeping and landscaping, then up to servers, cashiers, security as he worked his way to the top. There he posted OWNERS – INVESTORS. "I think this goes deep. What do you know about the top of the chart?"

"Now that you mention it, all I ever heard was the Ivory Winds was financed by a group of businessmen. I never looked further."

"Well, I did. There is a rule of in-depth investigations: follow the money." Mildred was stunned, that was exactly her new mantra.

Block didn't notice her reaction as he continued. "So I have gotten sidetracked. We gave the thieves too much credit. We are sure they had inside knowledge. That's what gave the impression of sophistication. However, this robbery was amateurish. Our one suspect has been sticking close to home. He hasn't connected with anyone except the attorney, and stays at his mother's playing video games. He is just a gangster wannabe and, with his record, it appears he is more of a hanger-on with no level of experience in something this big. The invasion really was a complete and utter failure. Lives were lost, and everyone involved was changed. There is something else going on. I wonder what the point of this was. Even dumbass thugs know there is sophisticated security at the casino."

Mildred added, "You're right. They only have to watch a movie or two to be prepared. They had made it through a couple layers of security, but when they got close to the big money – whammo! Stopped."

Block answered quickly, "I think we are onto something deeper than the robbery. Who would benefit the most from this fiasco? We have been looking for the inside man, but that might be looking too narrowly."

"Bingo. You think this was a cover, but cover for what?" Mildred asked. "I have to admit, I was working on something before this burglary, and don't know why it felt connected."

He looked at her quizzically. "What else?"

Mildred paused then said, "I'm sure you know my husband, Dick Petrie, committed suicide."

Block nodded his head and remained quiet to let her talk. "I'll bet you are wondering how I became a widow in a one-bedroom retirement villa, looking for work." Mildred continued, "Dick and I had not planned on jobs in our seventies, but after he died, I found we had been stripped of almost everything, and now I'm on the hunt for a loan shark." Mildred stayed completely honest and gave the names of the people who know of this investigation and her cover at the GA meetings.

After pondering for a second or two, Block spoke, "I'm very concerned about what you are up to, and how deep this could be going into possible organized crime. I'm particularly worried about your announcement at the Gamblers meeting."

Mildred answered, "Yeah, I know. I can't seem to divide the two cases."

He thought for a while and then started a new list on the board. After an hour of explanation and sharing of information, Block said, "Mildred, I have to agree. Even if these aren't connected, it is possible. I will monitor the Delilah email for information on the loan sharks, and stay in closer contact. I'm concerned about your working."

Mildred answered, "I'm not worried at all. When I'm at the casino, everything is on camera, and I have a team of black-shirted security at my bidding. I promise not to involve anyone else, and will let the secondary investigation get put on hold."

Block said," I also want notice of when you go in and check out. No more walking to work. And mix up your hours even more." Block reached over, taking her phone from the counter and programming his private cell number. "I also need your password information for the Delilah email."

Mildred wrote the information on a sticky note, gave him the extra key to her condo, and went to her bedroom and came out with the wig stands. "I guess you need to meet my personal assistants. This is Delilah Hopper. You will be working with her." She set down the first head and held up the slightly balding wig. "This is Mr. Oliver Brimstone. He also has a moustache and a wispy goatee, and I don't think you have heard of this one." Holding up the third head covered in a long, dark brown-and-grey wig, "Ms. Bambi Hunter." She dipped the head in a bow. "Honored to meet you, dirty copper."

"Charmed, I'm sure. I'll need photos of you in each get-up so I don't accidentally shoot one of your egos."

As Block shook his head, and wrote down the names of the disguises on his file folder, Mildred responded, "We wouldn't want any of us shot. Would we, gang?" Each head nodded as she gathered them back up. She continued to describe each of her characters and their particular talents.

When she returned to the kitchen, they confirmed her schedules, and Mildred advised she would go in for the 55+ gaming night as herself. It would be over by midnight.

"I want you to check out along with the crowd. Try not to be in the parking lot alone."

"Okay, I can do that," Mildred answered with a sigh.

"One more thing, Mildred. Try to avoid winning all of the grand prizes." Block checked his phone and gathered his materials. "This meeting is over, and the next one will involve Detective Hampton, too."

Once Block left, she chanted the mantra of *Follow The Money* while she cleared the counter. After she had chased the cat out of the evidence box, she repacked the Freeman case and settled in for a preparatory nap. As she was about to doze, she sat up straight in bed.

There was one name that showed up in all three cases!

Easy Night

She arrived at six for the 55+ Game Night that was scheduled to start in an hour. Mildred dressed in her favorite Kittens Playing Dice sweatshirt, which always helped her blend into the late middle-aged crowd. She signed in as she entered and went directly to the buffet. Not able to sit at her favorite table, she settled nearby. The view wasn't as good, but it would have to do. She started on the Caesar salad and then moved on to the creamy shrimp fettuccini with a side of buttery broccoli. She decided to avoid dessert, because she had been eating too many apple turnovers.

As she was clearing her dishes, she backed up and grabbed a chocolate pudding, easily justified as a need for the calcium found in dairy. That should help the shoulder rebuild. Able to see the main entry and some of the slot machines, she watched the crowd begin to arrive. This is the age group where the women roamed the slots, and the men went straight to the tables. It looked like it would be a good evening. It was nearly seven when she saw Judge McCaffie leave the elegant dining area and go to the glassed-in card room. She scanned, looking for his wife, but Brittany wasn't evident. At that instant, she made a decision and would have to get permission later. Mildred texted the office,

"Need a phone number."

"Okay, name?"

"Judith McCaffie"

As she was walking out on the floor for the best vantage point, the answer came in.

"Sorry, not listed, took some effort. Number sent to your phone."

"Thank you"

Mildred went to the women's restroom and made the call.

"Hello, Judith?"

"Hello. Yes, this is Judith."

"This is Mildred Petrie. I ran into the Judge and was concerned about you."

"I haven't seen you since Dick's funeral. How are you doing?"

The conversation stayed friendly, and Mildred arranged to meet her for lunch tomorrow. She returned to the main floor and settled in to observe. The Judge would be easy to avoid; he wouldn't leave the card room all evening. She then noticed Arnie was with a couple of unknown men dressed in the black security suits. *Must be new recruits.* When they passed her, Arnie winked as Mildred held her finger to her closed mouth in a suggestion of silence.

The slots were noisy and full of focused players, so she started a patrol to the shops, restaurants, and the hotel lobby. They were moderately busy, nothing of note. Mildred was sure most of her night would be in the gaming area with the activities planned for the event and went back looking for the best vantage point. She settled in at a slot machine, just as they announced a prize for the first person to bring a stuffed animal to the third crap table. There were trivia questions that moved into a scavenger hunt and costume parade as Mildred listened. There were drink coupons, prizes, and a trip to the Bahamas as Mildred watched. The night was silly and full of energy; the program director deserved the employee-of-the-month award. The casino had a line of taxicabs waiting at midnight for some of the most involved players.

Mildred was home before one a.m., and even with Popcorn trying to lounge on the keyboard, she got her report emailed to Bud before two. Still feeling alert, she typed up a few questions she wanted to ask Judith at lunch. She could not shake the common thread to the robbery, the loan shark, and the death of Lucas Freeman. She wrote *Follow The Money* on the white board, on the refrigerator, and on the box of the cold case, and only then did she settle in for the rest of the night.

− 48 −
Ladies Lunch

She drove into a landscaped circle drive, and a young man in a formal coat and tie greeted her. He called Judith to announce Mildred's arrival, held the door open, and then parked her car. Mildred felt self-conscious of her car and her clothes. She started to question what she was doing; this was not her element. Another man, also dressed formally, escorted her to a pleasant dining room and gave her a crystal glass filled with water and slices of cucumber. The table was elegantly set with fine china and silver. The server came with the beginning of their pre-ordered lunch. Unable to help it, she measured her small one bedroom in the subsidized retirement village off the interstate against this elegant gated community. Her whole condominium would fit into the dining room.

It didn't take Judith long to join her, casually dressed for tennis. Mildred's police eye took a quick inventory. Tan, facelift (maybe two), slim and probably physically active, she appeared younger than her seventy-plus years.

"Judith, you look fantastic."

"Thank you, Mildred; it has been so long since we spent any time together. I often reminisce about the old days with the Women's Alliance and the McGruff program. You and Dick were excellent representatives. I'm so sorry for your loss. Are you doing all right?"

"I am: busy with some volunteer activities, and my boys and their families." Mildred had decided last night to play this as an old, retired friend. She pulled out her wallet and shared photos of the grandkids. She had forgotten an old picture of Dick in his uniform was still in the plastic photo sleeve. His self-assured look gave Mildred more confidence. "This place is fantastic, you must love living here."

"It's fine; there are all kinds of activities and group trips. I can't complain. Oh, here is our lunch." The food came to the table on silver trays with a formal presentation.

"Wow, Judith, I'm impressed. This beats the grand slam at Denny's." Both women laughed politely, and a little more of the nervousness and years slipped away.

Judith smiled and said, "I do miss the Moons over My Hammy, and as much as I have tried, the kitchen here just doesn't seem to understand the processed meat, grease-to-bread ratio. What brings you here?"

Wow, right down to business. Mildred expected the question and was ready, "I ran into the Judge at the casino and I, of course, thought of you."

A sneer crossed Judith's face. "Was that skank with him?"

"If you mean the young chickie? That would be a yes." Mildred was a little surprised at Judith's tone.

"First of all, she is more of a viper than a chickie."

Not sure how to respond, Mildred answered, "So it was an amicable divorce?"

"By amicable do you mean a couple mil in hush money? I can't complain financially, but the humiliation of being tossed aside after forty-seven years also has its price." The malice dissipated as Judith stabbed a piece of fruit from her plate. "He is a miserable man and he deserves her."

Mildred spoke up, "I always thought you two were indestructible."

Judith put down her fork. "The vow of until death do you part became an impossible length of time."

"Well, she seemed to be miserable, if that gives you any solace," Mildred added.

Judith was silent, and Mildred could see an unidentifiable emotion before she spoke, "Not really. She only signed up for the money, and she is still pissed about how much it took to dump me. He is even angrier that I got Lucy."

"Lucy? I didn't think you had any kids."

"She is our peekapoo. Let me show you." Judith reached for a pocket sized photo album that had several pictures of a small dog. They gushed, Mildred shared stories of Popcorn, and told how the cat helped her recover from her a recent fall.

Mildred's silent mind repeated, *follow the money*. "So you said you were paid a couple mil. What do judges earn these days?"

"Good old Lawrence McCaffie invested well."

"Why didn't he teach Dick about investing?" Mildred smiled at the double-edged question, trying to keep control of the conversation. "Then again, it's well-known that Dick got into gambling at the end, and not on the winning side."

"I had heard stories about him. Are you doing all right?"

"Honey, don't worry about me. I have paid off all the debt and have my own place by the casino."

"The casino! I hate that place, but it does pay well." Judith looked out the window, and Mildred could tell there was an immeasurable bitterness still boiling in her.

Mildred added, "It only pays well with a proper amount of lady luck."

"Luck has nothing to do with my settlement," said Judith. *Bingo, there is a connection.*

"So that place set you up, and at the same time kicked my butt. Nice to know. Maybe in my next life, I'll be on the other side of the equation."

"It has to do with involvement. No one at the table will ever be a winner. The real money is behind closed doors," Judith revealed.

An elegant cart rolled to their table, and a young man in a flawless white coat and chef hat announced, "Dessert is served." Mildred decided on a crème brûlée and watched the dessert chef torch the top to a perfect crisp. Judith settled on a second vodka martini. They finished lunch sharing stories of Mildred's grandchildren and memories of the years gone by. Mildred reached for her wallet to pay, and Judith stopped her. "I've got this. Remember, Denny's will be your treat."

"Deal. And it will be soon. I don't want to lose our friendship." Mildred stood to leave, and they hugged an awkward goodbye. By the time she walked through the ostentatious lobby, the gold and etched glass doors opened in front of her. Mildred stepped out to the covered entry and her car was waiting for her.

The valet held the door to her freshly washed car, and she knew she was on her way back to reality. *Damn, this place is great.* She tipped the valet ten dollars, feeling like her usual one dollar would be an insult. As Mildred drove out of the compound, she felt like one of the chosen, *whatever the hell that means.*

Mildred went directly to the store, needing to replenish her stock of Pepperidge Farm turnovers and coffee. Once home, she called and left a message for Block, then went to the closet and wrote on the white board, "LMc" under the owner heading. Next, she settled with her computer and started a new search.

Night Shift

It didn't take long for Detective Block to call back. "Hey, Double-Oh-Seventy-One, what's up?"

Mildred said, "Well, I can tell that you've been talking to someone at the casino. I thought my deep cover ID was secret."

"You aren't the only one who is working on this. Your Delilah email has had two hits, nothing of any substance yet, but I'll keep you advised."

"I noticed a little something. Every one of the cases has one person in common."

"Really? Please go on."

"Judge Lawrence McCaffie's name came up in all of the investigations, including the cold case."

"Damn, that's an interesting observation. Now that you mention it, McCaffie is the one who approved our current suspect bail."

"He also dismissed the possible murder case of Lucas Freeman, and he was a close friend of my husband before he died, drenched in gambling debt," Mildred added. "So I met his ex-wife for lunch earlier today."

"MILDRED! There is no reining you in, is there? You aren't supposed to step out like that without backup. What did you find out?" he asked.

"They were married for forty-seven years when he took up with the new wife. Judith, the Judge's ex, mentioned getting a couple mil as a divorce settlement. After the second martini, she suggested it was hush money. She also said that the new wife, Brittany, was upset about the divorce settlement. She hinted the Judge may be one of the owners of the casino, and she mentioned business investments in the Bahamas or Caymans, one of those tax haven islands. I've looked for and found the new wife's last name to check her affiliations, but that is just a gut feeling."

She could hear the clicking of the keyboard as Block answered, "Always listen to your gut in these cases."

Mildred said, "I hope I don't have many more of these investigations. I'm retired, you know."

"Yeah, right," Block snorted. "You need to join a knitting club or something."

"The reason I know Judith is from years ago. The Women's Alliance sponsored the Officer McGruff, and we worked together."

"No telling where old associations will come into play." The two detectives settled into more of the details and nuances of her meeting with Judith. Mildred supplied an address and the information she had found on Brittany Caprio-McCaffie. She was about to conclude the exchange when he said, "Bingo! Ms. Caprio has a record. I'll run a full background check, and be back in touch."

"Great. Do you want me to respond to the Delilah emails?"

"No, we have it under control for now."

"I'm working tonight; Thursdays are the first day of the weekend in casino life. Later, boss."

He started to say goodbye, but she had hung up.

Mildred decided on Bambi for tonight. She had benched her, but with her shoulder doing so well, it was again possible to put on the tattoo sleeves. Jeans, boots and biker vest, and she was out the door a little early. Lunch was elegant, but she needed to eat bigger food before she hit the floor.

"G-ma on the floor."
"U R early, this is Belinda"
"I'm hungry."
'Meet you at the café in ten."
"Back table, I M biker."

The café wasn't busy that time of night. Most of the crowd wanted an elegant dining experience or the buffet, so Mildred was able to get the table they met at before. Belinda was there within minutes. "Good evening, ma'am. May I join you?"

Mildred looked up to her friend's incredulous expression. "Yes, that would be delightful."

Belinda whispered, "Your answer is out of character."

"Shut up and sit, Bitch. Is that better?"

Belinda smiled and nodded as she sat. The two women ordered burgers and salads. Mildred continued with her hyper-vigilance, watching the security team for any suggestion of involvement. Now she felt comfortable with Belinda, and this meeting made a pleasant start to the night. Belinda talked about her husband's job and their hope to have another child. She voiced concern over insurance, which caused Mildred to relax further. This meeting was about friendship and not work.

"Belinda, I've been out of the loop. What events do we have this weekend?"

"Some old rockers from the Neolithic era, Herman's Hermits."

"Herman's Hermits! They are part of the theme song of my life. I need a new outfit."

"I'm really not familiar with them. What would you wear?"

Mildred started to quietly sing. "Mrs. Brown, you've got a lovely daughter..." and then slipped into "I'm Henry the Eighth, I am...." Belinda joined in on the second verse, and they ended in unison with exaggerated British accents. Mildred was joyous with the memories of the band, and Belinda basked in the familiarity of the songs her parents sang in the car on vacations. "This is the tragedy of new generations; you think everything came from Sesame Street."

"You have until Saturday. They are doing two shows. I'll get your passes, and Arnie will deliver them to you later tonight. Anything else you need?"

"Are you kidding? I can't think of a thing other than a granny dress."

"That is something I can't envision. You should enjoy the show, since we have the pickpockets under control. Hey, I don't know your name today."

"Bambi. Bambi Hunter, at your service, Ms. Belinda."

They finished the light-hearted lunch, and Mildred started her patrol as Belinda left for home.

She noticed the hotel concierge watching as Bambi walked into the gift shop off the main lobby. She considered the mixed blessing of being unrecognized, but being noticeable. They paid almost no attention to her in the lounges. She spent time surveying the game rooms from her lookout at the Hip Hop Hippo slot machines. Then she moved on to the table games and lost some at craps. She radioed in a slip-and-fall and identified a possible shoplifter as the evening passed.

She closed out the shift in the nightclub and called security with a domestic dispute; the usual Thursday night. The crowd quieted into the late night patterns as Mildred checked out at midnight.

"**G-ma out.**"

"**Thx – C U tomorrow – out.**"

– 50 –
A Break

Mildred woke to the ringing cell phone. Rushing into the kitchen, she pulled it off the charger. "Good morning," she croaked.

"Sorry to call so early. But I've got something." It only took Mildred a moment to recognize Block's voice.

"Sure, Boss, what do you have?"

"Your lead on the Judge may have some merit. Brittany is an alias, and her record was washed before 2010. When I searched her name, my computer was blocked by an FBI notice and given a number to call."

"Did you call?"

"What do you think, Mildred? I am a cop, after all."

"So spill it, Detective."

"Only so much I can say, but this took me to the organized crime department. They are sending someone out to look over our files. I'm keeping you out of this as long as possible."

Mildred whispered, "Thanks?"

Block continued on. "Do you have a gun?"

"Hell, no. Do you?"

He ignored her sass. "We are getting into some dangerous waters, and I want you safe."

"Safe is an abstract term. When Dick and I retired, we turned in our guns and started a new chapter. Chief Nelson offered me one at our first meeting for this job, and I'll tell you the truth, I don't want one."

"I want you to think about it seriously," Block said.

"I'll think about it. Now, what did you learn from the FBI?"

"Not over the phone. Do you have any more apple turnovers?"

"I will by the time you get here; I've started buying them by the case. Give me a few minutes to get dressed and heat the oven."

"10-4. See you in a half hour."

Mildred rushed to wash last night off her face, and the shower would wait. Sweatshirt and jeans on, she was ready when he arrived, and the baked goods were cooling on the counter top. He slapped down the now-familiar folder, which had grown in size. He poured the coffee as she plated the hot turnovers. They settled into work.

"There are a lot of questions on the owners of the casino. The story had been 'a group of businessmen,'" he said, placing air quotes around the phrase. "I have one of the cyber tech officers working on it. At first, it looked good, but the more he dug, he found shell corporations and fake names. The forensic accountant has researched, and you were right, they found probable accounts in the Cayman Islands, and the judge is involved in the recent data breach papers that came out a couple months ago."

"It's always the money, isn't it?"

"Money, drugs, or misguided affection every time. The amounts change, but it nearly always goes back to dollars and cents."

Night Crawlers

"911, what's your emergency?"

"Someone tried to open my door, and now they are messing with my car," Mildred whispered.

"You said someone is tampering with your car? Are you at 23022 Casino View Drive?"

"Yes, I'm unit 102B. It is four units in on the right past the office. My car is a 2001 Mazda Protégé, blue."

"A car has been dispatched. What's your name, dear?"

"Mildred Petrie. I'm sorry, I need to stay quiet, don't want them aware that I heard anything."

"I understand. Can you see them?"

"No, but I can hear them or him. Hell, I don't know who is out there."

"Mildred, the unit is in the parking lot now; they are coming through slowly."

"I can see the headlights off the curtains."

"The officer will check in with you before they leave."

"Okay, thank you. I'm hanging up now." Mildred sat intently listening for movement. She heard a vehicle door close, and then more silence. Finally, she heard footsteps, a muffled conversation and a gentle knock on her door.

"Mrs. Petrie, this is Officer Gutierrez."

She had to stand on her tiptoes to look through the peephole and then opened the door. "Thank you for coming so quickly."

"That's our job, ma'am. We didn't find anyone, but my partner is taking a walk through the compound. We found what looks like brake fluid under your vehicle, and it appears the line was cut. We can't tell if there is anything else, so we have requested forensics." He was very calming and professional.

Mildred went to make coffee, and she heard the other officer enter. They spoke quietly as they walked into the kitchen. "Mrs. Petrie, this is Officer Chin. We have made a list of vehicles on the lot, nothing looks obvious right now, pretty quiet out there.

We will run them to see if there is any out of place. Do you have any enemies that you know of?"

"No, I don't know of anyone in particular. I work with Detective Hampton at the casino occasionally and with Detective Elton Block on a couple open cases."

Both officers looked at her with puzzled expressions, and Gutierrez responded, "Interesting. I will flag them on the report, and they will have it by morning."

The younger officer spoke up. "In the 911 call, you mentioned they tried your door?"

"Yes, I did. I was on my way back to bed when I heard the knob turn."

"Did you look outside?"

"No, I went directly to call you and stayed away from the windows. Do you want milk or sugar in your coffee?"

The older officer accepted the cup with both hands, dismissing any additions. "We will fingerprint the door and after the inspection of the car, I suggest you have it towed to a shop."

She could tell that Officer Chin wasn't a coffee aficionado by what he added to the cup. Clearly, he only drank it to get through the night. She pulled open the tea canister, and he smiled and shook his head no. He took his cup outside and checked the door for prints. He continued to patrol, sipping the hot coffee and approaching some of the doors where lights were on.

Mildred opened the drapes and watched as the community came alive with curious faces peeking out. She had to smile: *We elderly don't sleep as much as we would like. It is a life of naps and it's hard to get away with anything without lonely, bored eyes peeking out from every door.* This would be the talk of the community for days to come, and she decided to follow up personally with the neighbors who may have seen something.

As the night sky faded into the morning, the police van arrived, and Officer Gutierrez left the computer he had been working on in the patrol car to greet them. The police lit up the parking lot with bright lights directed at her car and front door. They moved efficiently, not wasting time or risking the loss of evidence. By the time the sun slid over the horizon, they were finished, and the entire community was watching. Several of the neighborhood men stood along the parking lot. Mildred could hear them ask questions, offer theories and make suggestions. *Men! There is no understanding men at times like this.*

The results were inconclusive, as Mildred's door had multiple prints, some of which belonged to their own detective. Officer Gutierrez gave her a business card with a report number handwritten on the back and again suggested she have the car towed.

Mildred nodded in agreement as she accepted the card and handshake. "Luckily I've been a member of Triple-A since 1974."

"You did the right thing, calling us and not confronting. I've cc'd Detective Block with the report. He will probably contact you when he gets in." As the officer spoke, her cell phone rang.

She looked at the screen. "Well, he is pulling an early shift. That's him now."

"Good, I'll leave you to it." He tipped his hat and walked back to his car.

"Hello, Elton, is that you?"

"What the hell is going on, Mildred? I opened my computer to this report. Why didn't you call me?" She could hear the agitation in his voice.

"I've been kind of busy, and it was the middle of the night." Mildred snapped, "Jeez, don't yell at me. I'm the victim here."

"Okay, okay. You are right. I'm just concerned, and I have a hundred more questions. I'll be there once I talk to forensics and the investigating officers."

"That will give me time to get showered and dressed. You have caught me in my pajamas too many times already. I'm calling Triple-A to move the car to Eddie's and get some repairs going."

Mildred awoke in her chair to a knock on her front door and the smell of scorched turnovers in the oven. She called out to Block, "Just a moment," and she ran to turn off the oven and the water still running for the shower.

When she opened the door, her cohort stood grinning, holding a McDonald's bag of egg sandwiches and two cups of coffee. "Smells like dead pastries in here. It was a good idea to drive through for us on the way over. It felt like we would need protein this morning."

"Is it still morning?" They walked to the kitchen, and she turned on the fan to remove the gathering of smoke. He laughed and teased as they sat down to work. There was another knock at the door. They looked at each other, and Block got up to answer. She heard a familiar voice, and Bud followed Block into the kitchen. He had a fresh coffee cake and more coffee. Mildred went to get another plate, shut off the coffee pot, and dumped the dregs into the sink.

"Good morning, Double-Oh-Seventy-One. Smells like you had a fire on top of the other criminal activity. Hampton is on his way." Bud started to move everything to the small dining room table, and Block texted Detective Hampton to pick up more Egg McMuffins. Within a few minutes, they all settled in to work out the facts and speculations of the night before. Hampton was the first to mention what the men were thinking. "Has anyone suggested a safe house for a few days?"

It was evident Mildred would not agree. "No one, and I mean no one, will drive me out of my home."

Block spoke immediately. "Why don't we leave the offer open, and if she changes her mind it can be ready quickly."
Bud finally spoke, "She could stay at the hotel."

Mildred spoke through a clenched jaw. "Can't you men see I'm sitting right here? No, listen to me when I speak. No, double no."

While the two detectives tried to calm Mildred. Bud stepped away, when he returned he spoke, "Here is another option. I've arranged for maintenance to come over and install new locks on the condo. Someone will be here later this morning. Do we want to order a heavier door?"

Mildred pointed out the obvious. "Oh, sure. With the picture window next to it, a heavy door would be a brilliant security investment." The observation brought laughter into the room. "In case no one has noticed, almost every resident in the complex creeps around at night searching for gossip and hoping for sleep."

"We did have a couple of witnesses. This wasn't random vandalism, but an attempt on your life." Hampton was serious and double-checked that she had his cell phone also programmed into her phone.

Mildred's sleep-addled mind was not sure what was decided as the men left, and the cat finally arose from her third nap demanding food. Popcorn seemed completely unconcerned about the excitement. Mildred dismissed the thought of getting a dog as she went to bed. Dogs were high maintenance when all she needed was a bark and a bite.

Kind of a Hush

Mildred woke up later into the afternoon to a ringing cell phone.

"Hello."

"Did I wake you?"

"Who is this?"

"It's Arnie; I heard that you don't have a car. I go in at nine, so I can pick you up earlier if you like. Bud doesn't want you walking over."

Mildred checked the clock. She had planned to go to work at seven, but there was no way she could be ready. "I wanted to go in at seven, but nine would be all right." They talked for a few minutes, and he agreed to pick her up at eight so she could get something to eat and attend the nine o'clock concert.

Mildred had to smile at the good friends she had made since taking the job. Everything felt like a new incarnation. And she was confident that she was no longer the woman she used to be.

Mildred pulled herself together quickly, deciding on going as Delilah and dumping the walker for the sword cane. She was confident she would never be able to release the sword faster than a bullet, but it would remind her to stay alert.

Arnie arrived five minutes early, but she was ready. He laughed when he saw her, recognizing the disguise and the memory of the first concert. He asked, "Please keep the water balloons in place until after the show." He dropped her off at the main entrance and left for home. He would check in when he came on shift.

"**G-ma on the floor.**"

"**Check.**"

The brief response assured Mildred that her story from last night wasn't public with the department.

"**Is Bud in?**"

"**No left. Need something?**"

"**I'm good.**"

Mildred walked over to the snack bar and bought a hot dog and a bag of chips. She had just enough time to eat and walk over to the concert. Looked like a good crowd. As usual, Belinda had arranged for an excellent seat on the aisle near the front. This would be what she needed to get her mind back on track. She wasn't seated very long, when the lights dimmed and the instrumental sounds of a recorded version of "There's a Kind of Hush All Over the World" started. Quietly and slowly the curtain rose as the band joined in. Mildred tried to remember where her albums might be stored as she slipped into the reverie of Peter Noone. She had loved the joy in the Hermits' music since 1965… or was it '64? Where had the years gone?

The band spun the magic of simpler, happier times. The concert ended with "I'm Henry the Eighth, I Am," sending the crowd into the casino singing joyously with the required horrific accents. Mildred texted security,

"Concert over on patrol."

She found the restaurants filled with concertgoers and watched others buying cheesy souvenirs and T-shirts. Mildred planned to keep moving for a couple hours, but everything was calm. With the older group for the show, the customers dissipated after the initial rush. No mean drunks, no arguments; it was a lovely night.

She saw Arnie approaching on a direct line to her. "What the hell, Arnie?"

"Shut it, Delilah. Quiet tonight. Why don't you go home? I've got a break coming and can give you a ride."

"Sounds like a plan. I'm ready." He walked her out to the car, and she yammered on about the concert, extending sadness for the generations that came after, not having the wealth of '60s music. They sat in the car for a while as they argued the British Invasion against Disco and then Punk and Hip Hop. He waited for her to unlock her door, then he walked in, turned on lights, and finally waved her in. Mildred was confident she won the music argument.

– 53 –
Scare Tactics

Once in the door, Mildred found it unusual that Popcorn did not greet her with the usual rubs and total look of indifference. A feeling of foreboding took over as she searched the condo. Mildred was startled when the silence was broken, but it was the air conditioner kicking on.

Popcorn must be under the bed. Why was she hiding? Stop it, there is no evidence anyone has been here. Paranoia doesn't solve a thing.

Everything was in place, and she breathed a sigh of relief when she sat on the bed to kick off her shoes. Next, off came the wig, and draining of the breast balloons into the bathroom sink. Mildred turned with a strong feeling of resignation.

She got the key out of her jewelry box and entered the walk-in closet. In the back was Dick's lock box. She had let its existence slip from her consciousness over the last three years. They had argued after he turned in his side arm at retirement. He had insisted on buying a new one. Mildred may have been a cop, but she hated guns. Once the box was open, she looked at his weapon and slowly removed it. No surprise, it was clean and oiled, with no evidence of the passage of time. She loaded it and then decided it was an over-reaction, doubting she would use it. She put the gun back on the shelf, but didn't close the box. Mildred returned to her preparations for bed, placed the Taser on Dick's side, along with the cell phone, and unsheathed the sword cane.

She was surprised she slept well, considering her concern of rolling onto the assorted weaponry. She woke late in the morning and slipped back to her usual routine. Popcorn nudged and begged for breakfast.

Calmed by sleep and familiar household tasks, Mildred put the cane away and charged the cell phone and Taser. She gathered the trash from the kitchen and bath and walked out to the dumpster, where the manager approached.

"Hey, Mrs. Petrie."

"Good morning, Aggie. What's up?"

"I'm getting some questions about the police patrols ever since the other night."

"Questions? I don't understand. Someone vandalized my car, and I called the cops. Have there been any other incidents?"

"I wasn't sure what happened, but there has been a buzz going around the community. We had some vandalism a couple months, maybe a year ago. I wonder if the same ones are back."

"That's probably it." Simplicity was always the best cover.

"The police promised to kick up the patrols, and that should rid us of that problem." It was apparent Aggie had more questions.

"Nice talking to you, I have to dash." Mildred quickly dropped off her recycling and left.

Relief washed over Mildred as she closed the door. She was aware of the increased police patrol, and knew she needed to thank Block. Returning the trash and recycling containers to their usual locations, she noticed the red flashing light on her phone. There were three messages. A quick press of the button:

Message one…"Grandma, we haven't heard from you. Daddy wants you to check in." Beep

Message two…"We know who you are and where you live." Beep

Message three…"It's Sunday Grandma. Daddy said to tell you to call, or he is getting you a life alert." Beep
End of messages.

Mildred was stunned for a moment, then decided to call Richie first. She had to think about the second message for a moment. Her first worry was for the grandkids being in danger, but decided not to mention anything to her son. After a pleasant conversation with the middle granddaughter, she mentioned her car was in the shop. Amelia said she would ask her mother to come over to take Mildred to the pharmacy. As the conversation ended she sent a text to Block.

"Threat on answering machine."

Her telephone rang immediately. "Threat? What kind of threat?"

Mildred repeated the message, and Detective Block responded, "This is serious, they doubly made it clear they know your involvement. And now there is a threat. Whoever this is, they are dangerous, and you are in their sights."

"Yes sir. I'll pay attention."

Mildred could hear the aggravation in his voice as he spoke.

"Don't use the landline anymore today. I'll have a tech team in contact shortly. I'll also send over an officer to stay with you."

"I told you before, I don't need a guard. I can stay at the casino if it is necessary. Do you want me to bring the answering machine in to you?"

"Answering machine? I didn't even know they still made those."

"Shut up, Elton. Someday you will be old too, with all kinds of antiquated electronics that work better than your prostate."

"Well, snap! G-ma, guess you told me. I'll get my ole decrepit self on the phone to the station. Don't unplug anything; they will probably work through your line. I don't know exactly what they need. Do you have your meeting with Security tomorrow?"

"I work tonight, and we meet around eleven tomorrow at my place."

"Save your turnovers for another time, I want you and Bud to come to the station. Bring that cold case you have. We don't need to confirm your involvement with detectives by having guys in black suits showing up at your door. I'll set it up with Bud to have you picked up."

Mildred's first thought was I have to fix this. Lindsey is on her way over now, and David and Katie will be here next weekend for the honeymoon. Will the grandkids help me eat a case of assorted turnovers? followed by a chuckle. Funny what goes through this old brain."

Moving Forward

Bud arrived early so they would get to the police station before eleven. He helped her haul the cold case to the car. The aroma of fresh baked goods greeted Mildred as she entered the car. "I can tell you have been to the bakery already. Do you go there every day?"

"I'm convinced we have some of the best bakers in the world at the Ivory Winds. Do you think we should stop for coffee on the way over?"

Mildred didn't take any time to respond. "Every police station in the country has a minimum of one pot of coffee in every room."

"True enough, but is it good coffee?"

By the time they stopped talking about coffee quality, they had arrived. The desk officer showed them to a meeting room with a long table and a standing white board. At the head of the table was Block's expanded file folder, and they added Dick's cold case box. With a quick scan of the room, they took seats together on the left. Bud laid out a large package of treats, and Mildred poured two cups of cop coffee. "This is fresh, so no complaining, Bud."

Mildred started to lay out the folder she had brought when the door opened, and Arnie held it for Q and Block. Arnie put down his file on the right, and Q sat across from Mildred. Q whispered to Arnie, and he immediately left the room. He came back and put a pot of water on the second burner of the hotplate, and held one tea bag for Q. Mildred smiled and tossed him a baggie of chamomile tea she had brought from home.

Arnie looked at the assembled group. "Anyone else need something?" The rest of the team opted for coffee.

Once they got over the niceties, the team went to work. Block turned the board around, and the info was already broken down. "Okay, team, we have two investigations going on: Robbery and Loans. Let's look at the robbery first." He taped a photo of Butt Munch under the heading, and below that a shot of Mildred and the Ninja. There were three blank spaces for the people that escaped. Under Loans, there was nothing written.

Q reported, "I met with Detective Handsome. He interviewed the night housekeeping crew."

Detective Block stifled a smile, "His name is Hampton, but I have heard him called handsome before. He was supposed to be here, but was called out on another case. I have his initial report with what he has gathered on the loan shark allegations." He stood at the front of the table, and scanned the pages. "Thanks to the housekeeping crew, there were some potential names. We don't have anything solid, but will continue with the follow-up. Looks as if we have some descriptions, and he plans on going over these with Arnie."

Arnie nodded, and spoke up. "I have a list of possibilities and gathered some victim IDs."

Mildred scanned the list, but there was no Richard Petrie. It almost broke her heart as she reached for the chain that held the wedding rings around her neck. There was an immediate feeling of comfort knowing that it was her husband's band against her skin. *Maybe on payday, I'll buy a real gold chain.*

Block noticed Mildred seem to drift away from the meeting and clutching a necklace. He wrote Dick Petrie at the head of the list, and continued speaking, "The Gambler Anonymous emails have a couple of strong hits, and we are working those. Let's take a donut break, and I'll be right back."

The break helped Mildred compose herself.

By the time Block returned, they were talking and picking at the fresh baked goods. Mildred noticed he had a police report.

"Folks, here is something that took us a while to find. Retired officer Richard Petrie had filed this report about six months before his death. The sergeant who took it in had filed this as ORC." Block explained that meant Old Retired Cop, and said that many of the retirees had a hard time leaving the job. The practice is to take the information and then drop-file it, with no follow-up.

Mildred was surprised when Bud opened his own folder, and had additional information on the loans. This had been a secondary investigation for the past year and a half. She was unaware of the additional file. Mildred felt as if a light came on when she said, "Has anyone checked the Pay Day Loan Company?"

"No we haven't. We had been working the casino angle." Bud wrote furiously on his tablet.

Mildred continued, "I heard a few people speak at the GA meetings as if they were a cog in the debt cycle. Can we find out who manages or owns it?" They all agreed with her realization that the problem may not all be with the casino.

Bud added, "Especially with the close proximity. They have a satellite office across the street from the Ivory Winds shopping center."

Arnie and Block both opened laptop computers and started tapping. The room was energized. The door opened, and in came Detective Hampton. "Sorry I'm late. I was actually working." He poured a cup of coffee and topped off the other cups. "What did I miss?"

Block stood up. "Hold it, guys, we need to chase this down after the meeting. We have so much to do. I'll turn this part of the investigation over to Handsome, er ah, Hampton and the group that has been working the loan cases."

The team mumbled in agreement. Block continued, "Now to the invasion. We have some background for Waller and he has a rap sheet."

Mildred spoke up. "That is Butt Munch, right?"

"Yes ma'am, you are right. We pulled his full juvenile file and found a series of minor crimes. There was nothing to suggest he would move up to something like this robbery."

Arnie said, "There must be more. Did you find any affiliations?" That possibility was too glaring to ignore, and they fell into a discussion of the increase of drugs and prostitution.

"I called the gang task force for a meeting later today; I think we need to include them." Block turned the white board around.

"We need to organize this better. Let's break down some work assignments and scheduled the next session."

Everyone started to talk at once, volunteering and suggesting work to be done. Mildred spoke up, "My son will be here with his new wife next week, but I can still make a meeting."

Block made a note. "Good to know in advance, Mildred. We will try to handle things and let you have a break."

Bud said, "Your son is staying at the casino, right?"

"Correct. Belinda helped set it up."

"Why don't you stay there too, especially since someone messed up your car? In fact, you could move over today."

"Seems like I told you before, no one is driving me out of my home. Besides, my son doesn't need his mom on his honeymoon."

"It is only an idea, G-ma. Think about it. We won't put you in the same room," Bud countered. "Also, the casino wants to install an alarm on your car, it will be paid for in connection with your job. Give me the name of the shop it is at, and we will arrange to have that done."

"No problem on that offer." Mildred dug through her purse. After a prolonged search, she pulled out a wrinkled business card and handed it to Bud.

Hampton took control of the meeting and called in the tech officer. "We have worked through Mrs. Petrie's phone records and found the contact for the message that had been left." He summed up the results in two words. "Burner phone. We would like to request your permission for a tap on the home number and a camera for the exterior door."

Mildred answered, "That is great. What do I sign? The front door is the only access."

The tech officer gathered the permission, and handed her a box. She opened it to find a pink watch band. "I know this isn't particularly your style, but it is set up for audio surveillance, and has a panic button. See, right here. This is still experimental, and you have the first one."

"Thank you. I especially appreciate your suggestion that I might have a style." Mildred strapped on the watch. "Best to be prepared too soon than too late."

The men mumbled in agreement. As the meeting closed, Block asked, "Hope you aren't feeling like bait, but with the threats…."

"I thought of chump, but that is just another name for the same thing. Whatever it takes, we are going to get the bastards."

Mildred and Bud decided on lunch and drove back to the casino, and the café. They both signed in when they arrived. Bud by phone and Mildred by text.

"**G-ma on the floor.**"

"**Go home; this is your day off.**"

Must be Belinda at the monitor, "**Only want food. Good, C U Weds.**"

It was almost two before Mildred was home, and her son Richie was already there, teasing the cat with a laser pointer.

"Well, there you are. Certainly get around for a retired woman with no car and a gimpy hip."

She walked over and kissed him on the forehead, "Oh, honey, it is great to see you. I've been over at the police station, working on the investigations."

"Mom, you don't know how that doesn't make me feel any better. I'm worried about you. David is getting married Sunday, and I've arranged for a video chat so you can be there. I can pick you up so we can watch on the computer."

Mildred answered, "What time and I'll be ready."

"They have it scheduled for three at the church, and don't forget the time difference. We'll pick you up around noonish." Richie responded.

"I already arranged the flights, and I have them a suite at the Ivory Winds as my gift." Mildred was obviously excited. "Oh, and a reception room and food. I turned the party planning over to Lindsey. Don't you talk to your wife?"

"WOW! That is great, and yes, I talk to my wife, but didn't know you had them a room. Now that I think about it, maybe

Lindsey did tell me; you know how that goes. This will be a great surprise. David is planning on staying at our house."

Mildred started for the kitchen. "You hungry? I've got some chicken for a sandwich."

"No, I'm fine. I've been here for a while, and already ate it." He blushed and stood up and took the plate to the sink.

"I love you, Richard Petrie, Jr."

"I love you too, Mom. I need to go now, but if you don't start checking in, that Life Alert will be strapped to your neck really damn soon."

"Yes, sir."

As her son was about to leave, a van with a ladder tied to the side pulled up. There were two men, who looked like a maintenance crew. One started to install two cameras, one for the door and the other for the parking area in front of Mildred's condo. The other officer came inside and handled the wiretap to her phone. She signed a scrap of paper that appeared to be a fast food receipt on a clipboard and announced loudly, "If this doesn't take care of your leak, give us a call."

Richie whispered to Mildred as he got into the car, "Since the cops need a Life Alert on you too, I feel better now."

– 55 –
Unchained Melody

Mildred opened her eyes, disoriented in the darkness and cold. The smell reminded her of dust and grease. Her head raged with a painful dullness, and she couldn't tell if her eyes were open or closed. Her arms wouldn't move, and she panicked with the thought of a stroke. Unsure of the symptoms, she started to take a physical inventory. The memory of the poster at the retirement village meeting room played through her mind. *F.A.S.T.* F is Face – drooping? Can't see it. She could stick out her tongue without any pulling to one side, but there was a dull headache at the base of her skull. A is arms. They won't move, S was speech and she cried out with a panicked prayer, "Help me, call 911."

Almost immediately, a light came on in an adjacent room. She couldn't see clearly through the grimy window. It looked like an office of some sort, no way to be sure. Nothing looked familiar. This must be a dream.

"Where am I?" Every sound echoed, which made her head throb. In the vague light, she realized there was duct tape wrapped around her body and legs, securing her to a wooden chair. No wonder her arms couldn't move, they seemed taped behind the chair. Disorientation started to fade as she took an inventory of her surroundings. There was no memory of how she got here and no idea where she could be. She would have to worry about that later. Unable to hear any exact words from a mumbled conversation in the background, she decided it could be someone on the phone in the other room. She silenced her breathing and tried to calm her heart. It was obvious she had been drugged and kidnapped, but by whom?

This has to be to do with one of the investigations, I have to clear my head and pay attention.

With hope that her headache would go away, she began to deep breathe. Her eyes scanned, gathering information and trying to understand what had happened. Mildred listened intently. She was able to overhear a little of the conversation and could only pick out a few words from the conversation: coming – crazy – old – dem, or was that gem? Her first thought was to argue, "Shut the hell up, I'm not old," but she decided to stick with the word crazy. It was believable for women of a certain age. Mildred looked for a weapon and realized that that was ridiculous. She was confident that the only way she could win any fight was with the element of surprise, and if the guard was a baby, or maybe a puppy. She would have to resort to diversion, and it must be believable. Insanity. Whoever was on the phone already said she was crazy. Once a plan was decided on, she knew the secret to a plausible lie: keep it simple, don't hesitate and stick to it.

The muffled conversation ended, and there was movement; no more time to think. Mildred thought of her boys and family, vowed to get closer to her sister and started to sing. "Happy Birthday to yoooou. Happy Birthday to yoooouuu."

The captor turned on a light and entered the room. *Katie bar the door, it's Butt Munch?* He held a gun at his side as he stood at the entrance. "This is freaking serious, you old bat."

She smiled and looked him in the eye, "Happy Birthday, you goofy gopher. Isn't it time you get us some cake? I'd do it, but my arms don't work." She committed every fiber of her being at that moment to the delusion, adding a hysterical laugh. "Don't you think for a minute I don't know what you want, Dick?"

"I'm not a dick, you old bitch." His reaction was fast and defensive. He moved at her as if to strike. This might work.

"Oh Daddy, it's been years since you tied me up. I don't know if I'm up to it, but if I can get out, I'll take you on a wild ride."

"What? You're nuts. I wouldn't…"

This jackass is going to be easier than I could have imagined. She smiled, moved her eyebrows up, winked with a cheeky grin, and then she sang, "I wanna hold your haaand, I wanna hold a gun." She continued with a montage of Beatle songs from 1964 forward, yowling from lyric to lyric, many with the same tune. He slapped her across the face and ran from the room as she started into "Please Please Me" with a lurid smirk.

Mildred knew she had him. The singing diversion helped hide her constant work on the tape, flexing her muscles and twisting, ignoring the ache in her shoulder. The concert continued with Dave Clark Five and a little bit of Stones.

She heard him make a call from the hall, and she dropped to a hum.

"I won't do this. That old whore wants to have sex with me, and she won't stop singing. Get over here, now! I didn't want to do this, and I'm finished. You are on your own." There was a pause then he answered, "She doesn't have anything on you, I already told ya, she's nuts." He then threw the phone onto the floor.

With a flirty inflection, Mildred called out, "What's a matter Daddy'o? I know what you want, but I can't get free, this tape isn't like the rope you usually use. Give me a little help and we can get down to business."

He walked back into the room, and slapped her across the face. "I told you I'm not Dick, and way not your Daddy. I don't want to be here, and you want to shut the fuck up." He lifted his arm to hit her again when she let her bladder go. "Oh my god, you old pervert. You pissed yourself."

"I know how you love it moist, sweet Daddy." She felt a little guilty with the ruse; she had to get him out of the room. She felt a strange presence and hoped her lost husband was there, providing some invisible protection. He would help, and that belief gave her strength. The tape on her hand was starting to slacken, but only slightly. She could see her purse, dumped on the floor and her cell phone shattered. Mildred continued to stretch and relax her wrists.

She then remembered the watch the detective gave her may still be on under the tape. With her arms still secured behind her back, she could only hope. A wish for the Life Alert Richie kept threatening her with was followed with determination to get lose. The panic button on the watch would be close. She tried to bang her wrist against the back of the chair, but she couldn't tell if it worked.

Mildred continued to sing. It was evident Butt Munch wasn't coming back, and she hummed a couple *Sesame Street* classics. The smell of her urine was bitter, but the dampness leaked down the chair, and she hoped the tape would weaken. Once she stopped singing, the room was silent, and she continued to listen intently. With the light in the hall, she could see a little, and she searched the surroundings. Maybe there is an escape route, or a weapon. She kept constantly working her wrists. Clearly, she was in a warehouse or some similarly abandoned building. There appeared to be some old tools in a box under a work table: possible weapons. This meant she was probably in the old industrial district by the river. There wasn't any noticeable noise outside, and Mildred struggled on. Yelling for help was ruled out; there was no one anywhere around. She remembered the duct tape escape move she saw on the internet, but her arms had to be movable. Finally, she felt her left arm move, only a little, but enough to free the watch. She knocked it against the back of the chair several time in a regular rhythm. Not sure if it worked, she went back to manipulating the tape. Mildred was sure that running would be the only option. I'll have to remember to weave, because evading a bullet could be tough at any age.

Whatever they drugged her with was still evident, and Mildred started to doze as her head nodded forward.

Mildred startled into consciousness, unsure how long she'd been out. The sound of a heavy door sliding confused her even more. The surroundings were distorted and cold. The muffled conversation made no sense when the noise of a woman's angry voice came through. Not sure what direction the sounds came from, Mildred tried to sort the nightmare from reality. The voices seemed to come closer as the woman continued to berate someone, probably Butt Munch.

"I told you to take care of her, but not like this. Why did you bring her here? You idiot."

Mildred knew it was time to get back into character; they opened the door to the song. "Who's the cat that would risk his life…SHAFT? Who's a brother that knows his mother, shut your mouth…." Mildred wished that Isaac Hayes and Richard

Roundtree would burst into the room and help her with more than the lyrics. Forced to repeat the limited verses she knew, Mildred continued to make up the song. The woman was careful to stay out of sight. "Who is the guy that would do-wack-a-do… Shaft."

"Can you shut her up? She doesn't make sense. You know I didn't want to do this. I'm out of here. You are as crazy as she is."

It sounded like a tussle, and the woman's voice became shrill and said, "You do what I pay you to do. Get it?" Suddenly the tape came loose, and Mildred reached down to tear the restraints on her waist and feet. She was startled by a loud clang and the sound of rhythmic pounding of boots with a military sounding cadence. Is a S.W.A.T. team too much to pray for, something like on TV?

There was a distant crash and loud voices. Doors opened violently, and whatever was coming, it was moving throughout the entire building. There was a gunshot exchange followed by an overwhelming feeling of relief. She wasn't quite loose yet, and needed to get away to hide.

The door to the room crashed open, and a flood of flashlight beams radiated throughout the room, blinding Mildred where she sat. Four, maybe five, dark figures entered with a trained precision, followed by Elton Block. As he entered, Mildred broke into the chorus of *Unchained Melody*, but she only got out the first line when tears took over.

Block shook his head with a huge grin, and his eyes were glistening. "Tick tock, you knucklehead." He cut her loose and had them bring a blanket. "The watch worked. Took us a while to track it, but we have the recording, and I might buy the album."

"It will be released at the gift shop on Friday." Mildred's sobs took over. She was more frightened than she'd thought possible. As Block walked her outside, she saw the police loading Butt Munch and another young man who looked just like him into a police van. They brought out the woman, and Mildred exclaimed, "That's Judge McCaffie's wife!" She wasn't the disinterested toy Mildred had met before.

Her focus drew to an older woman, being helped from a Mercedes. There was duct tape loosely on her wrists. There was something familiar about her, but she kept her face turned away. A second black and white pulled forward to leave. Mildred could see the reflection of the woman's face on the car window, and "Judith!" escaped her lips. The woman turned and their eyes locked.

– 56 –
Safe

Mildred spent the next five hours in the hospital emergency room with Detective Block. She only had minor injuries. Her shoulder was not reinjured, but they watched for any problems from the drugs used to subdue her. She had no memory of the kidnapping, but they worked up a full report on the events in the warehouse. The cameras at her home showed nothing and neither did the casino video. They knew she had not checked out at casino, but there was nothing that showed her being drugged or assaulted. They must have grabbed her someplace, maybe in the parking lot, but there was nothing on any of the recordings.

Block had called Richie near daylight, and when he and Lindsey arrived at the emergency room, Mildred could hear him shouting. She heard her daughter-in-law try to calm him before they entered the room. Once he was able to see his mother, and confirm her condition, his anger changed.

"Mom, this has to stop."

"Oh Richie, my love. I have never been more alive. Do you really want me sitting in that damn chair watching *Gunsmoke*?"

"That show was canceled when I was a kid," and the tension was broken. "I'd rather you watched *Gunsmoke* than smell like it." He collapsed into the chair as the nurse came in to check Mildred's vitals, and ended up taking his blood pressure. "Mom, you can't do this anymore. You are too old to solve all of the crimes in the county."

"I had plenty of back up and protection." She nodded towards Detective Block in the hall. It appeared that there were several more officers with him. "Oh, honey, could you go pick up my car? It's at the shop and should be finished. You know the place you use." He looked angry and frustrated, as his mother continued to divert the conversation. "The repairs were finished. The casino had an alarm system installed, and I need wheels."

Mildred looked away, and noticed Lindsey was watching from the hall with Block. Lindsey looked directly at Mildred and then waved for Richie to join them. Mildred watched them talk, but was unable to hear anything. Her son nodded his head in agreement, and then threw a kiss to his mother and left.

Block reentered the room and announced, "No more discussion, you are staying in a safe house until we get this straightened out."

Mildred started to argue. "But we caught them and you…"

"I explained this to your son, and he is in full agreement. Enough of your sassing. We don't know how deep this goes and who else may be involved. We are sure they were watching you, and once you met with the first Mrs. McCaffie, they apparently caught on that you were part of the investigation. I think they suspected you ever since you took Waller down in the bathroom. Apparently, they thought shutting you up would throw us off the trail. I don't know how they knew you were deep in the investigation. They didn't realize what we knew, and it is all more complicated than a burglary." He was still talking as she dozed off.

The nurse came in with release forms and roused Mildred to confirm her Medicare number. Bud and Detective Hampton had shown up by then, and it was obvious plans were made without her input. The three men kept the discussion hushed in the hall with their backs to her room.

Immediately after she signed the hospital discharge papers, Block left, and Bud came in with a carry bag. "Your daughter-in-law helped me pack a couple things. I'm so glad you are all right. We will get together tomorrow if you feel up to it. Take care, Double-Oh-Seventy-One, and get some rest." He was gone as quickly as he had arrived.

Detective Hampton was the only one left, and he came in right after Bud's exit. He wasn't putting up with any of Mildred's arguments. "We see you got the bag. Let me know if there is anything else you need. We will meet with you tomorrow morning. But first you need to get some sleep. With any luck, we should have more information by then. Block already left to start the interrogations. We had to wait for the three of them to be booked."

Mildred sighed, finally in agreement with the team. "Okay. I'll go along with this for tonight, but there is one thing I need to know. What day is this? Do I get breakfast, lunch or dinner? I'm so hungry."

He stepped outside for her to dress, and then helped Mildred gather her belongings. They left out a side door, and Hampton led Mildred to an unmarked car. He drove directly to the first drive-through restaurant he could find and bought her a double burger meal and a soft drink. Before they got to the house, she had him drive through another place and purchase a Meal Deal #8 and two #10s, a yogurt parfait, two brownies, and two salads. Mildred was hungry, but she hoped there would be enough to share with the officer staying with her.

Unfamiliar with the section of town they had entered, Mildred watched intently, trying to get her bearings. It was an older housing development, with rows of similar homes. They pulled up to a nondescript bungalow, and she noted a beat-up old Pontiac backed into a carport. Hampton had her wait while he went in to be sure everything was in order. Things moved efficiently as he transferred Mildred, her suitcase, and bags of food to the safe house. Hampton was gone in about a minute.

Bewildered and still hungry, Mildred stood inside the sparsely furnished room as someone approached from the kitchen. Her protection wasn't very big; Mildred had hoped for someone the size of a refrigerator. Then relief washed over her when she recognized the officer.

"Melody, what the heck?" They embraced, and the nervousness dissipated.

"Yeah, I scored my days off to hang with you. Thanks for the overtime. Oh, good food! I was taking a kitchen inventory and found six cans of ravioli and Hi-C fruit punch. Men certainly don't know how to shop." Mildred sat at the table, as Melody made a quick patrol around the house and yard to confirm no one had followed them, and double-checked the doors. Then they ate almost all of the food, leaving only a pile of limp fries and a wad of wrappers. They sat until it was almost dark, talking about everything Mildred could remember about the day before.

Melody seemed hopeful that more memories would come if they could talk about it more casually.

Mildred settled into a small bedroom with a secured window made of bulletproof glass and covered with dark curtains. Clean sheets and a blanket were folded at the foot of the bed. Unable to find the energy to make the bed, she simply smoothed out a sheet, kicked off her shoes, and laid down. With the blanket pulled up to her shoulder, she settled in.

She stared out the opening of the curtains at the vacant home next door and listened to Melody. She heard her pull a chair around the living room, and then Mildred was asleep. Melody had a second gun hidden on the other side of the room, a radio, and a magazine on the end table next to the couch. Through the night, Mildred would awaken to hear her protector move through the house checking windows and doors. With an unspoken trust, Mildred fell back to sleep easily, listening to the sound of a portable television and the cooking channel. She slept soundly until she heard her name the next morning. "Mildred, honey, it's time to get up. The men called and will be here in a half hour. You might want time for the shower before they arrive."

Her head was still foggy, but the shower was just what Mildred needed to re-enter the human race. Lindsey had packed her favorite pajama pants, clean underwear and a cotton shirt. There was no hair dryer, so she ran her fingers through her short hair and slipped on a little lipstick. *This is as good as it gets.* She could hear voices in the other room and soon the smell of bacon.

Mildred walked into the kitchen surrounded with the comforting smell of breakfast. Block was frying bacon and scrambling a dozen eggs. Bud was frosting some turnovers at the adjacent counter. Hampton had set the table with plastic plates and four large lattes. The men seemed quite proud of themselves as they hustled around the kitchen. Melody looked tired, and sat at the table caressing an extra-large paper cup of something they must have bought especially for her.

Melody moved her plate to the coffee table in the living room, keeping up her guard duties, and was close enough to hear everything. The five people enjoyed breakfast and light conversation. Once the dishes were cleared, they got down to business. Detective Block took the lead as they brought Mildred up to date. The kidnapping perpetrators weren't giving any information.

"We started the interrogations, and one, two, three, they each asked for an attorney. We have been able to have bail denied, due to your position with the police department." He looked to Hampton, and he added, "Due to Judge McCaffie's status with the court, and his long history, we have him under house arrest."

Melody called from the front room couch, "Are you sure about that choice? He might not like the ankle monitor."

Elton Block spoke up first. "We all know the judge, and he has been a pillar of the community for decades. The house arrest was as a courtesy and concern for his safety in lock up."

Hampton added, "You think cops have it tough in jail, try sending in a judge. Damn near a death sentence." They all nodded in a grim agreement.

Mildred spoke up. "I'd like to be there for the interrogations."

"That is questionable, Mildred, with you being the victim and all. We want to move strictly by the book, and extra careful not to compromise any of the cases."

"Oh, Elton, I do understand, but I need to be part of this. It was my investigation."

Bud finally spoke up. "Mildred, I'll be there. If you have any questions, I'll relay them. I'll keep you in the loop."

Hampton added, "We do understand you have been part of this, and are the one that tied it all together. We will keep you informed, I swear it."

Mildred wasn't happy, but agreed that would have to do. "You know I can't stay here any longer."

Melody answered from the other room, "Hey old lady, I take offense to that."

Mildred smiled, and said, "My son David and his new wife get here this evening, and I need to be home. I also have to feed Popcorn."

Bud jumped into the conversation. "Belinda and Lindsey have worked out everything for the honeymoon. When you get home, check in with the office. She will give you the details. We had everything cleared and management approved their stay."

"I wanted to help. I feel terrible," Mildred lamented.

Bud patted her shoulder. "Don't worry about a thing. Management is pleased to offer this token of gratitude." Mildred's eyes overflowed with tears. "But I...."

Block spoke up, "We want you to stay here one more day. We need to be sure we have addressed every threat to you." His phone buzzed, and he walked out to the living room. When he came back in he announced, "Hampton, we have to head back to the house, seems that the attorney has arrived and is raising hell."

Hampton added, "You went through a lot the last couple days. Just take the day to rest up. You have a full week ahead of you with your visitors.

The men could tell she was weighing possibilities before she spoke. "Sorry guys, I want my own bed, and Popcorn is home alone. I need to replace my cell phone, and I only have one pair of comfy pants here. If that isn't a good enough reason, too bad. I'll check in with my new number and make sure the phone takes incoming calls. No more discussion."

"Okay, Mommy. I think it has been thirty years since anyone spoke to me like that," Elton added.

"Well, tell your wife she needs to step it up; you have gotten a little too bossy, Mr. B. One question before you go. Did Judith McCaffie claim she was kidnapped, too? I just have this suspicion," Mildred queried.

Block was the first to respond. "I'm with you. Her hands were taped, but not securely, also she was sitting in the front seat of the car. Even the most inexperienced kidnapper would keep the victim away from the driver's seat. We put her in a safe house, but mostly to hold her until evidence could be processed."

Mildred added, "Something about Judith's eyes weren't right. She appeared angry and not frightened. I don't have anything else, just the cop gut thing."

Bud spoke up. "Don't worry, men. I'll clean the breakfast mess." Mildred went to gather her things, determined she would go home.

Melody entered the bedroom. "We canceled the next watch. I'm going home to bed and stay there all day. I'll check in with you in a couple hours. If you want me to stay with you tonight, I can come over."

"Thanks, I felt safe with you. Don't worry, I just know they have the leaders, and thugs don't act on their own."

"You have a point there. I think they are just worried about you. Elton felt guilty that you were taken."

Mildred answered, "Now that you brought that up, I'll bet it was a wild ride at the station that day." Melody yawned and stretched. "I can only imagine. I don't spend much time there." They hugged, and Mildred's security team of one left for her home.

Family

Bud drove Mildred home and did most of the talking. Mildred was surprised how tired she was; every muscle ached. They parked next to her car, and she was relieved that Richie had picked it up. He walked her in and went through the place to confirm it was safe. The giant cat ran from under the bed and almost knocked down her owner with the enthusiastic rubbing and an odd verbal flutter.

"All clear, Double-Oh-oh, Ms. Indestructible. Be sure to keep the door locked. Here is the remote access for the car locks. It has an alarm, so don't forget. There was a home alarm system installed too, and that key fob and codes are right here." Bud saluted Mildred and left.

She went to the kitchen to feed Popcorn and found the bowl full and water fresh. There was a sticky note on the refrigerator. "Call when you are home, Dad got you a phone". ♥ "U Glory."

A shock of dread filled Mildred when she realized that, while she was isolated in a safe house, they had let her granddaughter walk right into danger house to feed the cat.

Immediately, she kicked off her shoes, unhooked her bra, and made a call to check on Glory. There was no response to her granddaughter's cell phone. She then left a message for Lindsey. Almost as soon as she hung up, Lindsey's name came up on the screen.

"Hello?"

"Grandma! I love you so much."

"I love you too, Izzy. Is Glory there?"

"No, she went somewhere with her boyfriend."

"So she is okay?"

"No, she's a bully."

"Izzy, you know she isn't. Is your mom or dad there?"

"MOMMY, its GRANDMA."

Mildred thought she could have lost the hearing in her right ear after that outburst.

"Hello, Mildred, where are you? Are you okay? You looked grim yesterday. Can I get you anything?"

"I'm home and yes, I feel better; but I'm tired. I got a note that Glory was here. Is she all right?"

"She is fine. Why?" Lindsey questioned.

"Just checking to be sure." Mildred decided to minimize her concern and not cause any more panic than necessary. "What time do we go to the airport to pick up David and Katie?"

Mildred heard paper shuffling, and then Lindsey responded, "We are going in a couple of hours.

"Great, I have time to take a short nap before we go. Thank Richie for picking up my car."

"We dropped it off last night. We will pick you up at about seven to go to the airport. Your friend, Belinda at the casino, has been fantastic. She set most everything up. The casino is sending a stretch limo to pick them up. Rich and I think we may ride along in the limo."

"Oh, I didn't know. If you ride over, I'd like to go, too, but then again I must remember it is their honeymoon."

"True enough, but remember they have been together for ten years, and cohabitating for seven. The romantic isolation isn't as important. Otherwise, they would have gone to the Bahamas and not planned on staying in one of the girls' rooms at our house."

"I see exactly. I hadn't thought of it that way. Do they know anything?" asked Mildred.

"Nope, nothing. They only know of a small reception tomorrow night." Lindsey couldn't stifle the snicker. "I just love this whole thing, and the casino is handling most of the expense. It is going to be fantastic. Do you think you will be up for all of this?"

Mildred stopped and then added, "Oh, I will be ready, wearing bells. This is to be my gift."

"Then give them a savings bond. The casino comped everything."

"Oh Lindsey, how did Richie get so lucky to find you?"

"Sometimes I don't know. He has been a whiner about you, so go take a nap. I'll tell him you are home when he gets back."

So many of her concerns disappeared with the phone call, and Mildred went to bed, fully clothed. She slept soundly until she heard her door unlock, and then slam into the chain lock.

"Mom, you awake? Let me in."

"Coming, Richie, be right there." The soreness in her arms and back had stiffened as she slept, so it took a moment to climb over the cat and out of bed. She unhooked the chain and opened the door to a giant hug from her son. "That's enough, sonny boy. Momma is a little tender."

"Oh, I'm sorry. I wanted to bring you the new and improved cell phone. I also need to explain the alarm systems further. The casino bought the car alarm. It's worth about twice as much as the Mazda. The house one is simpler, and you can activate it from your bathroom."

"Is it from Life Alert?"

"How did you know?" He looked surprised.

"You have been threatening this since I was in my fifties and Daddy was still alive."

Richie blushed. "I didn't realize it had been that long. I'll bet you wish you had the neck fob, day before yesterday."

"Honey, it did cross my mind."

"Lindsey wanted me to tell you we are going to the casino at five-thirty to catch the limo. We are going to ride along to pick up David and Katie, and she said to tell you to be ready."

"I will be."

"I don't know much about makeup, Mom, but I'd suggest a little concealer on that black eye of yours. See you in a couple hours."

Black eye, I didn't realize I had a black eye.

Mildred went to the bathroom mirror and, turning on the light, she immediately saw the discoloration. It was great of Richie to notice and not bawl her out.

It wasn't extreme, no swelling, just a little bruising to both eyes, looked more like dark circles. Luckily, they should cover up.

By five-fifteen, Mildred was dressed and made up. She had just finished a sandwich and put the plate in the sink when the room lit up. The longest car she had ever seen was in front of her door. She saw Lindsey hop out, dash to the door, tap and ask,

"You ready?"

"All set."

Mildred was amazed at the inside of the vehicle. It was obscenely large and the elegance was excessive. There were flowers, chocolates and champagne with monogrammed flutes. Initially, she was embarrassed by the opulence, but then remembered it was for her youngest son's honeymoon.

Richie spoke up. "I hope you remember me when I get married again."

Lindsey cleared her throat and looked at him with a scowl.

"…to Lindsey again, you know, renew our vows. There is no one else, my darling. I was drunk."

They all laughed and watched out of the windows with the cooling air of early evening rushing in through the sunroof. When they arrived at the airport, the plane was already in. Richie took the sign from the limo driver and went to find his brother. He went to the baggage area with the sign that said PETRIE. The limo driver stayed with the women, and Mildred engaged him in polite conversation while they anticipated the arrival. In a few minutes, they heard the familiar voices laughing and teasing. The driver jumped out and went to open the rear door. Katie entered while the brothers wrestled with luggage.

Mildred spoke first, "Good evening, Mrs. Petrie."

"Well, hello to you, Mrs. Petrie, or should I say, Missuses Petrie. There is no proper plural, is there?" Mildred could tell immediately that Katie would fit in perfectly.

David entered, and they could have heard his roar on Mars. "Wow, Mom! This is a hoot! Thank you!"

"You two deserve it. Congratulations. Now open the freaking champagne, as it is arid in this place." They commenced to drink, laugh and talk about the wedding. There was one toast for their dad, but it was in celebration of the man who lived and not his death. The limo turned onto Casino Avenue, and Mildred watched David's face. She saw the thought of the fold-out couch skip across his face. When the town car turned left to the Ivory Winds Hotel entrance, both David and Katie were surprised.

As soon as they stopped, Richie jumped out, not waiting for the driver to open the door. "Thank Mom. This is all her doing, Davey."

"Wow, Mom. You shouldn't have. This is too much."

Richie added, "Don't worry about it; she has connections in high places." Mildred turned towards check in, but the concierge and his crew swept them away.

The suite was fabulous, just like in the movies. They entered into a sitting area and wet bar with a view of the city. The bedroom was behind carved double doors. Mildred felt severely underdressed, but she cast her insecurity aside. She had no idea the hotel had suites like this, and it wasn't even The Presidential; that one had two bedrooms. There was a table set up with hors d'oeuvres, more champagne, and two monogrammed robes in the bathroom.

They ate, drank some more, and shared old exaggerated memories. Mildred started to doze off around ten-thirty, and Lindsey gave her shoulder a gentle shake. "Do you want me to drive you home?"

"No need to leave the party, honey. You have been drinking a bit, and I can always get a ride."

Mildred took out her new phone and, with a little help, she was able to text.

"G-ma needs a ride."

There was an immediate response.

"Main entrance 20 min."

Just as she expected, Arnie was working, and the problem was solved. She kissed both her boys and their beautiful wives, with a promise of joining them for lunch. Mildred walked from the opulence back to the life she knew. Once off the elevator, she made a left from the hotel into the casino. The harsh clanging sound and background smell of cigarettes pleased her. Every part of the forlorn hope and cheesy décor was her life, and she admitted her work was important. She walked to the huge glass doors of the main entrance with the massive African sculptures and felt at home. The door attendant opened the door and in a richly accented voice said, "Have a beautiful night. We hope you come back."

"I've already had a nice night. Things couldn't get better."

"That is good to hear." He closed the door behind her. She stood in the garish light as the security van pulled up.

Arnie was smiling as she entered the passenger seat. "I thought you were off for a couple days."

"I was here with my sons."

"Oh, I heard something about a wedding, right?"

"David. Got married last week in Cleveland, and they came here for the honeymoon. The casino has been great and made it possible for them to have a beautiful suite. Belinda set it all up."

Arnie responded, "Great seeing you so happy. Glad to hear the Ivory has shown some appreciation, especially after the past couple of months. Are you doing all right? Were you hurt?"

"I'm all right, a little banged up is all. Guess I'm lucky on several fronts," said Mildred

He continued, "I talked to Bud. We are the only two who know what happened. We are keeping everything from the team and the press if possible. Besides, as you are aware, there is no telling who is who."

Mildred answered as she buckled her seatbelt. "I'm not going to think about it until Monday."

Arnie nodded and started the van. "I left you a message earlier. I found something, but we can talk later."

She nodded in agreement, "I didn't get the message. Do you think it was on my old phone? I'll text you with the new number. For now, I'm not letting the cases into my weekend reality. We can talk Monday."

He answered, "You texted a bit ago. I'll just go in and save the number. I spoke with the detective, and he has my data. So don't worry, the investigations have a life of their own and lots of help. Here we are. I'm going in first and do a quick check. I'll turn on lights, so wait here."

"Hold on, you have to stop the alarm. Here is the fob."

Reception

Mildred snuggled into the bed with Popcorn against her back. She repeated the vow that the ordeal from the past few days was a nightmare and not real until the visit is over.

Hours later, Mildred jerked awake and forced herself to focus on the love and joy of her family. The ability to compartmentalize was both a strength and a shortcoming. Until David and Katie left, the old habits would help heal her more than any drug. It was nearly noon the next day when she drove over to the casino.

Eventually, she learned Richie and Lindsey didn't make it home and spent the night sprawled out on the matching white couches. Her children had partied most of the night and were ragged and hungry by the time she arrived. Lindsey begged off lunch to go home. She had things to finish, preparations for the reception, and wanted to pick up her girls to help decorate.

After sharing room service, Mildred convinced Katie they needed new dresses for the reception. Mildred wanted something elegant with long sleeves, not mentioning it was to hide the red abrasions on her wrists. In addition, she was eager to discover more about this beautiful woman who was smart enough to win her son. It also gave the brothers time alone.

As they got in the car, Katie spoke up. "It is kind of a relief to get away from your sons, Mrs. P. They can be exhausting. I'm nervous to meet David's childhood friends and his college roommate."

Mildred smiled. "I wanted some time with you, I know we met you briefly at Dick's funeral, but the visit was so short, and not a good time to spend time."

So the women shopped, ate candy, and talked the time away. Mildred relayed stories of the boys and her own wedding. The early years were almost dream-like after the passing of so many years.

Katie shared about first meeting David, and the struggle in the first few years. Mildred was relieved to hear that, once her son decided he was in love, he was loyal and honest, just like his dad. Her face lit up as Katie told Mildred of the proposal and the cocker spaniel puppy he brought with a ring box tied to his collar. "We named the dog McGruff."

The statement made Mildred roar with laughter and sentimentality. Mildred's cell phone vibrated with a message, and she ignored it, refusing to allow reality to tarnish the day.

When they were on the way back to the hotel, Katie asked to stop at the grocery mart and Mildred waited in the car. She seized the opportunity to check the phone, and it was from Block.

"You Okay? – Break on the case. Meet Monday, Bud will pick you up six-thirty a.m. Have a good weekend."

She tapped out a quick response by text:

Okay, c u then. Try not to think about case. U invited to the reception tonight.

Katie opened the rear door and slid in a half case of Sparkling Cider. She was getting in the front passenger seat as Mildred's phone buzzed again.

Thanks, but no. Enjoy. C U Monday.

Katie looked flushed. "Do you mind if I confide in you? I'm so excited, and I need to tell someone before I burst."

"Always. I'm your mother-in-law, with the accent on the mother. You can tell me anything. I'm great with secrets." Mildred smiled gently.

"No one knows, but I'm pregnant," Katie squealed with joy. "WHAT! I had no idea. Does David know?"

"Not yet. I thought there was a chance, but I didn't know for sure until this morning. I wanted to tell Lindsey, but there was no privacy, and then she left so quickly. That is why I was dodging the champagne. I had one glass, but then kept adding ice, and finally ginger ale from the mini fridge."

Mildred was stunned with the thought and hugged Katie. The idea of another grandchild filled her heart. "This is huge! I'm so excited. Any idea when you are due? When do you think you will tell him?"

"It is very early, but I can't hold it in any longer. I might tell him tonight. I'll see how it goes. I got the cider so I can drink along with everyone and not mess anything up." Katie sighed and Mildred slipped into a contented grandma glow as she started the car.

Mildred's mind reeled with an idea. She dropped Katie off at the hotel and delivered the fake bubbly to the Congo Room. Lindsey was there, barking orders, and Mildred's granddaughters were busy decorating. She called her daughter-in-law aside and whispered, explaining the sparkling cider. Lindsey hooted, and then covered her mouth; the secret was safe with her. They plotted further, and Lindsey called Glory over and left her in charge with a list of instructions scratched on a napkin. The conspirators went to the storage facility and wrestled the 'surprise' into the rear of the van.

Once home, Mildred hung up her new dress and went to work. She dusted, sanded, touch-up painted, and finished the rocking chair. Once completed, Mildred gathered the shadow box of Dick's badges for David, and her mother's silver tray for Katie.

The reception was due to begin. She called Lindsey, who arrived in minutes with the van, and the two loaded the gifts. She had a large blue bow that they tied on the back of the chair. Mildred followed in her own car back to the casino. They carried the original two gifts into the Congo room, and Mildred was stunned how the granddaughters had transformed everything.

The girls glowed in similar-colored dresses. The younger two stood at a table near the left sidewall. They were in charge of opening and recording gifts. Izzy had already opened several packages, and Amelia recorded everything into a formal looking book and then set up the display with the cards.

Glory stood at the front door greeting everyone and gathering signatures in the guest book. Note to self, have Lindsey handle all events. David and Katie entered to a round of applause. Mildred and Lindsey tried (and failed) to stifle the conspiratorial snicker, and Lindsey gave Katie a wink and thumbs up.

The room filled with tinted lights and familiar faces. Mildred stayed seated at the end of the main table, sitting next to her sister, Sissy. "Mildred, you have been a terrible sister lately. You don't call, you don't visit. Luckily, the nursing home brought me over for the reception. Then they make me leave early, before I drink all of the good scotch."

Mildred bowed her head in shame. "I know, but I've been so busy with the job and all."

"Flimsy damn excuse. I'm the one that lied for you. Better start showing up," Sissy demanded.

"Yes ma'am, I will do better. How about if I come over on Tuesday afternoons."

"I'll hold you to it." Sissy offered a weak but sincere high five.

The two sisters continued to fill the time together with memories and laughter from long ago.

While they talked, Mildred watched her sons working the room, both animated and friendly, hugging or punching all who arrived. David kept Katie at his side and introduced her with the same swagger of pride his dad used to have for his family. Mildred visited with most of the now-grown children she had chased out of the house. They were husbands and wives. Where did the time go? It was strange to recognize faces that had changed drastically with the passage of time. The crowd lingered around the massive buffet, balancing plates of food and wedding cake, yet it appeared they were more starved to see old friends.

Richie started the production with a tribute to his younger brother that was both sincere and hilarious. Next, it was a multitude of mocking (and a few honest) tributes directed at the groom. It was a little after ten when Arnie and Q entered the party. An explosion of granddaughters in a community squeal greeted them. The girls ran to Q with armloads of hugs and kisses. Luckily, Glory intervened and escorted them to David for introductions. He laughed as Arnie made a remark about noise complaints and then shook hands, presenting a gift. The girls took the present to the table and unwrapped a dark clay Tandoori oven. Mildred smiled, knowing which of her friends had picked the gift. Arnie tipped his hat to Mildred and spoke briefly to a couple of people on his way out. This was the first time Mildred realized that the people she spent her time with were closer in age to her children.

Once the girls settled back to their jobs, Q came over and pulled up a chair. "As I have said before, some customs are the same no matter what country you are in."

"That thought gives me hope. I'm sorry you missed my sister, she had to leave," Mildred answered.

"Me also." They watched the festivities, part of the group, and yet on the outside.

Finally Q spoke again. "You look as if you are tired, have you recovered?"

"Not improving as quickly as I hoped, only soreness though, no real injury. I understand that there is a break. Do you have some new information?" Mildred asked.

"Yes, we do. However, it will wait. Mr. Arnie and I agreed not to talk about it until Monday. This moment is important for your family. It is family that we do everything else for."

"Okay, you are right, but the suspense is killing me."

"I promise you, Miss Mildred, you will not die. I must go back to work now. We wanted to pay our respects." Q slipped away before Mildred could express her full appreciation.

Music started filling the room. The guests with children began to make the rounds of goodbyes, with sincere promises to stay in touch. Mildred kept an eye on Katie as her husband asked her to dance to their song. They held each other closely, and the love between them was apparent. As they moved slowly around the room, she whispered a couple words to him. There was no description for the look on his face. He picked her up and spun her around the dance floor. He glowed as tears frosted his cheeks, and he kissed her lightly and then again deeply.

Lindsey waved Richie to her side, and the two slipped away. At the end of the dance, David went to the bandstand and asked for the microphone. "Ladies, gentlemen, family. There are no better people in the world that I could share this announcement with. My bride, my love, my wife, my Katie has just told me that we are going to have a baby."

Every corner of the party, including the band, broke into applause and encouragement. Lindsey opened the door, and Richie carried in the rocking chair. The same one Grandpa Dick's mother held him in, with both brothers cuddled to sleep in the rhythm of the chair. Even the granddaughters had been soothed in loving arms with the cadence of this chair. It was now his to continue the tradition. The silence in the room broke by the sound of a grown man's sob as he clung to Katie and stared at the chair.

A half-hour later, Lindsey and Glory walked Mildred to her car. They talked of the reception success and mostly of the emotional reaction for the baby. They waited for the car to start and waved as Mildred drove the short distance home.

As soon as she was in, she turned off the alarm and greeted the demanding cat, Mildred sent a text to Q.

"No wait to M-day, tell now."
There was an immediate response. "**Excited 2,"Found connection Block digging**

It would take a while for Mildred to calm down and sleep. There was so much to dream about tonight.

B-I-N-G-O

Mildred woke to a banging on her door, and a familiar voice.

"Come on, Mommy Dearest, time for breakfast." Before she could get up to answer, both of her sons jumped in bed with her, all remembering childhood. "Mommy, you are supposed to use the chain lock and reset those alarms."

"I'll do better next time."

Richie whispered in her ear, "You better, old woman."

"I know, I know. But right now, settle down, you monsters, ole Mommy has to hit the bathroom. No jumping on the bed." While she was in the bathroom, she could hear the sound of their whispering, and she choked on a mouth full of toothpaste.

"You don't have to get pretty for us. We've seen you at your worst." They both sounded like their father, but that was David. Her heart soared with love and shoved back the regrets of the years after the funeral. She slipped into her newest sweat pants and a long-sleeved T-shirt. She offered to make breakfast, but the two handsome men had other plans. She believed pride was filling every inch of air around her. They mentioned their wives had gone for a spa day and left the brothers to their own devices. They walked their mother to the casino and into the café. David ordered an apple turnover and Richie snorted into a nearly hysterical laughter. Mildred realized that her frozen pastry of choice was more of a very long-term habit. No wonder Block had started bringing an alternative.

They ate, laughed and drank extra cups of coffee. When Richie nodded at David, they both looked at her seriously. David began, "Mom, I know we have brought this up before, but Richie told me there was another incident. You explained away concern on one, but this is too much." He took out a piece of notebook paper covered with numbers. "Do you get any of the retirement from you or Dad?"

"That isn't important. I'm doing fine."

"Mom, you got your ass kicked and kidnapped because of this job. That isn't fine."

Richie interrupted David's tirade. "We only have one parent; we want her safe and strong…"

"…and sitting in my chair waiting to die? I don't care what the risks are. I'm busy and doing good work. I won't quit. We will be at the bottom of it soon."

David took back control. "We are not asking you, we are telling you. Rich checked with your retirement plans, and they informed him your policies were cashed out about the time Dad died. We also found Dad sold the house and bought your little condo. Where did all the money go? Do you know?"

Her eyes began to moisten. "You should have let me cook if you knew you were going to get all serious."

Richie reached over and held her hand. "But Mom, we only want the best for you, and in all the digging I discovered things were more critical than we understood."

She straightened her shoulders. "You two damn fools. I'm doing fine. I still have social security, the condo is paid for, and the police and the casino pay me. Now that I think of it, I'm doing very well."

"It's not well enough if you get killed," David added.

"I don't plan on getting killed. The investigation is moving quickly now. Besides, if I were killed, it would be easier than a life of television and computer solitaire. I have no plans on quitting as long as I'm able. End of discussion."

David was silent for a moment. "Here is the deal. We both can give you five hundred a month to replace the salary."

"Keep your damn money. Put it in a college account for your children. I already said 'the end of discussion.' Which word didn't you understand?" She was still their parent, and they knew from their youth there was nothing more to say.

"Anyone for pie?" David asked.

"I usually don't have dessert at breakfast, David," Richie added.

"I know, but I have to bury the conversation, and get us back." He looked at his brother and sighed.

Richie waved at the server. "Excuse me, may we have three apple turnovers?"

David raised his hand. "Can you make one of them blueberry?" They all laughed, ending the tension.

Once the turnovers were finished, they held warm cups and remembered more schmaltzy stories about growing up. Both men kept her laughing with often-told tales of being in trouble. "It amazes me how you two remember the same things differently, and both of you are still wrong."

The seriousness of the conversation dissipated as the men acknowledged her strength and control of her own choices. Clearly they had plotted the speech before they broke into her home. "Thank you. I had no intention of changing. And I do feel so much better having your support."

Mildred looked at her youngest. "David, I thought this was a honeymoon. I was under the impression you were to be romancing your new wife and singing love songs."

Richie rolled his eyes, "Yeah, Romeo, you have spent more time with your brother."

"Get off my back. The bride went to the spa with Lindsey. They are doing something with their feet and stuff. She is supposed to let me know when they are done, if that makes you happy. Besides, with the big announcement last night, she has already been romanced." David looked quite pleased with himself. "And..."

"Stop. Too much. No mother wants to hear the details."

Richie broke in. "Enough, you two. David, we were going to run over to the house and check on the girls and then hit the car show. I'll get the car. Meet me out front, and Mom can go with us."

"No, you two criminals can drop me off at home. You call them antique cars, but they are my life." While Mildred and David argued over the bill, Richie paid and left.

They walked hand-in-hand towards the main entrance. Mildred noticed an afternoon event and saw the slot machines were busy for this time of the morning. With a quick decision, her boys went on their way, and she signed in.

"G-ma on the floor."
"10-4."
"Who is this."
 There was a slight pause,
"Larry."
Mildred tapped **"Bingo?"**
"Good luck – call in."
 She put in her earpiece and rang the office. "Hi Larry, what's the deal?"

"Heads up for the afternoon event. They have moved the bingo from the parlor to the grand showroom. They are filming for some TV movie."

"Cool. Which movie?"

"They told me, but I don't remember. It's logged. We have a ton of reservations, the crowd is already growing, and it doesn't start for two hours. I'm glad you are here. I've called in some backup, but they aren't here yet."

"No problem, Larry old man. I'll check it out and will keep you posted. I'll need a ticket."

"I'll get you a pass over at Customer Service."

Mildred took a deep breath; it felt good to be back on patrol as she started through the gaming areas. It was crazy for a Sunday morning, mostly nicely dressed older women. The slot machines were singing with the high-pitched whirs and clangs. She strolled past the showroom and noted a crew setting up lights and cameras. Off to the gift shops. To blend with the appearance of the crowd, Mildred bought a glittery vest with puppies and dice on the back. This should go nicely with my comfy pants and help me blend in.

Most of the crowd was female, focused on the slots. Mildred picked up the badge that Larry arranged at Customer Service, but he had sent a security pass, and that didn't work for undercover. Instead of hassling Larry, and adding to his stress, she clipped it inside the vest. The walk and watch continued in alternating patterns.

The high rollers appeared to be at church, because the glassed-in card rooms were nearly abandoned. She checked for

Dick's shadow on the glass, but it only reflected her own image. Shocked to see how much older she looked, compared to how she pictured herself, Mildred sucked in her stomach, did two neck exercises and stood a little taller. She continued to the buffet in an attempt to shake off the image. Next to the cashier area. She was glad to see some additional security that she didn't know. Then back to the staging for the bingo event. It was close to an hour before starting time, and women were already lined up. They clung to hopes for front row seats, and to be discovered by the director. Mildred shook her head and continued toward the backstage access when she heard a recognizable voice. She turned and came face to face with a woman dressed in a nearly identical outfit. Mildred's mind embraced memories of iconic characters this woman had created. Mildred nodded to Lily Tomlin as if passing an old friend at church, and received a cherished smile in return.

By the time she reached the back employee entrance, Mildred had looked out towards the parking lots and then turned to start over. She reached the main entrance as a gravelly-voice announcement came over the Jumbotron. The slots began to clear, and the glittery crowd moved to the main stage. She smiled. The bingo crowd was different, and yet the same. Mildred fell in lockstep with the migration.

"Addl security here. Enjoy."

Mildred didn't want to risk being noticed and was going to respond later until she saw many of the waiting group were tapping on their own phones.

"10-4 going in now."

The line inched forward. Mildred faced the young man taking tickets and subtly flashed her security badge from inside her vest. The ticket taker's eyes scanned her face with a discreet acknowledgment and turned his attention to the next ticket holder. Mildred entered and found a seat near the emergency exit. Casino employees seated the avid bingo players. There were a few young interns, probably from the film crew, rearranging the mob. They moved some individuals to specially marked places. I'll bet those are actors. The confusion appeared choreographed by an unseen entity. Mildred noticed that her earpiece picked up some background instruction, possibly from the dark control booth. Startled by a tap on her shoulder, Mildred turned.

"Ma'am, could we have you sit in the front?"

"Ah, ah no. I'm fine here."

"He wants you over there," and the intern pointed to the front of the room.

Mildred leaned over and whispered, "No dear, I work here. I'm not moving." Then she flashed her security badge.

There was no answer as the young woman whispered into a button mic on her lapel and walked away. The intern continued to scan the ongoing stream of potentials. The whole ordeal fascinated Mildred as she continued her general survey.

It seemed like hours of fake bingo and retakes. Mildred sent a text to Larry and slipped out the back to the casino floor. She felt lucky to have the option to leave and checked off an old dream of acting from her bucket list. The filming was more tedious than anticipated, and Mildred decided she was too old for an acting career. It was good to stretch her legs as she walked toward the gaming areas, which had filled with the typical Sunday customers. The tables were picking up, and she saw the mixed crowd replace the bedazzled bingo players. Not needing to sit, she continued to the hotel lobby and gift shops. Her attention was drawn to a potential shoplifter. She stalled to look at sunglasses. Suddenly there was a warm hug from behind. Mildred was stunned to see David and his bride beaming at her. They were a little noisy, but so was everyone in the casino.

"We are thinking about eating."

"I hadn't thought about food since breakfast. Just one moment." Mildred watched the suspect take her bag over to the cashier and paid for all of the items. "Okay, now you mentioned food."

"We thought we would go to one of the fancy places here, and I'm buying. No discussion, Mom." David announced.

"I'm so sorry, but this is Italian night at the buffet, and that is the only place I would consider."

"Deal, Mom!"

The three continued with Mildred's patrol, and her son watched her disappear into the crowd. She was like a ghost keeping a persistent watch. She hoped he understood her need for, and the importance of, her work. She proudly showed him where she saw Daddy's reflection in the window, and the bathroom where she captured Butt Munch. It took a while to make it to the other end of the facility, where the warm smell of tomato and garlic drew them forward. The bingo fiasco was still filming, and the restaurant wasn't crowded. She directed them to her usual table and pointed out the view as they filled plates of comforting and exotic cuisine. She sent a quick text to Larry, signing out.

At the end of the meal, David looked at his spaghetti-spattered mother and his bride. Mildred could see the love he tried to hide. *This was the happiest I've seen him since childhood.* Mildred was thrilled to be part of it. He reached out to hold both of their hands. This moment would replay in her memory for years. She watched the light in his eyes as he looked at his new wife, silently acknowledging his hope and joy. No matter the reason, he had dismissed his guilt of the past couple years, and replaced it with gratitude. "You know, Mom, you have never really changed. I'm worried about you, but this is really who you have always been, if I'm honest with myself." His eyes scanned the room. "You are like this cannoli. The shell is crispy, sweet and yet strong enough to, to, ah..."

Mildred choked back the emotion. "Hold in the gooey parts?"

"That is it. Perfect." And the tense emotion was acknowledged and defused.

Mildred continued to expound on how that particular dessert would be responsible for world peace. The two women stood together and walked back to the counter. They returned with cannoli, two each. David ate the tiramisu and then Katie's second cannoli.

The young couple walked Mildred home in the warmth of the early evening, stopping to watch the sun slip beneath the horizon to leave a light show of yellow and orange. They turned off the alarms and checked to be sure her home was secure. Mildred held Popcorn and watched them walk away hand in hand, drenched in the purple of the approaching night. She went to bed early appreciating all of the years, good and bad.

– 60 –
Monday

Awake before dawn, Mildred caught herself singing as she got ready for the meeting. Bud was there at six fifteen and he looked haggard, apparently not a morning person today. She entered the car to the familiar smell of the casino bakery. They drove directly to the station. Recognized at the front desk, they were waved through.

The white board still commanded the room. Mildred noticed Detective Block's folders at the head of the table, now bulging with papers. Dick's familiar cold case box was also waiting. Her contentment of the day before and morning dissipated as she settled in. Bud opened the pastry box and put it at the center of the table. They took the seats on the left side of the room. Within minutes, Q and Arnie arrived, straight from work. A junior officer followed them in with a coffee pot and a pot of water and turned on the hot plate near the door. Mildred smiled and tossed the familiar baggie of chamomile tea to Arnie. He winked and poured two cups of water.

"Thanks, Mom, how is the visit going?"

"That is Grandma. It couldn't be better. Perfect timing, it helped me ignore the kidnapping and share romanticized stories with my boys."

Q dipped her tea bag repeatedly. "Thank you, Ms. Mildie and congratulations on your new grandchild." Mildred's smile lit up the room.

"I took care of the breakfast this time," said Bud as he pointed at the large white box exposing a variety of fresh pastries, still fragrant from the oven.

Arnie whispered, "Damn, no apple turnovers. Don't think I can talk crime without them." Mildred heard Q, "You are not a humorous man. You need to appreciate the hospitality extended to you with grace."

"Don't worry about him, Q; even my boys were teasing me about a lifetime of turnovers. I should have bought stock in

Pepperidge Farm. Arnie, you will be glad to know I've purchased a case of mixed flavors."

His guffaw filled the room. "I don't know why they aren't everyone's favorite anyway. You've got your fruit, your flaky crust and frosting. A balanced meal straight from the oven."

The co-workers laughed in unison as Detective Block entered the room. "Cheery group for this early in the morning. Sorry to interrupt, but we have work to do."

He set down a tape dispenser and another folder and rolled the white board to the front of the table. He taped a photo of Judge McCaffie on the left and wrote dollar signs under his name. Then a picture of Judith, labeled Wife #1, went up to the right and slightly lower, one of Brittany, Wife #2. Beneath #2's photo he wrote robbery, kidnapping.

Block then announced, "They will be referred to as Judith and Brittany, or One and Two." He drew a black line down the center of the board and at the top center he taped another photo labeled T. Conner, Esq.

"Isn't that the fancy attorney that got Butt Munch out on bail?" Mildred asked.

Block answered, "That's the same guy. His firm stepped in for all three McCaffies."

Bud jumped in. "I've seen his name for years in the news. He is always on the big cases and wins, too. Is he that good?"

Block answered, "I've been talking to some other departments, and there is another investigation going on. What we, our group of misfits, have done, is to bring together several units. We have tied them together. We believe a renegade group from the much larger organization executed the burglary. We have DNA back from the van, and it ties to a homeboy brother of Waller."

"Two Butt Munches? Tell me more. Where are they?" Mildred asked.

"That boy is locked up with no bail, and he is starting to cooperate. Conner and some of his minions have been down in holding all weekend. Luckily, we put the fear of all that is holy in young Waller before his representation arrived."

Everyone agreed, and Arnie started a rotation of high fives and congratulations. Q's eyes lingered on Mildred's bruised wrists, but said nothing. She gently reached across the table and patted Mildred's hand. "You Americans confuse me. There are so many jokes over serious things. I don't know if I will understand." Arnie answered her, "You will understand when you get your citizenship papers." Mildred simply rolled her eyes and shook her head. "We are getting ahead of ourselves. First, we need Qaseema to give us her report."

Q stood up and spoke, "Yes sir, I have sent information to you with my new email address. I have it written down if you need it." Block nodded and she began, "Four trusted members of the housekeepers are paying attention to conversations. Maria saw the Mr. Conner speak to the judge. This was while Mildred was in the kidnap. Maria has requested she not be involved for personal reasons. I have promised she would not be called to the court. Maria heard Mr. Conner tell Mr. Judge to rein in his women. Mr. Judge looked scared and said he did not know what they were doing. Mr. Judge promised that he would fix it."

While taking notes, Block asked, "I wonder if he was aware his wives had met each other? Q, did you send me Maria's contact information?"

"No. Maria would only speak to me, and I respect her fear and concern. Maria is unyielding; she will do no more. She said Mr. Conner looked at her very harshly."

Mildred spoke up, "Can this just be a lead from a reliable source? You know, like on Law TV?"

"No other choice. I have a feeling that Conner is more than the legal counsel of record," Block said.

Mildred added, "Is he involved with both sides?"

Block drew lines from Conner to the judge and to the women.

After Q sat down, Arnie stood, and Block spoke up. "We don't have to be formal; this is just a give and-take while we try to work up the bones of this mess."

"Right." Arnie sat and said, "Hampton, do you have the connections on the Pay Day loan business? I'll bet it is possible money laundering. Am I right? Is this why we are here?"

Hampton searched through his papers, not finding what he wanted, then he stated, "That is how it appears."

Arnie continued, "I followed up with our poker and baccarat supervisors. We have learned that some of the dealers have been handing out business cards from the loan store, and are paid a kickback based on referrals."

Bud added, "We are setting up new training, and will be eliminating this practice."

Arnie nodded and went on, "That should slow it down, but won't stop it. There is always someone wanting or needing to supplement an income. However, that is a great start. Hampton, do you have any results on the owners?"

Detective Hampton moved purposefully to pick up a thin, blue folder. "This is where things get complicated. The research into these Pay Day Loan stores opened a market to the lower income population."

Arnie broke in. "Yeah, we know. They have been in the news for a while."

Block continued, "The companies are usually franchises, but there is an independent in their midst. We are into a mire of foreign and bogus companies. Nothing has been confirmed yet, but the forensic accounting sections have seen this type of thing before."

"Follow the money," Mildred whispered.

"We do have attorney Conner as the representative for the owners," added Hampton. The team responded with nods and agreement.

A uniformed officer entered the room and whispered to the Detectives. "Hold on, folks, have some more coffee. We have a situation in holding. We'll be right back." Hampton and Block left quickly.

The four finished the donuts and the pot of coffee as Mildred retold the story of her kidnapping. Q went to refill the teapot at the water cooler in the waiting room and rushed back in. "There is only one officer out there, and I overheard him on the radio speak of suicide in holding. Do you think it is our cases?"

Mildred was stunned and looked from face to face to see the same concern. "We don't know everything they work on." They sat in silence, waiting.

It was another half-hour before Hampton finally returned. "I'm sorry; we had a problem downstairs."

Arnie was the first to speak. "We overheard it was a suicide. Did it have anything to do with our group of reprobates?"

Hampton chewed on his lip. "Yes, it was Number Two with a sorry attempt to hang herself. She is fine, and Block is with her waiting for the attorney. Therefore, we have to finish up quickly. Basically, the money lending works back to Conner, not sure if there is anyone else. We found McCaffie has taken bribes for years. I personally think he was being blackmailed, and it got out of hand. Mildred, we found indications that your husband may have been on to it and got close with the Freeman case."

Hampton continued to stack the paperwork as he spoke. "The other side of the line, the wives, we don't have any details yet. Number Two was claiming to be framed, and that they promised her money."

Block rushed into the room. "We have a break. Number Two wants to fire the attorney, and we are bringing in the WITSEC for a possible deal. Depends on what she knows. She complained that Number One framed her. She won't talk until the prosecutor and the Marshal Service arrive. I'm not sure how they caught on to Mildred's involvement." He rushed out as quickly as he came in.

Mildred looked about the room, and everyone was stunned and silent.

Hampton took back the control. "There is something more, because they cut your brakes after you met with Number One. I believe your lunch confirmed suspicions. Mildred, you could still be in danger."

Mildred addressed the whole team. "I've known the Judge and Judith for over twenty-five, maybe thirty years. I worked with her on the McGruff events, and he was friends with Dick.

They were close, more of a business association. We would talk and sit together at different events, but they didn't come over to the house or anything." Her tone was apologetic as she continued. "Since starting at the casino, I've seen him and Number Two several times. He is at the card room a lot. I've made a point to avoid him. The last time we spoke, I wonder if he had noticed me other times. I was so busy watching, I never thought about someone looking back."

Bud started to speak, but Mildred continued. "He introduced me to the wife. She seemed totally disinterested in everything."

Bud added, "I have had some interaction with the Judge a couple times. He is a big investor and is on the Ivory Winds board. We have never shared Mildred's position with anyone except the few who work with her. I wonder if this involves someone in security."

Arnie spoke up. "I'm sure she has become general knowledge in security. I've overheard questions about who she could be on any given night, and they had bets trying to ID her. Bud, it's up to us to check further into our teams."

Hampton took over. "Mildred, I need you to stay very close. I know better than to tell you to stay home, but please only go to the casino when Bud or Arnie are working. I'd suggest using your disguises, too."

"Okay, boss." Mildred saluted, but privately she was scared.

Bud answered, "I double-checked with Human Resources, and they will have the requested employment and background files over here by tomorrow. Hey, now I understand why you kept me on the whiteboard." Mildred shrugged and giggled guiltily.

A uniformed officer came in and whispered to Hampton, who then looked up at the others in the room. "I'm so sorry, but this meeting needs to end.
Carry on, and keep us in the loop, no one is to take any risks. Please keep everything private. I have to get over to the hospital."

All quietly gathered their reports and folders, and left. They met in the parking lot, and everyone had ideas but no answers. The team dispersed in multiple directions. The ride with Bud was quiet. "Please take some time off," Bud pleaded once at Mildred's place.

Mildred smiled gently, "Hell no. No one scares Double-Oh-Seventy-One." He watched as she unlocked her car, and then relocked it. "Oops, I get them confused." Finally, he watched her open her front door, disarm the alarm system and wave goodbye as a giant white cat ran up to rub against her legs.

Company

Mildred sat for a while, brushing the demanding cat in the summer swelter. As much as she didn't want to stop, the body heat was too much. Mildred extricated herself, leaving Popcorn draped across the arm of the chair. She propped open the front door, and the fresh air drifting through the screen helped lighten the heavy thoughts.

A walk would help, and Mildred left to stroll around the community. Most of her neighbors had their doors and windows open, and the drone of mindless televisions and radios floated through the air, along with the smell of muscle cream and tuna casserole. Her mind reeled with a series of scenarios, and each one only created more questions.

Have you heard more from the detectives? What if, what if, what if? Follow the money, who benefits? Why would they take Judith? It makes no sense. How did Butt Munch fit in to both the burglary and the kidnapping? He couldn't have taken Judith, he was with me. What is the common theme?

She walked around the circular neighborhood, mumbling, thinking and scheming. After a half-hour, the frustration was too much and instead of screaming, she sped up her walk back home.

Upon re-entering her bungalow, Mildred went straight to her computer and composed an email to Detective Block:

"Was it Number Two trying suicide? Has Butt Munch explained his connection to Wife Two? Who was the guy with him, was he part of the break in? Do they have any organized crime affiliation?

"Check the financials of both wives. What did your forensic department find at Judith's kidnapping? Why would they take her? Did you search the Mercedes? Something isn't right."

She went into the closet, erased the board and stared at the blankness. She held the marker, motionless, unable to start again. She heard the screen door open and called out, "Popcorn, what are you up to?" Mildred exited the closet and came face to face with Judith McCaffie, standing at the open door.

Mildred greeted her, noticing a gun in her right hand. "Judith, so glad to see you. Are you all right? Did the kidnappers hurt you?"

"That is bullshit and you know it. I'm out of here, but I needed to tell you first. You aren't so smart. You're too stupid to take a simple message. Back off. We are on to you and your little investigation. This is the last warning. The next visit will be with your family." "Please, Judith, this isn't necessary. I was a victim in this. I still have questions. Sit down and I'll make tea." Mildred's response seemed to confuse Judith. "Where are you off to?" She turned to go to the kitchen, where her cell phone was charging.

"Stop! One more word out of you, old woman, and I'll answer all of your questions with this." She pushed the gun forward towards Mildred's face, and she stepped forward.

At that exact moment, Popcorn tried to weave through Judith's legs, causing her to trip and fall back. Mildred dropped the marker she had held and jumped onto Judith, kicking the gun into the living room. Mildred straddled the intruder and held her arms down.

"That wasn't much of a struggle, was it, dear?" The cat began to rub against Judith's head. "Two against one, doesn't seem fair." Mildred had the advantage, but neither of them could reach the weapon, and Popcorn refused to fetch.

Mildred called out, "Help, call 911! Help, Help!" Due to the heat, most of the neighbors had their doors open, and no one jumps on a 911 call like the residents of a retirement village. Within minutes, a fire truck arrived, and the first responders ran up to offer aid. There was a spectator on nearly every stoop of the village.

"We can take this from here. What seems to be wrong with her?"

"I need the police, this is an arrest. Could you please pass me the gun from over there, under the coffee table?"

The EMT picked up the gun, and then stalled. "Sorry, no. I don't know who you are and who should be on top."

Mildred smiled and had to agree. As the first paramedic held the gun on both women, a second firefighter blocked the door, and a third helped untangle the two combatants on the floor. Judith finally spoke. "My husband is a judge, and you need to arrest this woman. She assaulted me."

Mildred responded, "You just don't quit, do you, Judith? I'd suggest shutting up right now, or maybe even better, just keep yapping. Who do you think is in control of this fiasco?"

"I don't know what is wrong with you, Mildred. I have to leave, and I can't be late. Please, take that woman to a hospital. I think she has had a breakdown."

Mildred crossed her eyes and stuck out her tongue.

"Real mature, Mildred. Just wait," said Judith.

Mildred answered, "The cops are on the way."

The wait seemed longer than it actually was, but several black and whites screamed into the lot with lights flashing. The officers jumped out of the cars at full speed and ran to Mildred's door. She recognized Officer Gutierrez as he came in, then she noticed the unmarked SUV right behind. Relieved, she saw Elton Block running up to the door.

He started barking orders while still on a full run. The firefighters stepped aside, and the first EMT turned the gun over to the detective. They spoke briefly, and Block thanked them, sending them back to the firehouse. When Block turned, he saw an elegant older woman sitting on the couch, with the start of a bruise on her cheek and a trickle of blood from her nose. Seated in the chair was the associate he thought he knew, holding the cat. The look of victory and strength made her look years younger than she was. "Nice work, Double-Oh-my-gawd. What happened now?"

"I guess you could call it uninvited company, trespassing, assault, animal cruelty, and I'll press charges."

"Okay, Mrs. McCaffie, you're going downtown. Cuff her." Once restrained, the uniform officers stood her up and started towards one of the cars.

Mildred looked directly into Judith's eyes. "Not so much to say now, is there, girlfriend?" Once outside she could hear a demand for a call to her attorney.

Mildred sat back and listened as Block arranged to have the Mercedes impounded and towed to the yard. Block picked up Judith's purse from the floor and could see an airline ticket, but he simply slipped it all into an evidence bag, not daring to compromise anything. He scanned the room and noticed the black marker on the floor as it bled onto the carpet. He picked up the pen using a small plastic evidence bag, and put it with the others. He then went to the kitchen and returned with a roll of paper towels, the Murphy's Oil Soap from under the sink and carpet spray cleaner. The two of them knelt together scrubbing the black ink that initially seemed to spread but finally lighten. Mildred knew it would never completely disappear. "I'd like to file some additional charges: that bitch ruined my carpet."

"Seeing who went downtown in the back seat of a police car, looks like you have proved the marker is mightier than the…"

"Stop right now, Elton. I will not allow you to stoop lower with that metaphor. The entire team has asked me to tell you that humor is not your strongest trait."

He faked a hurt expression. "Well, Ms. Mildred, it's time we went to the station. I need your formal statement. You want to drive or ride with me?"

She smiled as she reached to the table, picking up her keys.

"I'll drive. I like to have an escape plan."

"Then you need to get a place with a back door."

– 62 –
Clean Up

When Mildred arrived at the station, she walked through the front waiting area. The desk sergeant buzzed her in, and the door opened to greetings of approving nods, winks, and a few high fives. This continued as she walked to the rear offices. No obvious remarks, but it was evident her takedown tale had swept through the precinct like a virus. Mildred felt like a one-woman parade and was proud but embarrassed by the attention. She wiped her eyes as she entered the office. Block sat at his desk and Hampton stood behind him as he flipped through papers and photos.

"Good afternoon, sirs. I notice you don't keep secrets."

"There she is. You almost need a desk here." Hampton walked over to her and patted the top of her head. "Didn't expect this kind of a break on the same day I tell you to take no risks."

"Yeah, what a surprise. I guess I do need a badge so the fire department doesn't arrest me." They all laughed, briefly.

Block gathered up the files and moved everything to the conference room. The cups and crumbs were still there, and the board had not changed from the previous meeting.

"Have you called any of the team?"

Block said, "No, I'm keeping this with us and not risking any contamination. I can't discuss some of the new information we have outside the department. We don't want to compromise the cases."

"Especially since they like to pick on old women," Mildred sighed.

"Lots of things I could call you, but old woman isn't one of them," Block nodded in agreement with Hampton. They then slipped into suppositions about who, where, and what when Block's phone beeped. He looked at the message and said, "Folks, we are moving. The Marshal is here, and I don't want to miss anything Number Two has to say."

They rushed to the interrogation room, and all three sat behind the two-way glass. A man and a woman, both in Kevlar vests marked MARSHAL, sat across from Brittany, Wife Number Two. There was a court reporter in the corner, busily recording everything in addition to a videotape. Brittany looked tired, dirty and her eyes were swollen, probably from crying. The prosecuting attorney for the state was doing a lot of talking when Hampton flipped on the intercom. They listened intently, and Block handed Mildred a notepad for any questions.

It sounded as if the negotiations were finalizing. The attorney said, "We agree to drop charges for the break-in and the kidnapping, if the information you provide proves to be true and brings the suspects you mention, Judith McCaffie, Lawrence McCaffie, Thomas Conner, Joshua Waller, Milton Waller and Jax Britter, to charges and trial. You will also provide the location of the body of Lonnie Downs, the fifth burglar who apparently was shot at the casino. You will be provided with a new name and location, but you must, and I repeat must, testify."

One of the Marshals pushed what looked like a contract to her. The nervous tremor was visible as she signed the agreement.

The attorney tapped on the glass and waved for Block to enter. "Now we get down to details. First, let's start with your relationship with each of the parties involved."

"I have been married to Lawrence McCaffie for the past two years. Thomas Conner set me up with him. He used a couple prostitution charges I was facing to convince me to manipulate the judge. It was easy to marry him, he is old and kinda horny, you know. I couldn't see anything wrong with it, and I got a new name and a clean record. Besides, the old man has lots of money. Hey, I could use a Diet Coke."

The attorney tapped on the glass. "Could we get some drinks in here? Make sure one is a Diet Coke."

Hampton hopped right up and left the room. In a few minutes, there was a tap on the door and Mildred watched a hand deliver soft drinks to a Marshal. He came back in with two more soda cans, giving one to Mildred. They all took a moment to open the containers, consume a universal drink, and settle in for an extended interview. Mildred noticed what looked like a red burn on Brittany's neck.

By the end of the day, Mildred's muscles ached, and her head was ringing. Brittany admitted to masterminding the burglary with the Wallers, Britter, Downs and the help of Davis.
Mildred sighed, "Aww, Lena Davis, my Ninja."

She learned that Brittany and Lena knew each other from the old neighborhood and Number Two thought the money would be an easy take. They had watched *Ocean's Eleven*, and *Twelve*, in preparation. "Maybe we were giving them too much credit," whispered Hampton. They had found floor plans online, and then Wife Two worked the Judge for additional information on the counting room procedures. She had convinced Lena to get a job there, so they could determine the major deposit pickups.

Several times Brittany played dumb, but Mildred could see the manipulation. Brittany was no one's fool. She gathered some of the material by digging through the Judge's private records when he was off at the card room or asleep. Everyone was stunned when she explained that Judith McCaffie and Thomas Conner had had a long-term sexual affair.

"I was surprised when Judith McCaffie made contact with me and offered a million dollars if I would get the old man's account numbers. Ya', I'd be a fool to turn down that kind of bank. They opened me an account somewhere in the Bahamas, and it was all supposed to be electronic." Number Two claimed to have turned over the bank account information, but they had only paid her half of the agreed amount. Brittany continued, "The trouble is, the job kept getting bigger, with no additional money. That woman has it made, but for some reason she can't get her wrinkled old claws on enough money. I would have been okay with the shit pile she generated in the divorce." Number Two went on about how Judith and Conner came up with the money laundering for some business partners. "Guess seeing all the money rolling in, they got greedy."

Mildred leaned over to Hampton and whispered, "Who is 'they'? Does she know we arrested Judith?"

He shook his head 'no' in response and wrote on the tablet, "Don't know."

Mildred wrote, "Cool beans."

They continued to listen, and the two made notes and slipped questions under the door to Block. It was well into the night when they finally called the interview. Brittany left for her last night in holding. "Oh, one more thing you might want to know. I overheard something a couple years ago, when Conner told Judith to never cross the Eastern something, maybe. someone out of Chicago, it would be worse than death."

Mildred drove home, confident that she was safe, since all of the players were reported to be in custody, or in Chicago. She expected to miss some sleep trying to make sense of the new information, but she was wrong. Her mind finally had some answers.

Double Turnovers

Mildred's first thought was of the closed case. Does Lucas Freeman's case have anything to do with all of this? Oh, let it go; not everything can tie up so neatly. She promised herself that she would visit Freeman's wife, just to check on her and the children. She went ahead and showered, put on her best pajama pants, scrambled two eggs, and toasted an English muffin. She had brought out the white board and leaned it against the other stool. As she picked at breakfast, Mildred started to write each of the names and their involvement, when there was a knock at the door.

Mildred looked out the window and could only see the back of a man. She finally learned her lesson and stood at the door, and spoke. "Hello. Who is it?"

"It's Brian Hampton."

Mildred threw open the door. "Brian? I didn't realize you had a first name. What's up?"

"Elton had me stop by. Don't you answer your cell phone?"

"Oh, I forgot about it. I went straight to bed last night and didn't plug it back in. Do you want an egg?"

"No, I'm good. We called a meeting for today with the team. It will be at one o'clock."

"Sure, no problem. Do I need to bring anything?"

Hampton laughed heartily. "Please don't go out of your way. It should be short."

By twelve-thirty, Mildred was in a pair of her gray elastic-waist dress pants with the matching jacket, thinking it best to look professional for once. She put the double batch of turnovers in a plastic container and left for the station. She drove with a strong feeling of success and satisfaction.

She was first to arrive, as usual, and put the baked treats in the center of the table. Q came next. She had finished her class for the semester that morning and would have her medical degree soon. They chatted until Bud and Arnie came in together. They both grabbed a snack; Arnie said, "Must be important to have fresh turnovers. Break in the case?"

Mildred smiled knowingly as she poured coffee. "Guess we have to wait and see."

The two detectives entered with big smiles. Each took a cup and a turnover, then greeted the casino security team. After a couple moments, Block smiled with a little icing on his cheek.

"Well team, we have a couple breaks in the associated case. Mildred, did you tell them of your visitor yesterday afternoon and the big bust?"

There was a group exclamation of surprise and all eyes turned.

Bud sighed. "Not again. What happened?"

Mildred started the story with exaggerated details. They all gasped when she related that Popcorn took down Judith McCaffie, and Mildred jumped on her to restrain her. They laughed about the firefighter holding the gun on both of them until Block could arrive and straighten it out. Then she turned the floor over to the detectives.

"We have arrested all of the involved suspects. Two of them, the Wallers, were also involved with Brittany McCaffie in Mildred's kidnapping. Someday we will all listen to the tale of Double-Oh's award winning performance."

Q looked puzzled. "I do not understand the Double-Oh. Is that Ms. Mildie?"

Bud spoke up, "It is a reference to a series of movies. There was a spy who worked with a boss named Q, so you are involved in the joke, too." Q smiled and blushed.

"I'll rent one of the movies, Q, and we will watch it together," Mildred added.

Her face was still confused, but Q nodded and smiled.

"Back to business. We haven't cleared Penny and Tim Dumple. The prints weren't in the system. We could find no ties to anyone in this case. We could find no criminal affiliations, only a questionable fashion sense."

Mildred was surprised how happy she felt that she would get to keep her new friend.

Blocked continued, "Wife Number Two has negotiated a plea agreement, and with her testimony, we have also arrested Thomas Conner." The room was stunned, quiet.

Arnie was the first to speak. "Isn't he the lawyer of choice in this mess?"

Block continued, "We have found a connection to an Eastern European crime syndicate. Looks like he and his mistress went renegade on them."

Mildred spoke, "Sorry to interrupt...tell them who the mistress is."

"Wife Number One!" He went on to explain how Conner and Judith McCaffie skimmed off the Pay Day Loan Store and handled the larger loans. "We have closed it, for now. The forensic squad is working through the books, and we brought in their accountant."

"Why were they so hot and heavy on Mildred?" Bud asked.

"Well, we learned a little something Mildred doesn't know. Thanks to Bud, we found the employee from the robbery, Lena Davis, was the leak."

Bud jumped in. "Remember, she was the one that helped stop Butt Munch."

Mildred seemed disappointed. "I still am resistant to involving her."

"Bud had a hunch. Hampton followed up, when she quit soon after the reopening ceremony. We weren't sure of the connection until we brought her in. Her mother worked for Judge McCaffie as a housekeeper, and grew up with Brittany. Lena was being blackmailed by Number Two. Her cashier job provided the deposit-timing information. Once we picked her up, she sang like a soprano in church. She was the genuine amateur in this whole ordeal and a victim.

They all high-fived, back-patted, and toasted with coffee cups. As they were about to leave, Mildred turned to Block. "Elton, do you know where the Freeman cold case fits? I'd like to go visit the family."

Block stood and scooted the box to the center of the table. "Looks like your husband was suspicious of possible bribes, and he was closing in on the judge for taking payoffs. FYI, we have reopened the cold case of Freeman."

"Can you get me a phone number, please? The old one is disconnected. I'd like permission to take her the news." Mildred picked up her pen.

Block nodded and continued. "We would also like to request the medical records for the new investigation into the suicide or possible homicide of Major Dick Petrie."

Mildred was stunned. Finally, all of the emotions exploded into an exhausted sob. Block put his arm around her shoulders, and Hampton handed her a folded white handkerchief. "Mildred, we have too many questions left. It is never as neat as one hopes."

– 64 –
Early Shift

It was a beautiful sunny Wednesday when Mildred arrived early for her regular shift. She parked and walked toward the main door in the warm summer day. She walked past a van with the logo of Village Green Senior Home on the side. Mildred noticed a slight motion near the sliding door. She walked around to the side and found a middle-aged woman struggling with the door.

"Can I help?"

The frustrated woman answered, "I just dropped off the seniors, and when I shut the door it locked, and my skirt is caught in it."

Mildred tried the sliding door and it was locked. The van was still running, and Mildred opened the front door, ready to get the keys, but tried to flip the door lock first.

Almost immediately the driver called out, "That's it! Thank God, thank you."

"I'm glad to be of service." Mildred bowed slightly.

"I'm so embarrassed, but there was a breeze just as I shut the door. It locks automatically. I was just about to tear my skirt off."

The driver hugged Mildred and then they both walked into the casino lobby. The driver walked over to the coffee shop and bakery, waving one more time. By habit Mildred texted:

"**G-ma on the floor.**"

She walked directly to the Ivory Winds buffet, and her evening shift began. She entered the buffet, collapsed into her booth of choice, and noticed it was Festa Italiano night.

There is no way I could leave this job. Not as long as I can walk and text.

– About the Author –

Toni Kief never planned to write a book, until she was sixty. Born in the Midwest, lived in Florida, she presently calls the great Northwest home.

She continues to resist writing an autobiography, because of her odd incarnations and the tendency to catch a bus and leave town.

Much of her creative energy goes into women of certain age. Toni calls her work OA, Old Adult, as she focuses on the ability to grab life full force and face unidentified dreams. Working with the Writers Cooperative of the Pacific Northwest, she has started her third book.

Made in the USA
Columbia, SC
12 July 2021